C   ADA

The Ledge

Also by Blánaid McKinney
Big Mouth

The Ledge

Blánaid McKinney

Weidenfeld & Nicolson
London

A PHOENIX HOUSE BOOK

First published in Great Britain in 2002
A Phoenix House Book

Copyright © 2002 Blánaid McKinney

A CIP catalogue record for this book is available from the British Library.

ISBN 1 86159167 5

Typeset by Deltatype Ltd, Birkenhead, Merseyside
Printed by Clays Ltd, St Ives plc

Phoenix House
Weidenfeld & Nicolson
The Orion Publishing Group Ltd
Orion House
5 Upper St Martin's Lane
London WC2H 9EA

Dedicated to Lilian Isabel McKinney (née O'Sullivan)

1

The old woman stared at him from the depths of the bed, with a feral, red-faced contempt. She was supposed to be dead and they both knew it. She wasn't supposed to be hanging on like this, like a malignant sprite, as if the trajectory of her life was a freeform thing, to be flirted with and staggered. There were medical rules, for Chrissakes, and those rules said that she should be dead. He also had the distinct impression that she wasn't hanging on in any desperate, wracked sense. She seemed to be almost enjoying herself, as if she was some kind of dreadless, bitchy pilgrim who knew exactly where she was going. As if she knew something he didn't. That bothered him. His experience as a doctor seemed, here, to count for nothing, and the civilised farce of her not dying was becoming a joke amongst his colleagues. What was the point in all that effort, all that expertise, if at some point it wasn't brought into sharp relief by the fact that the bloody patient actually, eventually, died? Not that he was an unkind man – far from it. But everything has its own reasonable end. The nice, fatty carnality of what we are has its welcome banishment – and this old cow wasn't playing by the rules.

So they stared at each other for a little while, the mighty background chit-chat of the hospital gently clogging up their ears. He smiled. She didn't.

John

John Kelso was neither teetering nor wavering. He wasn't doing much of anything, just hunching on the ledge, staring at the building on his right. It was a pastiche of something but he wasn't sure what. He rocked gently back and forth and closed his eyes, face upturned to the sun. It was a beautiful day. The sky was streaked with just a few dribbling clouds and a slight breeze tickled his hair. Fifteen storeys up, the noise of the traffic was reduced to a sweet, dinky sound, like an old tin-toy struggling at half-steam. John took a deep breath, exhaled slowly and opened his eyes. The windows of the building, hundreds of them, twinkled deliriously in the sunshine, almost blinding him. Just then, a peregrine falcon flashed past him, mere yards away. John almost laughed. When it came to pigeons, Westminster Council was off on its latest wheeze. He watched the falcon swoop high, then drop like a stone behind an office block. One less ragamuffin pigeon, probably.

A nightingale had taken up residence outside his bedroom window the previous month. There had been six males, all arrived on the same evening. And so battle commenced. John spent the night propped against the window, fascinated. They sang and sang and sang. All night they competed for the franchise, for the territory, creating a meltdown of vitriolic sloganeering, a cacophonous squall of call-and-response, eight hours of come-and-have-a-go-if-you-think-you're-hard-enough. An aural salad of tetch and shrewdness. The almost mathematical ugliness of the sound nearly stopped John's heart. Demented treble notes were swamped, drowned, tantrumed out, and all those swooning phrases mangled in a goofy jangle of sheer noise.

Then, one by one, towards dawn, the other contenders gave up, dropped out and flew away. Gradually, the air thinned of racket and gibber until only one nightingale was left. The winner, the new tenant, the glam king. He celebrated every evening, from dusk till dawn, calling and cajoling a potential mate, singing his heart out, and it was the most beautiful sound John had ever heard. Compared to the feeble manifesto of other birds, this lad's technique was unstoppable. Every night.

John quickly discovered that, throughout its adult life, a nightingale never repeats a musical phrase. Never. Its song is a bottomless vortex of ringing, mesmeric complexity. And this went on every night.

Brightly, beautifully, and three feet from his window.

Every night.

Three weeks later, in the late evening, when he'd looked down at the air pistol in his hand and realised that he didn't even care, John had begun to cry. And didn't know that he was crying. All he knew was that this had to stop.

He had been hunkered there for a couple of hours. He'd brought out with him onto the ledge a shoebox containing a half-bottle of whisky, four cans of Stella, ten Benson & Hedges and a box of matches, toothpicks, dental floss and an emery board. He had forgotten why he felt the emery board was essential, but since he had it, he'd spent the first half-hour filing his nails. The off-licence was run by a retired soldier named George. Every time people bought alcohol, George made it plain that he didn't approve, to the point where customers were going elsewhere, just to avoid his harrumphing and frowning. The man was putting himself out of business, but he just couldn't help it. John took a sip from the bottle and looked out over the river, the London Eye on the left, Hungerford Bridge on the right. He counted ten seconds between a pod's movement from one point to the next, and concluded that the wheel had been speeded up. About ten per cent more revenue, probably. Gradually, the pod's occupants stopped taking pictures of Parliament and started training their binoculars on the man perched on the ledge.

John had long stopped being surprised when tears came, and he wasn't surprised now. Through his tears, the windows on the adjacent building became an insane wash of pixellated light, the clouds pneumatic and drenched. He could hear a voice screaming at him, its accent Scottish and familiar. He looked down, down the fifteen storeys and thought to himself, *'Now's as good a time as any, I suppose.'*

Two Years Earlier

John climbed into his car and drove to the studio, a happy man. As far as he was concerned, he had the dream job – film critic with his own nightly show on a cable station. He was privileged and he knew it – having a nightly show was unheard of, but he was good at it, and he knew that too. And not just movies, but pretty much anything he fancied. He'd recently done a lengthy piece on (terminally unfashionable) eastern European animation – and the studio had just let him blather on to his heart's content about Czech and Yugoslav and Bulgarian animation, with their heartfelt political allegories and their occasionally brilliant but, more often than not, ludicrous style. Stick-like and brutal. Some of them still had the power to make John hold his breath. Since the censors were too thick to worry about cartoons, the animation guys were able to get away with all sorts of subversive bullshit, while serious and worthy film directors were being thrown in prison. Jutriša, Parn, Kijowicz, Goleszowski. The names were so ugly and the frames so nice.

And of course, there was always Jan Svankmajer, who went around humiliating and scaring the bejasus out of practically everybody in the trade, simply because it had never occurred to him not to. Some of the late-night fans may have gotten it. Some wouldn't. Kelso took one phone call from a woman in Lewisham who claimed to be seven months pregnant, and threatened to sue him because she'd been channel-surfing and had accidentally happened upon Svankmajer's *Dimensions of Dialogue*, and had been so shocked, she'd almost gone into labour.

Kelso laughed so hard in her face, or rather her ear, he could barely talk. That was the sweetest piece of footage he'd ever shown. What was wrong with some people? Besides, there were few things more barbaric than your average *Tom & Jerry*, and they had won Oscars, for the love of God. Mind you, John reasoned, they deserved it.

It took eighteen months to produce every five minutes of pure violence. A year and a half. Most people didn't believe him. Which was fair enough.

Just don't get me started on Scott Bradley or Carl Stalling, thought John. He thought that same thought pretty much every time he opened his eyes of a morning, actually. (It was just a bad habit. He knew that he would piss everybody off these days if he said it out loud.) So Bradley and Stalling were musical geniuses, and there was something, and enough, of the jubilant and guttersnipe fan in John Kelso to let himself get carried away so totally by such things. It was just that when he tried to transmit this serious nonsense to anyone else, he felt like a moron. Or dangerous, even. And nobody argued.

Since his show aired at 2.20 a.m. none of the station executives was seriously bothered. John's show was considered cult viewing – it wasn't profitable, but it probably didn't do any harm to give him room to pander to that particular demographic which loves nothing more than to be in a minority. Students, usually.

Which meant that John was able to talk about absolutely anything he liked.

And so, he filled his hugely enjoyable evenings at the studio writing scripts he didn't stick to anyway, digging out footage of favourite children's shows (it being a truth universally acknowledged, he discovered, that if you put half a dozen 30-somethings together in the same room, sooner or later the conversation will turn to children's telly in general, and Parsley the Lion in particular . . .), and generally educating his tiny audience as to how some or other *oeuvre* (a few quite brilliant, most positively toxic) was the key to the universe. Subtlety was not the show's main ingredient, but John was consistent in his thesis that it didn't have to have a budget of $50 million-plus to be at least of some interest.

So, he would blather on into the small hours about how *The California Dolls*, despite featuring acres of female flesh in the wrestling ring, was a proto-feminist tract. It had to be. The blessed

8

Peter Falk wouldn't involve himself with anything untoward. John was convinced. Just look at *The Brinks Job*.

John also let it be known that, apart from *The Rockford Files*, the best thing James Garner did was *The Americanisation of Emily*, the wittiest anti-war movie ever made (plus it had Julie Andrews as a bit of a trollop, and you don't get to see that every day).

And speaking of Julie Andrews, he opined, *The Royal Hunt of the Sun* featured a deeply camp (and yet weirdly heart-breaking) performance from Christopher Plummer as the Inca king Atahualpa, with Robert Shaw as Francesco Pizarro.

Of course, he had his favourite actors, so he would mouth off about Robert Foxworth in *The Questor Tapes* and *The Black Marble* (that Russian folk music!), or Alan Arkin in both *The Defection of Simas Kidurka* (according to John, officially the best foreign accent ever attempted by an American actor – ever) and *Freebie and the Bean*. ('Brilliant. Vulgar. Crude. Brilliant. Off you go.')

And although most other critics didn't pick up on it (because all they could think about was below-par spaghetti westerns), for John, the end sequence of *Mr Billion*, with Terence Hill (playing an impoverished Italian, heir to a fortune, blah-di-be-blah, gotta make deadline, yah-di-yah) galloping in slow motion past a truly beautiful, 400-yard public mural charting the history of the working class and immigrant culture of San Francisco, was one of the most thrilling things he'd ever seen. Okay, part of it was probably Hill's amazing, ice-blue eyes, but mostly, he was stunned by this cheap, populist, American movie's positively *socialist* agenda. He got a few dodgy phone calls about that one, and he didn't give a fuck. In fact, he was delighted. (John obtained a fair proportion of his tapes from America. It never occurred to him that most of his viewers didn't have access to, or couldn't afford, NTSC video players.)

Sometimes, when he'd had a few drinks John would mither aimlessly on about such things as censorship. Or the war. Or the war, censorship and Betty Grable. Or just censorship. That was one that just got his goat. (Which was strange, considering the fact that the first time Kelso got his hands on a proper, black-boxed porn video at the ripe age of twenty-nine, he had almost died of embarrassment. After ten minutes and one orgasm, he was bored. Bored, but more than anything, embarrassed. And he was alone.)

The classic WWII Grable pose. Kelso never understood that one, though. Okay, Monroe had a nice, pointless chunkiness to her, but John had never been able to disassociate Grable's cheesy smile with the piled-up hair on top, and the nothing-special legs below, from some kind of sexless gormlessness. It just did nothing for him. Then again, he had not been a soldier in the forties, far from home and terrified. A soldier who was never going to run up against the kind of video which featured, close-up, three people for four hours, fucking each other fifteen ways from Sunday.

For some reason, Audie Murphy would crop up now and again in John's repertoire. He wasn't certain why, but assumed that it was almost certainly a childhood, Saturday afternoon matinee thing. Either that or a war-medal, decoration-type thing. He didn't even like Audie Murphy.

He preferred his heroes a tad *less* self-deprecating and low-key; a smart-ass Fred MacMurray or a less humble Jeff Chandler would've done just dandy.

A touch of braggadocio never went amiss. Keeps the ladies on their toes. Yeah. Right. As if he was an expert.

But John did like his old-ish movies. He had a few battles with the studio over his attempts to get some silent stuff on the air but he never won. Never. But it didn't do any harm to tussle. Hedy Lamarr and *Ecstasy*, directed by Gustav Machaty. (Or Hedy Kiesler and *Symphony of Love*, as she, and it, were originally known in 1933). Now that would have made interesting viewing for the post-pub lot. An up-close, ancient, black-and-white and utterly silent picture of a woman's face. A woman in the throes of orgasm. And before that, the same lassie swimming nude in a lake.

Nude. In 1933. Needless to say, it got itself banned all over the place.

Hedy Lamarr. A grand and smart girl, and lovely too. Sometimes censorship made sense.

Good actors in bad movies. And bad actors in good movies. That was Kelso's other delight. Or bad performances where you least expected them. Or bad actors turning in unexpected pieces of brilliance in truly awful movies. Or bad actors being just brilliant in mediocre movies, or mediocre actors being fantastic in fantastic movies. And great actors being just great. In something that just didn't work, for some reason or other. Or rotten movies that had a tiny spark from actors who would later acquire greatness in average movies. Then perhaps, later, good movies.

Kelso found himself, periodically, trawling through his video collection for the evidence.

Dick van Dyke – crap in *Mary Poppins*, and brilliant in *Cold Turkey*.

Dick Powell – tough and scary in *Murder My Sweet*; merely scary in *42nd Street*.

Dwight Schultz – decent enough in *The Shadow Makers* but fantastic in *The A-Team*.

Anthony Edwards – fabulous in *Miracle Mile* and utterly superfluous in *ER*.

Farrah Fawcett – a bimbo in *Angels*, a muddy and excellent whore in *The Substitute Wife*.

Raquel Welch – same thing, then *Walks Far Woman*.

Steve McQueen – sleepwalked his way through everything he ever did, except the glacial, gorgeous, penultimate *Tom Horn*.

John Astin – great and lovely in *The Addams Family*, but just hysterical in *Evil Roy Slade*.

Michael Keaton – an icy Batman but a weak, heart-breaking fucker in *Clean and Sober*.

Christopher Lee – nice as Dracula, but even better in *Captain Invincible*, as the campest villain on the planet, tormenting poor Alan Arkin, the world's first alcoholic superhero.

Rock Hudson – brilliant and brutal in *Hornet's Nest*, convincingly terrified in *Seconds*, and rubbish in fifty per cent of everything else.

Ginger Rogers in *Roxie*, a better comedienne than *he* ever was a dancer. (And in everything else, a better *dancer* than he was a dancer, since she had to do everything he did. And she had to do it backwards and in two-inch heels. John never understood why she wasn't a bigger star than Astaire.)

Jesus, even a piece of lumber like Chuck Heston had *The Omega Man* going for him.

And so on and so forth. Ancient, modern or mid-century, Kelso would come up with a notion that required repeated viewing, or investigation or just some people to badger. He would pioneer the cause of movies that were never going to set the world on fire, no matter how good they were. So as soon as he started in, his friends would roll their eyes and smile and move away, spilling their pints in the process, while John just blathered on happily about such gems as *Kill Me if You Can*, starring that nice Alan Alda as a convicted rapist and murderer on Death Row, and that wasn't something you got to see every day, either. Or the same Alan in *Isn't it Shocking?* – the definition of a neglected classic. Okay, John would say, the film was low-key, low-stream, low-budget and as mad as a box of frogs, but that was no reason for people not to see it. And only James Garner, in *Barbarians at the Gate*, could make a tobacco company executive look like a hero.

And his friends would sidle back, usually, not because they were interested, but because they liked him. They just wished he would stop being such a trainspotter.

In the mid-seventies, he was convinced that there was going to be a mighty renaissance for Canadian movies. He was right, but the renaissance consisted of one film, and even *Skip Tracer*, a piece of chilly, humane and melancholy brilliance, couldn't carry the thing by itself. He revived that one on his show, years later, and got a brisk response in the postbag and on the website. Made no difference.

Sometimes, Kelso wondered to himself if he liked lost causes because they were just that. He had had, although not very often, that delicious and horrible *frisson* of seeing his favourites rise from obscurity to prominence, thanks to some style guru or other who had nothing better to do.

Kelso had always known that he was a wee bit of a snob. He just wasn't absolutely certain if there was a huge amount more to him than that.

Other nights, he would try to stick strictly to a theme – say, science fiction – and invariably end up wandering all over the shop. So he would start with twenty seconds from an original *Star Trek* episode which featured an extremely rude bit, just because the prop guys couldn't have foreseen the advent of video, and by the end of the show he was ranting on about how *The 5000 Fingers of Dr T.* was the best political allegory ever made, and screw *Dr Strangelove* while we're at it. And speaking of William Shatner, John would demand, why hadn't *Incubus* been released on video, seeing as how it was the only fucking movie with dialogue entirely in Esperanto, eh? (Except he didn't curse on television.)

Or how *Mr Sardonicus*, which he saw when he was nine, gave him nightmares until he was thirty. (That was actually true; John tried to neither lie nor exaggerate on his show. After almost thirty years, he'd recently acquired a tape, and was almost reluctant to watch it because he knew that the power the movie had over him when he was a child would be gone. That he would probably snigger and sneer at it, and be adult and unafraid. He popped it in the video player and, because his memory of it was a little askew, he wasn't ready for the moment when the Doctor's hideously deformed face first appeared. John screamed, jumped about three feet out of his chair, and spent fifteen trembling minutes sponging vodka out of his carpet. He'd been scared shitless, just like when he was nine. Fantastic.)

And so it went, night after night. One man talking to himself on camera, in a world of his own, a one-man Greek chorus, with his cheap, taped vignettes, his fair-to-middling movie reviews and his badly bored and tiny tribe, watching. Watching and, on the odd occasion, badly in love.

Occasionally John felt regret at the fact that he had never pursued his original dream of becoming a film-maker. That had been his ambition ever since he was a child. And now here he was, hopping around on the sidelines, heckling the real players. Still, he was permitted to conduct his own unfussy critical skirmishes, something that dragged a little grubby applause from the insomniacs, a small dose of vagrant energy from the students.

So here he was, late thirties, unmarried, busy, happy. Done and dusted.

He'd made a few half-hearted attempts in his early twenties, while at college, to write a screenplay but, after a dazed chug-a-lug of demented characters (mainly sweaty, despicable types with guns, and yelping whores), he gave up. It was over-populated, it was unmanageable but, mainly, it was garbage. A couple of years later, he tried again, with an updated version of Hans Christian Andersen's 'The Tinder-Box'. In his version, the soldier and the witch were reinvented as business partners, the tinder-box was a ground-breaking piece of encryption software, the dog with eyes as big as teacups was a nightclub bouncer, the one with eyes as big as millwheels was the club boss, and the one with eyes as big as towers – well, he never got as far as that with the story, so he gave up. Again. John gradually realised that he was no good at the hard-nosed stuff, but was repulsed by the possibility that his real talent lay in 'relationship-oriented' material. He wanted his work to be pestilential, not *amiable*, for God's sake. And so it went. He would start a story, be gripped with several outstanding ideas, write like a maniac for two months, and then, as on one occasion, watch his pet project disappear into a morass of his own lousy dialogue, plagiarised plot devices, situations of implausible nastiness, one-dimensional blokes, stratospherically stupid bints, and lots and lots of guns.

John knew no one like that. He'd grown up in a huge house in Bromley in Kent, and with every keystroke felt more and more of a fraud.

Another story had involved time travel. The idea was that an endlessly benign twenty-second-century culture had perfected the process, and was conducting a series of experiments whereby famous figures from the past would be transported into the future, to dispense wisdom, clear up historical misunderstandings, and generally have a good time until they were sent home (with, of course, no memory of the entire episode). The main protagonist in John's story, a conscientious soul named Luke, is given the job of snatching Leonardo da Vinci and, amongst other things, showing him the marvels of the modern age. Well, poor Luke has no idea where to start – I mean, what do you show a genius? Does one start small with, say, the typewriter, before gradually moving on to such wonders as the telephone, the television, the movies, computers, the internet? Luke decides to go for the revelatory propulsion option, and takes Leonardo for a 110-miles-per-hour trip in an open-top sports car on the Santa Monica freeway. At this point, Leonardo, whose previous top speed would have been whatever a gently trotting donkey can manage, has a fatal heart attack, and Luke is severely reprimanded by the management.

And it was at this point that John's story ground to a halt. He had just killed off Leonardo da Vinci. In the future. Did that mean that he was still alive in his own time? Or had never lived at all? Thinking about the chrono-permutations just gave John a headache, so he abandoned that story too.

His final attempt never got beyond twenty pages. It concerned an Oscar statuette, stolen by the winner's drunken rival, tossed in an LA skip, found by a bum, sold for a 40-ounce, melted down and fashioned into . . . well, he never got that far either. The possibility of a very expensive dildo slithered across his mind for a couple of seconds, then he closed his writing pad, slid it under his bed, pocketed his pen and gave up the idea of writing anything ever again. He was twenty-two, just out of college, and the thought of a welcoming, alchemical nothingness – not the warmth of death, but similar – was already creeping up to him.

*

As a child, John Kelso had always melted into the wallpaper. His parents seemed to be only vaguely aware of him. He could spend all day, from morning till dusk, outside and running the roads, traipsing around abandoned quarries, jumping bog-holes five miles from home, swimming in stagnant lakes, cutting the wings off dead seagulls for his bedroom wall, and neither his mother nor his father would have a clue where he was, or what he was doing. For two summers in a row, he and three friends conducted a ferocious and utterly pointless turf war with a gang from a council estate six hundred yards away. It consisted exclusively of stone-throwing, and they became possessed of the kind of pin-point accuracy snipers can only dream of. He could still remember the hot, dark evenings, hiding behind hedges, diving over fences, whooping and hollering to his comrades, then launching a volley of rocks at the enemy.

They would straggle home with cut faces or hands and stinging skull lumps, covered in filth, and John's parents wouldn't even notice. John loved it. He wasn't a brave boy, and every foray terrified the life out of him but, as the leader of the posse, he couldn't back down or show weakness. The strange thing, John remembered, was that he became the leader not because he was the biggest or strongest, but because he was the smartest. And because he was funny. He was the boss because they liked him.

His gang. Jesus, what a bunch. There was Jason, twelve, whom he recently saw for the first time in twenty-five years – on television, on the roof of Strangeways Prison. And Linda, Jason's fourteen-year-old sister, who had the worst stutter on the planet but who, when it came to winging stones, had an eye like a travelling rat. Her crippling stutter provided endless hours of amusement for the group and, as far as John could tell at that age, she found it as funny as everyone else.

The awful thing about Linda was that she was so gorgeous. Her mesmerising face was engaged in a constant, twitching battle with the stutter, her marvellous, distraught eyes saying one thing and her semi-paralysed mouth another.

Bruce was eleven and skinny beyond belief. In the five or six years they hung out as kids, John never once saw him eat. Not once.

Benny, the youngest, was a baby-faced, effortlessly sociopathic nine-year-old who could barely speak English. He wallowed around under a crusty, grey layer of something-or-other, and could behead a sparrow at one hundred yards with a bent nail.

His gang. It wasn't much of a gang, but over the years it was more family than family. They went on ludicrous raiding parties into enemy territory at midnight, when their own parents were in bed, and all that John could remember was the night-time heat, the stupid shouting, the dodging and flinging, the knowledge that no one, on either side, meant any real harm. It was all rabbit punches along the high street, wobbly war strategies on the grassy field and running, screaming and idiotically happy, from fed-up shop-owners.

One weekend, John got knocked out by a huge rock, thrown from 70 yards by the rival kid-boss. He was thirteen and had never known pain like it. His gang picked him up after he came to, and deposited him on his own doorstep. He sneaked into the house bleeding, after midnight, up the stairs, past his dog, past his nervy elder sister's room, and past his dreaming parents, content and oblivious and dreaming in their huge room.

He swooned into his bed, drifted, woke, drifted again and, in the thinning moonlight, saw the lovely pattern of blood from the cut on his head swirled on the pillowcase, an incendiary, snazzy Rorschach.

That same night he dreamt of bleating, weeping women, and his mother too, perched over his prone form, with immaculate hairdos, and wagging fingernails indicating their bilious disapproval. In his dream, huge, benign figures clumped around him, sterile confections of his parents and his sister, all moody and fizzy at the same time. They shouted, in the dream, and sounded tinny and a bit pissed off. But they loved him, and his choppy, daytime mishaps were forgiven and, with a big bundle of soothing hair-strokes, he was once more the boy in the big picture. He was the wettest, most wondering creature on the earth. He was just so cute and curious. He was six again and credible.

The following morning, his mother snatched the soggy pillow from under his head, smacked him hard across the forehead with her palm and, with a laugh, bounced off to the laundry room. John wanted to know what kind of dreams kept both his father and her so placid and so happy.

*

The man John admired the most was Don Martin, the *MAD* magazine cartoonist. He would reel at the sheer brutality of his work, wondering how the hell the man got away with it. Probably because he was funny, John concluded. Strange, but most liberal newspapers nowadays wouldn't touch his stuff with a barge pole. As a teenager, John collected cartoons (in the eighties, when he acquired a VCR, he graduated to animation) and wallpapered his bedroom walls with them; some were from political satire mags, some were Lowrys from the *NME*, some from kids' mags. He had thousands more in a box, but the ones on the wall were those that still made him laugh, no matter how many times he looked at them. His absolute favourites. When he was fifteen, he realised that he should've copied them first, since he couldn't get them off the wall without ripping them to shreds. He was a lot more careful after that. About everything.

About his singles collection, his comics (every issue of the major *Marvel* silver-age characters, the more interesting DC graphics like *Dark Knight*, all of 2000AD, *Judge Dredd*, *Crisis*, *V for Vendetta*, *Watchmen* and just about anything else Moore turned out, *The Bogie Man*, *Skreemer*, *Mister X*, *Love and Rockets*, and dozens of others), his cuttings from the newspapers, which were filed both chronologically and by subject-matter – Celebrity Obits, Foreign Affairs, Theatre, Language, London, Naval History, Books, Women, Essays (Misc.), Nancy Banks-Smith, Essays (General), Third World Debt, the Gulf War, Islam Misc. (Spec.) and Misc. (General) – his photographic gallery, his collection of stars' portraits dating from 1911 up to the present, every issue of *Empire*, every issue of *The Face*, *Blitz* and *Smash Hits*, his theatre programmes, his postcards, his stationery, and his collection of highlighter pens.

The highlighter pens later became increasingly important as a means of cataloguing his huge video collection; yellow for comedy (with the exceptions of *Frasier* and *Steptoe*, which were in red, *Porridge* which was in blue, *Rab C. Nesbitt* which was in green, and *The Jack Benny Show* and *The Honeymooners*, which were both in orange), green for science fiction, including the *Batman* anima-tions (this covered *Buffy* and *Max Headroom*, which bothered him a little, since they were more fantasy than sci-fi, but his purple pen had run out, so he improvised. The green also took care of *Mork and Mindy*, which really should have been in yellow), blue for *M*A*S*H* and *Nightingales* (which should also both have been yellow), serious drama and *Have I Got News for You*, and finally, red for all things *Star Trek* (which should've been green, but it was an early run . . .). *Moonlighting* and *The Rockford Files* he just underlined in red biro, so they were always a bit more difficult to locate.

And finally, there were all his movies, labelled in big, black capitals.

At the time of his kidnapping, at the age of thirty-eight, John had thirteen thousand tapes. Fifty-two thousand hours. Every sitcom, animated feature, sci-fi series, drama and documentary worth their salt. And nine thousand movies.

John was not a geek, and he was not stupid, so he was perfectly aware that all this collecting and cataloguing might have struck some people as a little obsessive. But for him it was simply heaven – the sense of order, of completeness. Everything in its place, its home; cosy, identifiable, easily plucked, easily slotted back again. He was the perfect archivist/consumer. He was never sure which, and he didn't care.

At fifteen, his friends thought he was knowledgeable and cool. He had no idea what his parents thought. His bedroom was inviolable, a stacked teenage museum that grew and grew. More pictures, more comics, more tapes, more tapes. They just kept giving him his very generous allowance and paid no attention to what he did with it. His mother was, by turns, aloof and suffocating. At that age, John wasn't to know that very few manage to be both at the same time.

She would slide by with a glossy compliment, then not speak to him for three days, scrape his arm with a potato peeler and draw blood, then wake him up at 3 a.m. and talk about homework, and pandas, and Elmer Fudd, and her father, and Ralph Nader and poker strategies and God knows what else, until the starving dawn, until John wanted to either die from tiredness, or just lunge out and cover her mouth, cover her lips and stop the breath altogether.

But he would simply keep his head down, and weather this regular, atonal mini-squall, and eventually she would float off to her own room, spring-heeled, lupine and chirpy, while his dad made muffled, swampy noises in the background. He was her teenaged constituent, and he would put up with whatever damned tomfoolery she came up with. But, he thought to himself on his seventeenth birthday, it would be nice to have something else on top of this – this shameless, loony, stoned salsa, every fucking week. A quiet, thirty-second chat about his school-work would've been nice.

John got kidnapped twenty-three years later. He had been doing his show for three years, and had established himself as a favourite. He was smart without being annoyingly so, reasonably good-looking, and had a slight waywardness when it came to studio conventions, which his band of followers found endearing. His main asset, however, was his unadorned enthusiasm. He loved his job and, even on those nights when he couldn't sleep because of some inexplicable feeling of dread, or when he slept and awoke with his face wet, he still considered himself a lucky man. In fact, his popularity had been growing to the point where some of the executives were thinking of moving his show to an earlier timeslot. John would've hated that. Apart from having to cater to a wider and, to John (who could be as snobby as the next movie fanatic), thicker audience, they almost certainly wouldn't let him do the show live which, apart from those special, five-minute video segments, was how he did it now. For the moment, though, he was content.

At around 2.25 a.m. on a Tuesday morning, John left his studio chair and nipped out to the bathroom. He'd left running a ten-minute piece on Bill Plympton's animation, specifically *How to Kiss*, so he had plenty of time. From the bathroom, he wandered out to the fire escape door, which overlooked the car park, for a quick cigarette. It was a coldish, drizzly type of night. He caught a whiff of aftershave and alcohol and turned to his right. A thin young man with dreadful skin, and a gun, was looking at him as if he was God almighty, shivering and asking him, with some kind of accent, if he wouldn't mind doing as he was told. The man was wearing a T-shirt which read, '667 – The Neighbour of the Beast'. That struck John as rather a good joke, and he smiled. The man returned his smile. Then, with a firearm stuck in between two of his ribs, John did as he was told and walked down the fire escape to his car. He thought it fortunate that he'd jammed the keys in the back pocket of his jeans, rather than leaving them in his jacket, slung over his chair.

When the staff couldn't find him after fifteen minutes, one enterprising researcher stuck in a tape of Plympton's *How to Quit Smoking*, which runs for about ten minutes, then *The Tune* (well over an hour, so it had to be cut short for the music video chart show and the news), so the show didn't suffer too much of a continuity problem. They had a bit of an argument over who was going to get to say that their host had been indisposed, but finally Sally, who was new, went on camera and projected a lovely, hair-tossing combination of professional concern and next-item insouciance. She had her own work-out/makeover show within a year.

And it was brilliant.

The old woman closed her eyes and took a breath. The sweaty, decent doctor was gone, him and his bossy doo-dah. The ward smelled of a chilly cleanliness. Three months of glut and doomed synapses. If she wasn't careful, she was going to have to put up with this shit for all eternity.

Tom

Tom was a thief. Not brilliant at it, but good enough not to have to do much of anything else. He'd never been arrested; it's just that whatever he stole wasn't worth very much, or was difficult to shift, or so irresistible that he just had to keep it himself. Vinyl and books mostly. Tom knew that most self-respecting burglars wouldn't be seen dead staggering down the road with a cardboard box full of 45s and hardbacks, but he just kept doing it. The market indicated a demand for white goods (if portable), CD players, DVDs, televisions. Tom just couldn't work up any real enthusiasm for that kind of thing. He had broken into an empty house in Eltham (the river posed no totemic divide for him) the previous week. Turned out to be a pensioner's. Rummaging around in the upstairs bedroom, Tom discovered a box of papers under the bed and spent the next two hours reading. There were photographs, postcards, letters, all dating from the war, a chronicle of a cracking romance between Lilian and Charles. And a telegram of condolence, and a couple of medals. He couldn't find anything in the rest of the house worth selling, so he kept one of the medals for himself, just to have. Then he made some tea and toast, watched an hour's worth of daytime telly on the tiny set, and let himself out the back.

She could've walked in on him at any moment, but Tom knew he was lucky that way. It was a karmic thing, he was convinced. When he wanted to, he had invisibility by the bucketload, the ability to slide right by, unnoticed, unbothered, safe and sound. He did not avoid troublesome places – he'd spent half his life in terrible pubs – but he had never once gotten into so much as an argument, much less a fight. Swinging a punch at Tom would have been like wrestling smoke. Tucked into his wallet was a cutting he saw in the paper a few years ago. A shopkeeper in Milan was held up by two armed men and suffered a massive heart attack; one emptied the till while the other gave the shopkeeper CPR. Then they took off. But he made it to the hospital alive. Tom liked that story. He liked to think that maybe being a thief didn't make him a complete bastard, that perhaps he would do the same, given the circumstances. He'd once watched an elderly man being given mouth-to-mouth on the Strand. A medic was working frantically on him, but there was no sign of life. Every few minutes a colleague would take over while he retched and retched to one side, saliva and mucus stringing from his mouth. The man was grey and most likely dead. Gradually, the circle of people drifted away, sorrowful and punctured and disgusted. The medics carried on for another fifteen minutes, hammering righteously and angrily, breathing furiously for him, until their heads swam. Tom was the last to walk away.

When he was growing up in Fermanagh, the summers seemed to last for ever. He devoured books like a man starving anyway, and school didn't seem that important, so one O level in Geography was quite an achievement. The old saying held true: 'For nine months of the year, Lough Erne is in Fermanagh, and for three months of the year, Fermanagh is in Lough Erne.' It is the wettest, soggiest county in Ireland and, like everyone else, Tom could swim as soon as he could walk. The lakes have hundreds of tiny islands, most of them unpopulated, and he spent endless summer days rowing out to them with his friends. One island, bigger than the rest, was owned by the descendants of some rich Anglo-Irish family or other. The big house had been beautifully restored and the owner had, over twenty years, created an exquisitely ornate garden, with a huge maze that attracted tourists from all over. When he was fourteen, Tom rowed out to the island by himself, tied up his dinghy at the small pier beside the tourist cruisers, and sneaked into the grounds. Surrounding the garden proper was wild, dense undergrowth which the owners had left untouched. Tom squatted in the brush, sweat pouring off him, and peered through the tangle of branches. The garden was incredibly beautiful. He sat there for hours, staring and stunned. He rowed out every Sunday after that and, when the other visitors weren't looking, stole as many flowers as he could get his hands on. One day the owner, a posh and interesting man, caught him red-handed, and made him a deal – he could have a job if he stopped stealing the blooms. That was Tom's first summer job. Maze attendant. It took him an afternoon to learn it inside out.

Tourists would land at the jetty and, after a traipse around the garden, dive into the maze for what they thought would be twenty minutes of fun. They had no way of knowing that this maze, although not the biggest, was actually the most difficult in Western Europe. Tom had the homing sense of a pigeon, and it was his job to go in and bring them out. It fascinated him to watch these poor people, all poise and purposeful braying, enter the maze full of confidence and, five hopeless hours later, admit defeat with an undignified, frantic bleating. When dusk began to fall, he could detect real fear in their voices, as if they thought they would be lost for ever. This was not a maze made for fun. It was deadly serious. Tom found it comparatively easy, but he often wondered why the owner had paid a designer what must have been an awful lot of money to construct a maze which provided nothing in the way of fun or indeed, challenge (since everyone was defeated, except Tom).

That summer he spent his afternoons greeting cheerful families, who delightedly wandered around the grounds and the manor, and his evenings delving into the maze and pulling out distraught, trembling couples and their weeping children. All cut knees and no confidence left at all. The worst affected were the young professional types, especially the men, who could not bear the thought of being bested by a big hedge.

The maze acquired a terrible (in other words, terrific) reputation, which pulled in even more visitors, many of whom came to see it as an enemy to be clobbered rather than a nice, meandering couple of hours. And, nine times out of ten, Tom had to go flying in, round and about, sluicing through the green corridors, the magnetic homing device in his brain tingling, to find whole families gibbering and fed up, if not actually crying, and lead them out, handing out hankies to the kids and distracting football talk to the fathers. That was Tom's favourite summer ever. It was warm and long; he got to spend most of his time either working, or lounging amongst the flowers on the island, or fishing from his dinghy on the way there. He fell away from most of his chums round about then, although they stayed civil at school.

A couple of years later, when he was working at another job, he heard that a child had died in the maze. It had been a bright, sunny afternoon and her parents, ten yards around a corner, were so busy getting into a quietly vicious argument about which direction to take, they didn't realise that, behind them, their daughter was silently choking on a mint.

The owner stopped the tourists after that and the island became off-limits to outsiders. In his three months as maze attendant, Tom had never spoken more than a couple of dozen words to the man, and he never understood why he had allowed all those people to march, loudly and stupidly, around his garden, through his gorgeous maze. All they ever did was gape without the sense to steal the flowers, or whimper in the dark maze without the nous to find their own way out.

The man seemed to be simultaneously stooped and optimistic, and he never provided Tom with anything approaching an answer.

Six months after that, the maze was burnt down. Hedges are tough, and the roots survived, of course, but it was not a maze any more. It was a dingy pattern of stubby, fire-fuelled growth that would have made no sense to anyone who wasn't in a helicopter. And perhaps not even then.

His next summer job was for Bertie, the bike repairer in town. The fat fixer. Oil eater. Bike healer. Tom spent seven stuffy, sweltering weeks in Bertie's repair shop. The inside was like something out of *Alien*. A long wooden corridor led from the front door of the shop to the inner sanctum where Bertie worked on his upended babies. Hundreds of old-fashioned, hulking bikes lay four deep on either side, most of them broken in some shape or form. Some had been there for years, the owners having given up, or forgotten, or bought a new one. Bikes hung from the walls, from the ceiling, from the beams, like bizarre, tubular, grotesque sculpture. There was barely room, or light, to work. Tom would fetch tools, take deliveries of the latest orders, deliver home those bikes which had been repaired. But mainly, he just hung around and listened to Bertie talking and wheezing and whacking the upside-down wheels until the air hummed. He would talk about his own young cycling days, when forty miles to a Friday-night dance in Donegal was no problem at all.

After six weeks, Tom stole a bike from the ludicrous stack, a good green racer with ten speeds and not much wrong with it. The following day he felt so bad he took it back. A week later, Bertie gave it to him anyway, to say cheerio. He'd fixed the slack chain first.

When he was seventeen, Tom moved to Belfast. He prevailed upon the hospitality of a couple of friends who let him sleep on their living-room floor, and got himself a job with a security firm. He wasn't big, but he had a kind of stillness about him that just seemed to calm people down. He played bouncer a couple of times, but in the summer open-air gig season he spent all his evenings standing with his colleagues in a line, facing the crowds, with their backs to the stage. It drove Tom insane. Here he was, three feet away from thousands of screaming fans, and he wasn't even allowed to turn around and have a look at the bands. Every twenty seconds or so, he would sidle around and end up practically bent double, gaping under his arm at Van Morrison or whoever. The boss got fed up after four weeks and fired him. From then on, whenever he saw them on television, Tom felt sorry for the policemen who had to hold back the crowds at premieres and carnivals and football matches. The poor bastards were utterly fantastic in their forward-facing discipline, and they never got to see a damn thing.

The week he got fired, Tom saw a bit on the telly about a Chicago cop who was retiring after thirty years as a decoy. For thirty years, he'd dressed up as little old ladies, vagrants, hookers and anyone else who looked as if they might be a pushover for criminal sorts. He had been attacked 265 times in the course of his duty. Punched, clobbered stabbed, maced, you name it. Tom had no love for the police, but he goggled at the TV, his forkful of chips hovering in the air, and he was astounded by this man.

He got a job in a brewery after that. The latest wheeze, in 1982, before the widget, was bottled Guinness six-packs that came with a plastic syringe taped to the top of the pack, which was supposed to be used to inject air into the bottles, thus creating draught Guinness in the comfort of your own home. It was Tom's job to tape the syringes to the packs.

Jesus, he thought, years later, *syringes taped to the top of your six-pack* . . . He couldn't even imagine how a bunch of pissed, after-hours drinkers might tackle that one. Or how the marketing folk would try to put it over, God help them.

The promotion lasted in the Republic for about two months, then died a death, never to reappear.

He truly didn't want to steal but supplemented his income anyway with some petty thievery, mainly from student households. Around this time, the political atmosphere was getting on his nerves. It was the anniversary of the hunger strikes, which ones he couldn't even remember, and Tom thought, *That's it, I'm headed out.* He himself was completely apolitical, but he resented the fact that, all of a sudden, he couldn't walk where he wanted. All his life, Tom had wandered at any time of the day or night wherever he pleased. The outfields at night, the back streets before opening time, the lough shore in the early morning. Open skies and chimneys, water-lap and drunk giggle, seagull and motor – he was both acutely aware of, and oblivious to, all of it. He'd just traipsed where he wanted and didn't bother anyone. Now, when he walked along certain roads, he found himself being asked by men who placed a sudden, gentle palm against his chest, where he was going and whether he thought his journey absolutely necessary. Their courtesy and gentleness disturbed him. Denied his wandering, Tom fancied a fight. But never did any of them show willing for a fracas. It was as if he was, not invisible, but just not fightable. As if it would never occur to them to hit him, not in a million years.

Tom's last job in Belfast was in a bakery. His boss, Martin, was a master cake-maker. Which meant that he was the most hysterical, bad-tempered man on the planet. He was also a genius. Little ten-year-old Sharon who loves her dog, Craig who's nine and is going to play centre-forward for Linfield, Patricia and her tennis racquet – they all got the most extravagantly beautiful birthday cakes Tom had ever seen. Two-foot-high architectural wonders, with marzipan animals and footballs and big Walkmans perched all over the place, and icing in colours he didn't know icing could sustain.

The day before Tom left, because it was Martin Luther King Day, Martin made a cake in honour of his namesake, and gave it pride of place in his shop window. It was an amazing work, with the words, 'I Have A Dream' curled around the top in green icing. The second layer of marzipan was jet black. Tom didn't even want to think about how he'd managed that. And then, while the housewives on the Ormeau Road were peeking and peering at this new creation, and wondering who the good-looking darkie on the cake was, Martin, who was fifty-six and an artist with exquisitely good intentions, lay down on the floor of the oven room and cried for three hours, his fat hands smacking the floor and sending up weird showers of muggy flour.

Tom patted him on the head, and patted and patted, and knew the poor bastard would be in an institution before the year was out. There was something seriously wrong with this guy.

Before he moved to London, Tom gave all his records and books to his Gran to keep for him in her loft, telling her he'd be back soon. He spent a week saying cheerio to his few friends, and tried to be sturdy and all chisel-chinned about it, but failed. At the airport, he was teary-eyed and hopeless.

In Crouch End, he slept on various floors for a few weeks, and got himself a bar job in the Haringay. But his accent put people off and soon he wasn't speaking much to anyone. An old school pal who lived near Finsbury Park tube introduced him to a couple of chaps in the Railway, and pretty soon Tom was into some heavy and profitable thieving.

No ripping off students this time. Now Tom was stealing from seriously well-off people: jewellery, DVDs, that kind of thing. But while he prowled around their homes, Tom still couldn't resist the urge to open their mail, go through their record collections, and read the inscriptions in their books. Over the coming weeks, he slept all day and worked all night.

In one guy's house, he scanned the bookshelves and found a Joyce first edition. Tom kept that for himself. Another had left divorce papers lying on the kitchen table. The place didn't show much sign of a woman's touch, but there were photographs everywhere of a delicate brunette and, upstairs, a box of letters ranging over fifteen years.

In another neat flat in Camden, he found a signed photo of Caruso sandwiched amongst a stack of hardcore porn, and in a box nearby, a replica Smith & Wesson M29 44 Magnum, exactly like the one used by De Niro in *Taxi Driver*. And in another, a replica of Arnie's Francki shotgun from *The Terminator*. The guy obviously had a thing about ordnance.

A huge Victorian pile in Brent was obviously home to a bunch of young professionals sharing the rent. Every room was different. In one a wardrobe contained a life-sized artist's maquette and three gorgeous trilbys. Another room reeked of dope. A third contained a well-fed and energetic white rat in a glass-covered maze, and a wall-sized poster of the A-Team, and two big pictures of John Saxon from *Enter the Dragon* (and none of Bruce Lee, funnily enough, thought Tom). A fourth had one of those stand-up cut-outs of Captain Kirk standing beside the door. The damn thing nearly gave Tom a heart attack when he crept in and turned on the light. *Fuck's sake, Bill* ... he thought, and swiped half a dozen random CDs out of sheer annoyance. The fifth contained hundreds of movie reference books. The volume open on the desk was a biography of Arnold Stang. The voice of Top Cat, apparently. Tom learnt something new every night.

One family in Islington had 207 computer games and no books. Not one. Tom was so astonished he didn't steal a thing. He spent 45 minutes tearing the place apart, convinced he would find a book somewhere. He didn't.

In a beautiful two-bedroom flat in Brent, he found a framed inscription on the kitchen wall – 'Nihil Amore Injurium' – and was happy to discover that the owners had a Latin dictionary in the den. There is no wrong that love will not forgive.

In the living-room of a flat in Muswell Hill, he found six VCRs hooked up to six tellys, another four hooked up together for duplicating, and six DVD players, all still in their boxes. For a moment, Tom thought the guy was a thief like him. Then he opened the door to the room adjacent and wasn't too surprised to see a fair few thousand videos lining the walls. This lad was obviously serious about the subject. In the kitchen, there was a small wall-hanging of war medals, some possibly valuable, so Tom rolled that up and stuffed it into his duffel bag.

Four doors down on the same street, Tom poked around for five minutes in the bedroom of what must have been a teenage girl. The walls were plastered with posters of at least half a dozen boy-bands. Tom couldn't tell them apart. Blond, nice teeth and not a wrinkle between the lot of them. But under her bed he found a couple of dozen A4 pages she'd obviously printed off from the Visible Human Project website. Tom had heard about it but he wasn't ready for the detail of these pictures. Prime-body, average-build, healthy, disease-free and executed Death Row criminal, sliced by laser, from cryogenically frozen scalp to chilly toenail, into thousands of millimetre-thin slivers; myriad, majestic cross-sections, each one singing its stupid, murderous, sad and silent song, all in the name of science. And morbid curiosity. Tom, again, knew that he should hoick up and hightail it out of this house, or risk getting caught as a scabby and rotten thief. But the pictures were the most beautiful thing he had ever seen, and the most horrifying, so, again, he sat on his arse in a stranger's room, leafing through pictures that didn't belong to him, absorbed in the near-molecular terrors sheafed on his lap. The photographs were a quiet and sophisticated tantrum against death, a dreadless and good-natured romper-room which denied the very possibility of such a thing. The spliced-up man was as dead as a doornail, and these pictures said that it just didn't matter. The photographs changed the nature of such things as might be difficult to see and transformed the dead murderer into a vision very nearly Christ-like, in his beauty and in his helplessness.

What was a teenage girl doing with photos of human flesh that looked more like slices of smoked salmon, with lividly white bones in? Tom sighed, tucked three of the photos into his pocket and snuck off. The rest of the house had absolutely nothing worth stealing.

The next place was a mystery. It was a small, split-level

apartment in Bermondsey, where one entire wall of the kitchen was covered in cartoons. Tom, squinting and frustrated, turned his flashlight off and the kitchen light on. He had a good look at most of them, and most of them were brilliant, high and low. He leaned in to smell the yellowing patches where the paper rectangles had absorbed tiny spots of grease. He stood on tiptoe to look at the ones above the window and he bent double to clock the ones Blu-Tacked to the skirting-board. He jumped up and down, and dropped to his hunkers and he laughed and laughed and laughed his arse off for about ten minutes. It didn't bother him that the neighbours might notice. Most neighbours don't give a shit what goes on next door. Unless it's too loud. Tom scouted the living-room and the den, but all he found of any interest was a big, coffee-table book about the architecture of the Underground. So he took that to keep for himself.

The five-bedroomed beauty in Swiss Cottage, three nights later, had a carpet throughout the likes of which Tom had neither seen nor felt, ever. He sank in it up to his ankles; he actually felt as if his feet were drowning or something. He swiped three badly hidden credit cards, and a ton of jewellery, fed and patted their hopeless Great Dane and slid out of the huge dog-flap giggling, and cursing the bastards for being so rich. He had opened the bureau and read the letters from the doctors and from the hospital, and he laughed and swore anyway. Whoever owned a house like that was neither frozen nor skint, so fuck them. He swaggered home, all by himself, of course, in a flurry of shy and skinny curses, and cans of expensive lager, enjoying the brief and playful sprawl that comes with being a good thief.

A week later, Tom broke into a lovely, sweet-smelling two-bed flat in Hackney, crammed with educational textbooks (dozens in Latin), and discovered that the owner had blown up a poster of Teller to twice A3 size, and stuck it on her scullery wall.

No Penn. Just Teller, besuited and neat, with a hi-hat gleam in those eyes, and a nice but viral smile. A smile that said the lights are on and *everybody* is home. On top of the poster was sellotaped a small and slim strip of paper, with the word 'TEACHER!' scrawled in black biro. Tom had no idea what the hell *that* was all about, but the huge and unexpected picture unnerved him a little.

He was used to saccharine pictures of family and friends, or movie star posters, or similar. Not silent and supple anti-magicians with eyes delicate, dense and full of something a little chill. Eyes so clever they made him feel like a moron simply by looking at them. And like something else besides.

Tom sneaked upstairs where, in the spare room on a dusty dressing-table, sat three old-time, gorgeous Airfix models – a Spitfire, a Hurricane and a Lancaster. Huge and painted perfectly. What was a teacher doing with this kind of stuff? Envy rather than greed got the better of him this time, so he tucked the Spitfire under his arm and hurried downstairs, back past the super-pixellated picture of the calm, glacial and, probably, kindly Teller.

Those eyes reminded Tom of an occasion three months previously. He'd been strap-hanging on the Tube and had felt a rough finger on his collar. He'd turned to find himself facing a huge, pug-nosed, violent-looking bastard. Tom squared his shoulders, expecting the worst kind of trouble.

'Your shirt tag was up,' said the huge, pug-nosed, violent-looking bastard, and Tom had barely been able to contain his shame. The big man saw it, and he smiled a stale and small smile that, in the course of his tired life, he had gotten down to pained perfection. The eyes of Teller were the same. Bemused, sheen, placable and only partly insulted. Tom stood in the absent woman's scullery and stared again at the poster's graceful pose, shivering for a bit, then he fled out the back door, freezing and with nothing but the Spitfire.

And now there was the woman.

He knew the owner was female; he could tell what sort of person lived in a house the moment he broke in, and he knew instantly that this woman was more than interesting.

It was a three-bedroom flat in Crouch End, not more than seven hundred yards from where he was now renting a tiny flat. Had he seen this woman down the Broadway, or in one of the pubs? From the mail, her name was Lynne Callier. He searched her desk for photographs, and eventually found one with 'me and andy sept 99. Calais' written on the back. It was of a pleasant-looking fellow in a

Breton-style sweater and a woman with dark hair, sitting on a pier, looking at the yachts and cruisers in the harbour.

Tom stared at the photograph for far, far longer than he would normally have called safe, then he put it in his pocket and began a wander around her house.

It was the best house Tom had ever been in, bar none. Of all the stuff Tom had seen and pinched and, more often, seen and not pinched, this was the loveliest. She didn't seem to own anything terribly expensive in the way of furniture, but every available space was taken up with the kind of world Tom never wanted to leave. The living-room was four tall walls of books and music, lots of it vinyl.

Her bedroom was small and immaculate and smelled of musk, but lightly so. The ceiling was studded with thousands and thousands of glowstars and when Tom turned off the light and lay on the floor looking upwards, he could have been in an open field, on a clear and frosty night. The luminous spots fanned entire galaxies in the darkness, filling his entire field of vision. He even recognised some of the constellations, such had been her attention to detail. He lay there in the dark of her room, until his eyes began to water at the pinpoint lightshow, and his head hurt. He left the light off and bumped his way out and into the second bedroom. Tom nearly fainted. It was an indoor garden. She had filled every inch of floor space with every type of small and bright indoor flower worth having. The walls were dripping with exotic ferns and brilliant flowering cacti. She had temperature controls and water regulators and humidifiers and every conceivable type of ornamental pot.

And taking up a third of the room on the left-hand side were twenty-seven mature bonsai, each in its mini-landscape. Twenty-seven bonsai trees. He counted. They were amazing. Tom felt like Gulliver, afraid that he might put a foot wrong and crush this tiny forest. For a minute, he stood frozen and didn't know where to put himself. There was a stack of gardening books on the windowsill. Tom tippy-toed his way over and picked up the one on top. It was a huge hard-back volume about bonsai, and judging from the contents page, it seemed to cover everything – the history, the philosophy, basic techniques, advanced techniques, maintenance, seeds, styles, profiles and all the rest about these small and scary creatures. Tom forgot about the time, slid down the wall, folding his legs under him, and began to read a little.

Apparently, the art of bonsai arrived in Japan from China in AD 1195 and was originally confined to the aristocracy. A bonsai is created from either seed or cutting, and is kept to the desired size by pruning branches and roots, by regular repotting, by pinching off new growth and by wiring the trunk and branches. Further, Tom learned, a bonsai tree should always be positioned off-centre in its container because not only is asymmetry vital to the visual effect, but because, symbolically, the centre is where heaven and earth meet, and nothing should occupy this space.

Another aesthetic principle, according to the book's introduction, is the triangular pattern of foliage, which is necessary for visual balance and for the proper expression of the relationship shared by the life-giving, universal principle (or deity), the artist and the tree itself, a reflection of the Buddhist reduction of everything to its essential elements. In short, there are three basic virtues necessary for the creation of bonsai – *shin-zen-bi*, meaning truth, goodness and beauty.

Tom blinked and looked up at the plants but, try as he might, all he could see was tiny trees, gorgeous and all as they were.

Further along in the book, some twelfth-century commentator wrote that 'To appreciate and find pleasure in curiously curved potted trees, is to love deformity.'

The man had a point, but no one was listening.

Tom read and read and, after a while, he just couldn't put the book down.

In ancient China, *pun-sai* was the landscape of the imagination, and trees were often trained in the shape of lions, birds and dragons. These days, there were two overall types – the 'Classic' (*koten*) and the 'Comic' (*bunjin*), and five basic styles – Formal Upright, Informal Upright, Slanting, Cascade (in which the tip of the tree, on a near-horizontal trunk, drops below the base of the pot) and Semi-Cascade (in which it doesn't).

And there were loads of root styles – clasped-to-rock, root-over-rock and a dozen others. Maples are elegant for Formal Upright but not easy; larches and spruces are best. Crab apple, cotoneaster and pomegranate are perfect ornamentals for Informal Upright, but conifers are a good stand-by. Conifers are perfect for Cascade (and the winding main trunk should resemble a babbling stream meandering down a snow-covered mountain, apparently). And the cherry, the cedar and the juniper are recommended species for the Semi-C.

And so on and so forth.

Ideal pots and containers (dark, with *unglazed* interiors! The author couldn't stress that one quite enough).

The proper use of ornamental rocks (a volcanic conglomeration, ibigawa rock, is best. Avoid at *all* costs both marble and quartz, because their glittering quality detracts from the natural effect of the tree, and frost will easily split sedimentaries such as sandstone).

The use of accent plants to complement the tree itself (Mondo Grass, dwarf bamboo), and a hundred ways with moss. And lichens. Using tweezers.

And various things to do with wires, bamboo-skewers, trunk-chopping, drainage and tapering. After twenty minutes of reading this stuff, Tom could feel a nosebleed coming on.

At the back of the book was a gallery of photos of the most popular species. Tom struggled to his feet, scanned the beauties on the floor, licked his thumb and checked off the ones she had. She had a Creeping Juniper (*juniper horizontalis*), she had a Kurume Azalea (*rhododendron obtusum*), she had a Phillipian Banyan Fig (*ficus phillipensis*), she had a Japanese Maple (*acer palmatum*), she had a Queensland Small Leafed Fig (*ficus eugenoides*), and a dozen others he couldn't quite identify.

One of them, a delicate thing with twisted, tiny and confused-seeming leaves, Tom definitely recognised as a Lilac. It was almost definitely a Lilac.

Or perhaps, according to the book's index, a Flowering Quince.

Well, it was either that or a Trident Maple. Or a Golden Bellflower. Or possibly a Crepe Myrtle. Maybe.

Tom squinted as closely as he could at the pictures, and then at the plants, and then back at the pictures again. The room began to swim in front of his eyes, in a glossy and thoroughly stupid panorama of green, tiny and adorable things. Small and pesky leaves all over the shop. Tom was not used to this brand of brutal and synaptic delicacy. He was not accustomed to pretty things wafting around in his field of vision, around and about, and up and above, as if loveliness could be a temporary tactic against the spooked and the miserable.

Why the hell couldn't the woman have normal-sized plants, like everyone else?

Tom dropped the book and almost indulged himself in a clump of mashed and unreasonable self-pity, nearly teary but not quite, thank-you *very* much.

Tom was not used to beauty. Now and again, in a ho-hum way, okay. But not often. And not often enough to make him weep, that was for *damn* sure.

One Acer must have been at least seventy years old. It was a complicated, gnarled and handsome bastard, about a foot high and with impossibly small leaves, each no bigger than a piece of confetti.

Tom picked it up.

Then he put it back.

Then he picked it up again, cursed under his breath, and put it back.

And contented himself with just looking at it really, really hard for a minute or two.

The third bedroom was filled with her comics, magazines (including dozens of *National Geographic* from the fifties and sixties, with the maps still intact) and, on the walls, six original oils. Abstracts. Too big to steal, thought Tom, grateful. And a green, ten-speed racing bike.

Downstairs, he stood on a chair and wobbled along the stacks of books, humming quietly with glee. All his favourite stuff. Gorey and Seuss and Dick and Dora. Goodis and Thompson. Canin, Bloom, Carver and Mukherjee. Tons of Stephen King. All the classics, and a lot of books on poker, for some reason. And thousands of others.

Then he had a go at the music. It was a Thursday night and coming up on twelve. She could walk in any moment. Tom sweated and scanned and sweated, and he just couldn't leave. Not yet. He tried to dive into the pile of cassettes without causing too much of a mess, and through the albums without breaking anything.

She had tons of old vinyl, hundreds of albums, most of them covered in snake-like streaks of dust, as if albums weren't her thing. But the 45s pile was higgledy-piggledy in the extreme, as if she'd been traipsing through them, as drunk as a lord. Sleeves were all over the shop, and a fair few singles were stuck together with what smelled like Tia Maria.

Swiping his way through it, Tom wasn't sure if she had bought the singles because she liked the tunes or because she just fancied the names – Tallulah Gosh, The Flaming Groovies, Flesh for Lulu, Blue Rondo à la Turk, Rip, Rig and Panic, Raymond Scott's Manhattan Research Inc.

Some of them he'd heard of. Most of them he hadn't.

Either way, he faffed his way through some of it, and the thieving instinct in him made him want to lift most of it too.

Tom had no idea that Anthony Perkins was a singer long before he became a movie star. The album, showing Perkins wrapped around a chair and looking about fourteen years old, was tucked at the back of the pile. She wouldn't know it was gone, not unless she went looking for it specifically.

He walked quickly around the flat, tidying up anything he might have disturbed, then slipped out the back door, the album tucked under his arm. It never ceased to amaze him how many people had no burglar alarm.

In the small hours, back in his own bedroom, Tom had a choice of four state-of-the-art sound systems. He hadn't yet decided which one he would keep. The Bang & Olufsen, probably. He reflected that one of the beauties of modern technology was that it made everything smaller and, obviously, easier to carry.

Side One was a litany of slightly sub-standard fifties lounge-songs. The first track was 'April Fool', an undemanding piece. The production was muddy and the vocals were drowned by a chunky, bossy piano. 'But Beautiful' was better, clearer, and the voice managed to make its point a little.

And then, five tracks in, came 'I Cling To You'. Tom, gently pacing with a can of Stella, stopped dead in the middle of the room. Perkins must've gotten himself a new producer. Tom had never heard anything like it, like that voice. It was the purest, most luminous sound he'd ever heard. Every sweaty, clanking pop song he had ever adored evaporated from his head, and he crumpled, imbecilic, into a chair. He played it over and over and over, then put the song on a good-quality tape and transferred it onto a rewritable CD. He put the disc on repeat, took off his clothes, climbed into bed and listened to the words until dawn. He was exhausted, but beyond sleep.

> I cling to you
> As flowers cling to sunlight.
> My heart knows but one light.
> I cling to you.
>
> I bring to you
> A love that has no equal,
> No end, and no sequel.
> I cling to you.
>
> I'll bring to you
> A heart that never falters.
> As incense to altars,
> I cling to you.

As lilacs cling to Maytime, as daydreams to daytime. As sailboats cling to breezes, as songs to reprises. After two hours and forty repetitions, Tom's eyelids were stuck together, and he knew every note and syllable and inflection.

Though to our surprise, new stars may gem the skies, though nations fall or rise, still my love is true. The lyrics were old-fashioned and sentimental, but Tom liked the clever rhymes, and he liked the voice. He liked the fact that he had his own place, where he could play his own stuff at any hour, where his own little aural shindigs didn't bother anyone.

For another three hours, he just let the song go on in its tangled, terse and unfathomable way, washing over him sweating in his bed, like a beautiful bruise, a wound laid properly and grammatically upon his ears. The noise wasn't that happy and it wasn't a winner. It was just a series of precarious, stunning moments in his head, glued together by his thoughts of Lynne Callier's face. It was a tiny, prized constituent of what he wanted his life to be about. Something not renegade and barking, but a thing fulsome and backcombed and polite.

He turned off the CD player at 10 a.m. and, after rummaging around in his jeans' pockets, stumbled back into the sack and fell asleep with her photograph in his fist.

The woman lay and daydreamed and tried to ignore the ward's peppery smell. She thought of her brother Liam, who'd made his living on the horses. He was a rough-looking individual, and the quietest man she ever knew. He hardly spoke all the time she was growing up, and then only in monosyllables. But he made enough money every week to ensure that he didn't have to work. He scared her a little. When he was well into late middle age, he opened a hotel in Carrigart, Donegal, which became renowned for its lousy food, indifferent service and cramped bedrooms. But it was the only hotel for miles in what is probably the most awesome coastal landscape in Ireland. So, Liam would charge English tourists a fortune, which they seemed happy enough to pay, for the privilege of communing with nature for three days, and negotiating the minefield that was the hotel menu. She visited him just the once, when they were both very old, just to say hello. Liam spent all his time propping up his own bar and talking about how we were being colonised all over again. Once it was spices and tobacco and sugar, now it was 'stress reduction' and 'cultural connectedness', as if the whole country was some kind of fucking spiritual Jacuzzi.

'Stop relaxing all over us!' he would snap at some poor tourist, and then charge him a fiver for a gin. Liam died of pancreatic cancer ten years later, a well-off and clever and lonely man. She felt a pang of shame for not visiting her brother more often.

But then again, he never came to see her, so to hell with him.

The woman turned over in her bed, very slowly, and carried right on thinking. Thinking and wincing and ashamed, because she wasn't as clean as she might have been.

Lynne

What Lynne Callier didn't know about both cosmetic and corrective surgery, you could get on the back of a postage stamp. She had looked at a thousand photographs of breasts, before and after. Cleft palates, burned eyelids, bee-sting lips, suctioned hips, strung-back eyes, mucus and bandage and all the rest. The guest on this afternoon's show was a woman who had been in a fire and, as principal researcher, it was Lynne's job to find out as much as possible about the surgical procedures involved in her recovery. The woman, whose name was Lydia, showed up beautifully dressed at the studio at 11.15 a.m. and was met at reception by Paul who smiled and chatted and smiled and showed her to Studio Three, then ran to the gents and threw his guts up. Paul was a polite boy but not strong of stomach. To be honest, thought Lynne, as she shook hands with her, although her skin wore that distressing sheen, with scabby interruptions, Lydia wasn't actually very disfigured. It was just her eyes. It was the way her eyes didn't seem to belong to her face. It really was quite frightening. It was like the tiny, quiet thing in a horror movie that has you jumping out of your skin even when nothing is moving, and the sound-track is being quiet and civilised.

Poor Lydia seemed to have learned this lesson, and kept her gaze fixed almost exclusively on the carpet throughout the interview.

Lynne could've cried for her. Lydia was a nice, funny woman for whom self-consciousness had become a way of life. She managed to get through the moronic questioning from her well-meaning hosts with a brisk and heart-breaking dignity. After the show, Lynne took her for a drink in a pub nearby, but it was just awful. Fellow drinkers kept sneaking looks, without meaning to, at

Lydia's ruined and fascinating face, and Lynne kept repeating herself because she couldn't keep her glance off their glance until, eventually, Lydia patted her hand and announced, with her eyes fixed on the ground, that she'd be off then, thanks.

Sometimes Lynne really hated her job.

Lynne was one of the best researchers in the business, and everybody knew it. There was nothing she couldn't find out and she didn't need the internet to do it. She simply had an unerring eye for interesting stuff and, more importantly, for how to use it. If the guest was some loud-mouthed, right-wing, refugee-baiting, fag-hating pundit, Lynne knew that you didn't get to him by asking why he was right-wing. You skewered him by asking why he used to be left-wing – everybody was – then you produced a brilliant photo for the hosts to wave around, showing said fascist loved-up, half naked and totally stoned, thirty years ago on the Isle of Wight or somewhere similar, surrounded by his equally spaced-out hippie friends. And then you tracked down the friends, who were now living ordinary, middle-class lives, and holding vaguely liberal views on most things, and seemed like awfully nice, civilised people, with their lovely kids and their Labour Party membership cards. And then, after all this cosy footage, you asked your by now jittery guest – what went wrong? Why did he alone turn out to be such a bitter, fearful person, lonely and a bigot and so full of hatred? What happened to his life?

Exit one deflated guest to huge audience applause, and, for two minutes, the hosts get to look like Albert Schweitzer and Simon Wiesenthal rolled into one.

According to Paul, he found one such casualty crying his eyes out in the loos. Lynne didn't give a shit. He'd be back at the same nonsense next morning.

That kind of gig was a doddle. What Lynne really enjoyed wasn't the political stuff, but the times when she was able to slide onto the agenda subjects which interested her. She would make a suggestion to the hosts, Clare and Robert, about this or that and, sure enough, after a decent interval they would decide they wanted it on the show, and if Lynne could do the groundwork, that would be great, thanks very much.

Last month, they interviewed the director of London Zoo, who was keen to talk about the recent raft of educational programmes the zoo had introduced in tandem with thirty-seven north London schools. It was a terrific initiative, welcomed by parents' groups, the local authorities and the press.

Then the poor man made the mistake of mentioning the pandas.

Well, at that Robert jumped in, armed with Lynne's personal text.

Let the panda go.

The director blinked several times, not quite sure what they meant. Let the panda go? This sounded positively blasphemous. And then the pair waded in with the statistics they'd fallen in love with, the kind of 'facts' that made them look rather groovy, and as dangerous as daytime telly can be:

The panda should've been extinct years ago.

The female is fertile for about fifteen minutes in April.

The male has virtually no libido to speak of.

The male panda's penis is about three centimetres long.

The panda subsists on one rapidly disappearing type of food.

And finally, whatever offspring is produced is often crushed by the mother.

So, asked Clare, why do we insist on shipping the damn things from international zoo to international zoo, from Berlin to New York, from Beijing to Chicago, when God and Nature are clearly trying to tell us something? Let the panda go.

The director put up a valiant and cogent defence, correcting their mistakes, and citing biodiversity and the possibility, long-term, of repopulation in some areas of South-east Asia, with the co-operation of his learned colleagues in institutions across the world.

But it was too late. The audience had begun to enjoy the *frisson* of condemning a species to death, under the guise of a spurious scientific determinism, and were now whooping the mantra 'Let the Panda Go' to the tune of 'The Farmer Wants a Wife'.

You had to hand it to them. Nothing fazed this lot.

By that time of the day, Lynne was usually at home in bed, her work done. She had absolutely nothing against pandas; she just found it fascinating – the way she could present an idiot with information which was essentially true, and then watch him use it to turn an amiable audience into a cheerfully baying mob, simply because he was able to read out a list and pronounce the word 'photosynthesis' without mucking it up too badly.

To Lynne, information was sacrosanct. As a teenager, she had lost friends because they couldn't identify this cartoon character, or that Korean premier, or the guy in the Milk Tray advert, or Zbigniew Brzezinski. Lynne pissed a lot of people off. She didn't know she was doing it. She just wanted to get her O levels. Which she did. Nine of them, in fine style. A couple of years later, the night she and her friends went out to celebrate her A levels, Lynne was having the best night of her life, until the DJ played Vanessa Williams's 'Save the Best for Last', and through her alcoholic haze, she actually started listening to the words. Well, that was the end of the brilliant night. Lynne started a drunken, ranting, forensic examination of the lyrics. That was one of her pet hates – sloppy song lyrics. Words that are stupid, or clichéd. Writers who inhabit a world where 'love' always rhymes with 'above', and 'baby' with 'maybe'. But the worst offenders, in Lynne's book, were the ones who just plain lied. Who deliberately got things wrong. And so, while her friends covered their faces in embarrassment, on what should have been the nicest night ever, Lynne staggered up to the stage, grabbed the microphone and took poor Vanessa to task for the hideous mistake of getting her facts wrong.

'Do you hear that? The very first line – "Sometimes the snow comes down in June", eh?' she squawked. 'Well, *that*, sweetheart, is total *bullshit*! Not unless you're talking about, maybe Australia, or something . . .'

She was losing the plot here, and her girlfriends cringed against the dancehall wall. A lot of people started to laugh.

'Well, okay, I don't like it,' slobbered Lynne, 'but I'm not gonna crucify the poor girl for it – maybe Vanessa's talkin' about some kind of freak weather conditions or something.' At this point, Lynne began to get the hiccups and thought she was going to throw up. But she carried on, regardless.

'*But* – the second line! The *second* line – Vanessa *really* kicks herself in the teeth! – "Sometimes the sun goes round the moon" – well I'm *sorry*, Vanessa, *but*, I think you'll find, *actually*, that it sodding well *doesn't*!'

The crowd, by this stage, wasn't sure if she was joking or not, which really began to upset her.

'For Chrissakes!' Lynne bellowed through a hail of feedback – 'The woman has taken the laws of God, man, physics and the natural universe, and turned them inside out and upside down! Just so that she can have something to rhyme with *June*!'

She carried on her tirade for another two minutes. Then she fell off the stage. And threw up all over her best friend's shoes. She kept most of her friends, but they all thought she was a bit odd. Nice, but a little intense.

Lynne had the perfect job for someone of her temperament. Her evenings were spent looking after her plants, and trawling the news stations and the net for possible items for the show. The voluminous files she kept at home were better than anything in the studio. She'd been keeping news, features, pictures and clippings on just about anything that struck her as interesting, for as long as she could remember. She had a hundred crammed files on everything under the sun. She knew every inch of her files, her flat, her stuff, her smells, her dust. Lynne had a sense of place, of order, of chronology, second to none.

And she didn't have to go looking for the album to know that it was gone.

*

Tom woke up, played the song again, had a shower and some breakfast, and headed for Lynne Callier's house, this time in daylight. He parked himself on a bus stop seat across the road and got comfortable.

Lynne was excited about work today. She had been given an interviewing assignment, and was due to meet him in the bar in Brown's. Now and again, they let her loose on a real human being, and the studio assumed that her career ambitions were the same as every other researcher's – to wind up on screen, presenting her own show. They were wrong. Lynne had no ambitions in that direction. She was perfectly content with what she was doing. Besides, she despised most of the presenters, and some of them could smell it in her chilly demeanour on the rare occasions when they crossed paths. No, Lynne simply wanted to keep on doing what she was doing for as long as possible. She had never chased after success. She had simply always run away from failure. Well, she had a satisfying, reasonably well-paid job, and that was good enough for her.

The interviewee was John Kelso, the minor celebrity who'd had his own late-night movie show on cable up until the beginning of the year. He didn't have his own show any more; he was better known these days for having been abducted and held hostage by a crazed fan for a week in January. And he'd written a screenplay, apparently.

The station bosses had almost fainted with pleasure – one of their minor presenters, a member of their own staff, could apparently generate as much obsessional interest as some diplomat in Beruit or wherever.

They issued a sombre, big-font internal memo to all personnel about the need for vigilance and security awareness. (Naomi, the canteen supervisor, took it very much to heart and hyperventilated on the floor for fifteen minutes, until someone gave her a paper bag to breathe into, and someone else told her that she wasn't a celebrity, and to stop acting like a stupid bint.)

When John was released and the lunatic arrested, the PR unit had gone into hyperdrive. It was a huge story for all of a month.

Clare and Robert thought that it might make a good story to find out what the cable guy had been up to since the incident, how he'd coped etc. and if there were any lingering psychological problems, or PTSD, and Lynne was just the girl to ferret it out. They hated cable, and weren't about to let professional courtesy enter into it.

Lynne wanted to do a decent and professional job, but somehow she dreaded trying to talk to this man about the incident, the thing. The incident. She knew what men were like, and she just knew that she would probably have to winkle the whole thing out of him, syllable by syllable. Like pulling bloody teeth. She had always been fascinated by the way people behave when they know they're being watched. Like the guy last year, whose wife disappeared. He appeared on television, asking for her safe return and, because his demeanour was so nonchalant, so laid-back, the police took *him* in for questioning. Turned out, it wasn't nonchalance, it was utter shock – the poor bastard was so traumatised by everything that was going on, he barely had the power of speech. Lynne was in awe of the liars too, the weepers who turn out to be the culprits, but the people who fascinated her the most were the ones everybody *knew* were innocent, who seemed to have lost any ability to feel. They would appear on the steps of some courtroom or other, and repeat in a passionless monotone whatever their lawyers had written for them, instead of roaring and screaming into the mikes.

And leaders at national tragedies. How do they do it? Major at Dunblane, Blair at Omagh, Clinton at Oklahoma. Not a break, not a tear. Lynne didn't blame them – upright and dignified control, that's what people needed at such times. It was simply that she didn't understand how they managed to get through it without collapsing in a careless heap of grief, while she sat at home, bawling and weeping and carrying on like a mad thing in front of her TV. Men were, in fact, mostly a mystery to Lynne.

John Kelso was a nice-looking man, and he sat slightly buried in one of the huge leather armchairs of the bar. He stood up as Lynne introduced herself and fetched her a glass of white wine from the bar.

And then he started to talk.

Not that slowly but with a degree of care and thoughtfulness.

He talked about some of the things that had happened at the beginning, between him and the skinny guy with the skin and the accent. John was dignified and hangdog at the same time. He spoke of the franchise of minor humiliation which seemed to have grown up around him afterwards, about the romper-room farrago that his life became. About fans who are more like cannibals than fans, with love and cruelty to spare.

He knew that what had happened to him could be called serious applause in the night, or minor sadism, depending. The genial funk of a dozen jokey newspaper articles was not going to deal with that in a hurry. And so on and so forth, he talked, deadpan, of deadened nerve ends and frazzling fear, and the kind of hysterical joy upon freedom that can do a body *nothing* but harm. Especially when you're not taken seriously. Especially when in some quarters it's seen as a rather good publicity stunt.

John talked about a quiet, chin-stroking little life with this interesting, corrosive pantomime attached.

About a life crammed with detail and quite, quite empty.

But although John talked well and easily, he didn't actually say a word about what had really happened in that week of his life. He swerved and quietly pondered other related issues, and it wasn't until afterwards that Lynne realised that she'd come away with nothing.

John drank his drink and looked Lynne straight in the eye, and asked her what was her favourite movie of all time.

Lynne, by now trembling a little, thought about it for three seconds, and told him.

Then they sat and just looked at each other for a little while.

The Doctor was now calling in on her several times a day. Hovering and talking. His voice was solicitous. But there was a trace of something else. An enquiring tone, a little something, almost like resentment, as if he had to bite his tongue, to stop himself from asking the question – why are you still here? She hadn't spoken to him, or the nurses, since she'd arrived in this place. They didn't seem to mind it so much. If they could keep her fed and watered and not have to chat, then so much the better. The ward was so bright. She longed for shadows, for a cool, kind darkness where she could drift and think about the past, knowing that nothing mattered any more. The faces of her sisters, of her mother, floated across her mind, and she thought she could hear the noises of a sunlit outdoors, of dogs and horses, and childish giggles on the breeze. All her friends.

Everyone.

Everyone she ever knew was gone, long dead. She no longer knew how old she was.

And still he hovered, his question on the back-burner. She didn't know why she was still here, but she knew she wasn't going anywhere. Ever.

Kenny

Kenny Duthie's family had worked the same farm forty miles south of Aberdeen for almost a hundred years. When Kenny was twelve, his father had a long bath, then went out into the barn and shot himself in the head with the shotgun he was always careful to keep locked away in its custom-made safe, especially when the kids were small. There was a lot of that amongst the farmers in Aberdeenshire, although most of them used a rope rather than a gun. The farms weren't viable any more. Annual income could be as little as £5,000, and that for a whole family. And then BSE and foot-and-mouth put the lid on it. Meanwhile, their fishermen neighbours were racing around in BMWs and Saabs. But with the EU quotas system, and disappearing stocks, things became pretty tight for everyone.

Kenny's elder brother was outside at the time when he heard the blast and, galloping to the barn, found his father's body. He wouldn't let Kenny over the threshold. Kenny had never been able to figure out whether or not his brother got over that, but he knew one thing for damn certain – he wasn't going to be a farmer. He would be an actor or a director or a producer or a scriptwriter. Anything to do with the movies would do him.

At sixteen, he got a job with a painter and decorator's firm in Aberdeen. Andy was a good employer, a hard worker himself, and wound tighter than a spring. Nice, middle-class couples would ask for a quote on a paint job for their living-room, and Andy would give them a ten-minute lecture on their lousy colour scheme, awful furniture and ugly children. But he was a laugh and he was a nice guy. Kenny actually got the chance to become good at something. A craft. A trade.

It was a neat team. One of the other guys, Douglas, was a part-time mature student in English Literature at Aberdeen University, and a semi-professional boxer. And a semi-legal boxer. He would disappear down the docks on a Friday, and show up for work on a Monday with gashes on his knuckles, a half-finished essay on 'The Nature of Obsession in *Othello*' jammed into the arse pocket of his jeans, and a terrible headache.

He's twenty-eight, thought Kenny, *he should have more sense*.

It was a miracle Doug didn't get himself arrested. He was a lovely guy, but obviously hadn't the slightest idea what he was supposed to be doing with his life. He had an ex-wife and a small daughter he hadn't seen in almost a year. When he got drunk, he was a weeper, but the rest of the lads didn't much hold it against him. They liked the fact that he was doing something close to clever and which didn't involve sweat and swearing. They didn't know that Doug was thinking of dropping his Eng. Lit. thesis, and writing a different one. One about the sociological nature of pain. About how a clever chap can be a sublime fighter, feted and cheered, then go home and write the whole thing up, spitting blood all over his pile of A4, and love every minute of it. Love the *concept* of pain, without actually enjoying the pain. And all the while thinking he's cleverer than he actually is. Doug knew it was foolish but, on a fight night, he generally got through three pages of notes before he passed out. He had more dental appointments than anyone Kenny had ever met.

What the crew most admired about Doug was that, four years previously, he had worked in the city morgue. They were constantly asking him questions about those nights when he helped with admissions. All Doug would ever say was that, on a Saturday night, the place smelled like a brewery. He never told Kenny that, on his second-last night there, he'd seen Kenny's father's body brought in. He'd recognised the name and parish when Kenny joined the team. The man had been dead for about eighteen hours but, strangely enough, even with the gross head wound, he didn't actually look that bad. He had been a lean, fit gentleman in his late forties. His fingernails were tidy and clean. His skin still smelled faintly of deodorant. He just looked dead and still.

Doug had seen quite a few teenagers, with two days' worth of driving licence under their belt, who looked a hell of a lot worse.

For seven weeks Douglas wanted to find out if Kenny had seen his father's body, and if he hadn't, to tell him that his dad had looked okay when they buried him, even though it had been in a closed coffin. But he never did. It's a difficult one to just drop into the conversation in the pub.

Besides, if he was honest, working in the morgue had been a huge laugh. One puerile prank after another. It was also the noisiest, most obstreperous place Doug had ever known. No respect at all. So he kept his mouth shut.

Kenny could count. He knew that Doug had been working there on the night in question, but he didn't have the energy to ask. He just made notes and kept his ears open.

He also found time, late at night before he forgot them, to write down Andy's lurid and lovely tales from thirty years' worth of commandeering other people's homes.

Kenny worked really hard and, every night in his bedroom, although he was exhausted, made notes for what he was sure would, one day, be his masterpiece.

The money and the three-piece snobbery. The artistic, supporting-wall triumph and the brick-dust ruination.

Andy and his brilliant gob. Douglas and his divided life and his lost daughter. The rest of the lads and the twinkling shambles that was their lives. The boss with his spirit level and his cowed clientele.

The splendid pub bullshit. The boxer. The morgue. Whatever.

He was using it all, all of it, in the screenplay he was writing in his spare time. This was just a dress rehearsal.

Kenny's next job was with a guy who worked mostly for the Council, removing graffiti from around the city.

Most of it was just talentless tagging, but some of it was astonishingly good. Kenny started bringing a camera with him to work, just so that he could record the stuff before the rest of the team got out the solvents.

There was one guy in particular, who painted numerous versions of his nickname – '*KNOWN*' – all over town.

God, this guy had talent coming out of his ears. Every piece was different in the range of colours used, but his stringy, ligament-like signature had an unmistakable dynamic all its own. He never simply tagged. His work was a luxuriant, glutinous riot of colours, styles and politics. Most graffiti kids base their stuff on what they hate. *KNOWN* didn't seem to hate anyone or anything. In fact, his work oozed love and nothing but. Daft caricatures of his heroes, cartoon figures, his own mother (although this one he skewed sufficiently for identification to be impossible), film stars – he did them all, on any surface he could find.

All his murals were thoroughly gorgeous, and the Council hated his guts.

Mark, the graffiti team boss, tended to avoid removing them for as long as possible, to his credit. Kenny suspected he was a fan, like almost everyone in town. In a way, the graffiti removal team became a bunch of art critics; if a wall piece was really good, they would agree to leave it alone for a week, so that Kenny could clean up around it and get some decent photos. Some were quite special.

But *KNOWN* was in a class of his own. Everybody in the city knew at least one of his walls. His bossy, beautiful signature, if he had the time, undisturbed in the middle of the night, would spiral off into delirious depictions of mermaids or unicorns or Seurat's bather on his feet and pissing, pointillist-style, into the Seine, or Noddy Holder in his mirror top hat, or Homer Simpson or, on one bizarre occasion, Franklin D. Roosevelt, complete with a wheelchair which appeared to be gold-plated. The latter was found on the gable end of a nursing home. It was eleven feet high and handsomely rendered. FDR appeared in a dignified black and white, and most of the elderly residents, some war veterans, seemed to like it.

Another of *KNOWN*'s better-known works was a huge, gun-grey picture of a submarine, sitting ten feet high on the side wall of the Council's Social Services building. It was an alarmingly realistic craft, but without markings; no one could tell if it was supposed to be German, British, Japanese or what. In the watery streams around it, blue and green, were floating bodies of all shapes and sizes. Some were cartoons, some not. Some of the blood was proper red, some silly-purple. The overall effect was Tex Avery crossed with *Das Boot*. The Social Services staff loved it. They would amble and dawdle in the car park and make obscene and ruptured jokes amongst themselves, and laugh like lanky hell and all get out.

The Council had no idea who this so-called artist was, and the Cleansing Director began to get the impression that his graffiti 'hit squad' wasn't as diligent as it might have been.

Kenny went right on that summer, taking photos and stealing stories, and the rest of the guys thought he was just great. Most of them were young fellows who would have been doing other things, given the chance, and while they liked having a decent job, they were not impervious to some of these paintings. One of them, David, was a nineteen-year-old marine biology student on a summer job, and he had just finished setting up a website dedicated entirely to Dan Castellaneta, so he was pretty fucked off when the director *demanded* the immediate removal of the Homer painting from the side of the Sainsbury's supermarket.

Kenny bought him several beers and took notes.

Visitors to David's web page later must have been surprised to come across, in amongst a biography, pictures, downloads, a filmography and links to other sites dedicated to Mr Castellaneta, an angry, drunken rant against the director of the Cleansing Department of Aberdeen City Council.

The next gig for the team was in a fishing village down the coast from Aberdeen, to remove some graffiti from coastal rocks. For years, the rocks just beyond the beach had been covered in three-foot-high, gloss-paint letters spelling out the names of different members of the same family. The Andersons. And every year, the Andersons added a few more names. Uncles, cousins, newborn babies. And the police did nothing. Kenny was stunned when he saw it. Six hundred yards of pure vandalism. Ruined rocks in red and yellow against a backdrop of the most beautiful scenery he'd ever laid eyes on. The tourists were disgusted, so the local council finally decided to do something. Mark's team set to work. Because the rocks were darkish, conventional sandblasting would leave them unnaturally whitened, so the team had to use sand mixed with coal slack. And they were at the mercy of the tides so, over two weeks, they worked both in the early morning and in the middle of the night. It was the hardest, filthiest job Kenny ever had, but the best result. Gradually, after a fortnight of back-breaking work, the vista of rocky outcrops was purified, restored.

When, on the fifteenth day, the team went to a local pub to celebrate a job well done, they were perplexed by the chilly reception they received from the locals. Apparently local folk had been watching their efforts with a growing sense of resentment. They didn't want the rocks cleaned up. It was part of local culture. The names had been there for years. At this, Kenny nearly choked on his beer. *Jesus*, he thought, *if you hicks are going to get protective over something, make it something* worth *preserving, for God's sake.*

He was on his fourth pint and didn't realise that he'd said it out loud, and by the time Mark discovered that the barman's surname was Anderson, it was too late. The team were dragged outside and beaten senseless. Just for doing their job.

From that day onwards, Kenny hated small towns. He hated the sea. He was getting out. David lost the sight of one eye.

Kenny moved to London a month later, still writing what he was convinced would be the script of the century.

He got a dream job as assistant manager with the Prime Time video store in Blackheath, having impressed the manager with his encyclopaedic knowledge of movies. He rented an okay, cheapish flat in Eltham, and just carried on writing. He didn't go out. He didn't socialise. He spoke to no one but shop assistants. He wrote longhand, he worked, he got cable and a PC, he wrote, he took movies home from work and despised them, he watched television, and he wrote, he tried new things for his skin, and he did not consider himself to be desperately lonesome.

Sometimes he had dreams about his father, and Douglas and the morgue, but it always turned into something ludicrous half-way through, like a Broadway musical, with his headless father in a tux, twirling a cane, or a boxing movie in which Douglas always died in a lousy heap. He stopped phoning his family in

Aberdeenshire after a few months. He didn't know why. Perhaps because it was too much of an effort, and he was dog-tired all the time. He never thought he would be the kind of man to just give up like that. But, well, there it was. He began to write letters instead.

That would have to do.

Very late one Tuesday night, Kenny discovered John Kelso's show.

After twenty minutes, Kenny was bristling with excitement. Here was a kindred spirit, someone who would understand what his story was about. Who could open a door, or give him a break, or *something*. He was tired of writing, with no end, no reader, in sight. John Kelso became his late-night guru. Kenny began to watch the show while taping it, then watch it again when he got back from work. And once more before that night's edition. Which he also taped.

Kelso was perfect. He wasn't a snob but he could've been. Kenny liked the way Kelso seemed to regard *Pepe Le Pew* as a cultural icon as valuable as Randle P. McMurphy. Perhaps more valuable. And there was absolutely no way of telling whether or not he was serious.

Kenny tried to phone in one night, and was told, frostily, by the receptionist that John Kelso doesn't *do* phone-in. For Kenny, that made it even better.

Sometimes Kelso treated big-budget, calamity movies and meat 'n' two veg movies with exactly the same degree of slinky rapture, or falling-asleep contempt. And sometimes he loved a film so much, from either category, he was rendered almost speechless. But, more than anything, John Kelso was in control. He knew his stuff, he knew his history, and that wee, salty audience, judging from the dozen or so websites, just loved him for it. These keen types even knew his car registration number.

Kelso managed to be stealthy and vain, a clever-clogs and miserable, all at the same time. Kenny realised that John Kelso was his best hope. Kenny was going to meet him, and he was going to read Kenny's script. Whether Kelso liked it or not.

One evening, when Kenny had been working at the video store for three months, a customer came in and asked for a refund on a film which Kenny had recommended.

'I didn't like it,' was his excuse. Kenny laughed, then realised the guy was serious.

'You can't get a refund on a movie just because you didn't *like* it,' replied Kenny with more venom than was necessary.

'That's not the point,' said the man. 'You're supposed to be the expert. I trusted your opinion. You were wrong. And I want my money back.'

His tone was even, non-threatening, polite. Kenny instantly hated him. The ignorant swine thought watching a film which disappoints was like buying a new shirt and finding a loose thread, or buying a bottle of wine which turns out to be corked. The cretin thought he could just send it back, as if it wasn't already in his head. As if the experience never happened.

The movie was *Hellzapoppin'*. Kenny thought it was funny and sweet and fresh. This guy thought it was incomprehensible. And it was old. Kenny hadn't told him it was so old. Or that it was in black and white.

It was made in 1940, you stupid fucker, thought Kenny – *what did you expect?*

Matters deteriorated and the discussion turned into a row. After a quarter of an hour, Kenny gave up and punched the man as hard as he could. He hit the carpet like a sack of spuds and scrabbled around on the floor, blood pouring from his nose. It was only when the other punters stood around staring, in shocked silence, that Kenny realised the man had his small daughter with him. She wasn't tall enough to be seen over the counter. Here she was, in a blue dress, watching her dad crying and bleeding all over the shop. She was about five and she was looking at Kenny with a look of absolute terror, the likes of which he had never seen in his life.

The manager sacked him about five minutes later, hauling him bodily but gently out onto the pavement, and whispering into his ear that if he wasn't prosecuted, he would be a very, very lucky boy.

Kenny knew he was not an unstable person. He hadn't hesitated when he realised, with crystal clarity, that the moment had come and this man simply had to be punched. He had let the discussion go as far as it possibly could go, and then he had acted to end it. And that's all there was to it. The guy was an idiot, so now he had blood running down his chin and a trembling child, but he was still an utter fool. But Kenny had loved that job, and he was good at it.

A week later he got another job in Our Price in Woolwich.

Two days after that he was fired again, because he got drunk at lunchtime and screamed five minutes' worth of the most awful kind of abuse at a schoolgirl who asked for Britney Spears's new single. No taste. That was the trouble with most people.

Kenny didn't care any more. He'd finished his story and he still had the handgun he'd brought from home.

He had three hundred and seventeen pounds in cash.

He spent fifteen pounds on canned food, twenty-four pounds on two bottles of decent Scotch, and a full day cleaning his flat, just in case ... well, just in case.

And thirty-three pounds on eight packs of Silk Cut. He didn't know if the man smoked but – no harm done if he didn't.

On the evening in question, Kenny printed out his screenplay, slid it into a sturdy envelope, put on one of his jokey T-shirts (it was the only one that was clean), his best jacket and some aftershave, and caught a bus to within three hundred yards of the studio. He had seven drinks in a pub nearby and, from closing time until 12.15 a.m., he just walked and sweated and wobbled in small circles around the studio car park, clutching the gun in his pocket, trying to think of a way of sneaking into the building.

Then, at 2.25 a.m., Kelso himself appeared at the fire escape door and stood hunched in the light drizzle, smoking a cupped cigarette, framed in the alchemical glow of a security bulb above the door. Kenny hid behind an old Vauxhall Nova and gawped like a moron. Kelso, at this distance, looked like a shivering, off-kilter thing, smoking and hopping from foot to foot in the cold. Kenny took his chance, his gun into his fist, his heart into his hands, and sneaked up the steps.

Up close, even though he'd gone pale with fear, John Kelso was a lot more handsome than he appeared on television. But smaller. And skinnier.

He looks a bit like a young Jack Nicholson, Kenny thought to himself, and then he remembered that he was pointing a loaded gun at the man's chest. He knew he was a bit drunk and he definitely didn't want to shoot the guy by accident.

Kelso looked at Kenny's T-shirt and he smiled. He seemed to like the joke.

Kenny considered this an excellent start. He told Kelso to get moving and the pair of them stepped carefully down the fire escape towards his car.

*

Tom watched Lynne's comings and goings from outside her house for a couple of hours every day for a couple of days. He noted her outfits, her timetable, whether or not she wore her hair tied or loose. Then he began to follow her wherever she went, and he did it without her knowing. He didn't get to be a fairly successful thief without learning to be partly invisible. He followed her to and from work, to the pubs she visited after work, to the salon at lunchtime from whence she would emerge exfoliated and mani-cured. Tom didn't know what had happened to him.

He didn't know why he was doing this. He was not the stalking type.

But he just knew that he had to be near her. He even sneaked back into her flat a fortnight later, on a Saturday afternoon after she'd left with two girlfriends, and placed the Perkins album right at the front of the pile, visible and brazen. And flopped down on her bed for half an hour while he was at it. As he lay there, he tried to remember the inky, starry night sky he'd bathed beneath, the pinpoints invisible, now, in daylight. He inhaled vague, clean musk smells and tried to remember the quality of the darkness, and the sheer, sweaty, tottering effort she must have put in to get all those stars up there.

He knew that this was insane, but he couldn't help it. He hadn't even showered. She would clock his presence right away, just by breathing in. And he knew that she would know there was something going on. A woman that smart, that organised – she must know. It was almost as if she was daring him to steal something big. Or do something noisy. She would call the police, or a nosy neighbour would notice him and tell her that there was this guy hanging around.

He wandered into her kitchen. Although it was daylight, he felt safe and unafraid, for some reason. Daylight was usually Tom's sleeping time, but he felt, here, wide awake and spun on his toes a little, with a gloomy brand of glee. This space was light and airy, with brilliant cooking pots and potted plants all over the place. He paced silently around the kitchen, opening cupboards and drawers and the conditioner slot of the washing machine, sniffing packets of rice, and checking the use-by dates on all her food, tinned, fresh and otherwise. That took him a while. She was okay on that score.

He stroked and watered, and said a few words to the plants that seemed to need it, but not many did.

Tom drifted and trotted, quietly, from sink to cupboard to window ledge, peering and poking, prodding her ornaments, scrabbling lazily through drawers full of cutlery and tin openers, trailing his fingers over and around Lynne's kitchen. He shook snowy, touristy paperweights up and around, he tasted bits of cold chicken from the fridge and carefully reravelled the clingfilm, he turned on the radio and windmilled around for a minute or so to Jimmy the Hoover, he rummaged silently in the cupboards and put the proper lids on the proper pots. He noticed that both of her yellow rubber gloves were right-handed and was tempted to turn one inside out so it'd be usable as a left one, and then he thought to himself – *no*.

Among her seven fridge magnets, there was a wooden, half-inch-thick likeness of Spiderman, an enamel Union Jack, a big, shimmering, aluminium dung beetle, and a small, red roundel, saying 'Mind the Gap'. On the wall beside the washing machine, she had hung a framed picture of Raoul Wallenberg and beside that, a huge black-and-white photograph of a near-naked Elle Macpherson prancing gorgeously around in the surf. He looked at that one for a while. Did this mean that Lynne might be gay? He turned around and, on the opposite wall above the cooker, was an even bigger, full-colour print of a half-naked Scott Bakula. Tom relaxed a bit. He washed her coffee mug and left it to dry on the draining board. He was about to wash the breakfast plate and the juice glass, and wipe down the surfaces, when a voice in the back of his head stopped him.

Before he made his way out the back door, he ploughed through her vinyl collection again, this time really taking his time. He pinched *Nashville Storyteller – The Best of Tom T. Hall*, Warren Zevon's *Bad Luck Streak in Dancing School* and *An Evening Wasted With Tom Lehrer*.

On his way out, Tom was tempted to break either a lock or a window, for the sake of professional pride, but he had neither the energy nor the heart.

Later that night, padding around his apartment in a quieter moment, he convinced himself that she wouldn't notice a thing. Everyone misplaces things, rearranges stuff, unbeknownst even to themselves. Books, LPs, scissors, pens, mugs. Nothing would seem amiss. She wouldn't notice.

And Tom's heart sank. He wanted her to notice. To notice and not be afraid, but to see and appreciate what he was at. And he didn't even know what he was at.

Nice way to impress a girl, Thomas, he thought. *Steal her albums and hope that she will swoon at your exquisite taste.*

Why the hell didn't she get an alarm system and stop acting like a damned tinker?

What the hell was wrong with him? Tom hadn't been with a woman since he'd left Belfast. Even back then, he had fallen hopelessly for any woman that was nice enough to sleep with him, and that wasn't many, before they scuttled away from him because he was so intense. Sometimes he loved living in a city, and sometimes he missed the Fermanagh countryside so badly it made his chest hurt. He'd tried to tell his couple of friends about the Marble Arch caves in Fermanagh, about how magical they were, the biggest underground caves in Europe. But his friends mostly shrugged and didn't care. Tom knew that the landscape of his childhood was only in his head, that everything changes, that the significant, grassy, mucky points of his memory were all gone, probably. Paved over, developed, drained. Only the River Erne itself would have remained unchanged, its island-dotted lunacy and utter lack of purpose.

That was one thing Tom liked about London – the river, and especially the aerial maps, showing its less than stately progress through the south-east. Half the time, the Thames doesn't have a *clue* where it is going. More than once it turns back upon itself, meanders all over the place for ten miles, before finding its bearings again and heading east towards the sea, as it should. And at the Greenwich peninsula, it actually heads north/north-west for a while, then manages to catch a grip. That map actually made Tom laugh out loud. It reminded him of the Erne. The river held a sensible route from Fermanagh north-west to the Atlantic, but the two loughs, Upper and Lower, with their insane patchwork of islands, made a joke of any type of coherence mapmakers might have tried to impose. So up until the fifties, they didn't bother. The longer he stayed in London, the more Tom missed being surrounded by a watery landscape of grass and rain. He missed the loughs. He missed the caves.

Lying in his bed, he remembered the first time, when he was ten, his uncle took him to see them. The weirdest things he'd ever seen. After tramping down two hundred steps into a lush ravine, and then onto an unsteady punt, he and his uncle and the other tourists were transported into a huge and high cathedral of rocks and stalactites and stalagmites, expertly backlit in mauve and red and gold. The vaulted caves were freezing and the walls dripped loudly on all sides of the boat. This massive, echoing space had its own soundtrack, a soft, wet boom, with accompanying human whispers and the slap of oars. Around every corner was another grotesque piece of tall, stony brilliance. The rocky shapes were huge and twisted and extraordinary, and the colours left him breathless.

Tom tried to climb out of the punt, to investigate the nearest stalactite, and claw and slide around the slimy dips, and he shouted like a mad child, all over the caves. His uncle had to get him hard by the throat and pin him down on the bottom of the punt and slap him across the head for a bit.

For a long time afterwards, Tom wanted to be a geologist, and pestered his teachers to tell him how to get there. Some were cruel and laughed, and some were kind and laughed.

Tom lay on his bed in his Crouch End flat full of stolen sound systems, DVDs, videos, TVs, and big boxes full of jewellery and large-denomination notes.

He never set out to be a thief. Or a man foolishly in love with a complete stranger.

He stayed in his bed for three days, playing the stolen records now and again, and not really singing along. He dozed and dreamed and crooned to himself, occasionally reaching out for the crisps and nibbles that hadn't gone stale.

He wondered what had become of the boy who thought that drowning would be a boy's best destiny, who knew, even at the time, that his uncle wasn't trying to kill him, who believed that stealing stuff would be a temporary, funny hobby. He wondered what had become of him.

On the evening of the fourth day, Tom hauled himself out of his bed, tidied himself up, taped the albums, sneaked back into her flat and left them on display, yet again. He wanted to stay in this space so badly it was almost like a pain in his guts. He tootled around miserably in the dark, smelling her air, then decided to go out for some minor therapeutic thieving.

Three doors down. First house, first room, and the bastards had a bonsai tree. A gorgeous, foot-high Satsuki Azalea with root-on rock, second to none.

Tom left in a quiet blur, took nothing, went to the pub, got blind drunk and staggered home crying.

This was ridiculous.

The Doctor read an article once in the Herald Tribune *about a Chicago hospital. He couldn't remember the name of the hospital, but he remembered the statistic. Eight grannies. Eight old women being dumped at the hospital door every week. That was back in 1991. The figure must have been well into the teens by now. Dumped at the door, usually in the small hours. Probably by desperate and impoverished families at the end of their tether. People who just couldn't cope any more. He still thought they were scum, to do such a thing. Bastards, to give up like that. It wasn't like that with this one. She didn't have any family. Every friend, relative and acquaintance seemed to have died years ago. Which was a little unusual. The authorities couldn't even identify her, which was, frankly, fucking ridiculous, and because she couldn't, or wouldn't, talk to anybody, he had no terms of reference. He hadn't known where to start with her. No small talk. No tender gabble about children or visiting hours. She was just* here, *like a hard pebble in your shoe, staring from beyond the horizon of the sheet, not making a sound, without a past. And old. Impossibly, impossibly old. No one could be that old and alive. But here she was. He was starting to take a dislike to her – no, it wasn't a dislike.*

She was beginning to frighten him a little. She was too old to be possible.

She lay and she slept and she breathed less noisily than most, and she ate a little softened food with the slow delicacy of a big spider, and her condition stayed exactly the same. Day after day. Blood pressure, heart rate, everything. She got no worse and she got no better. She moved cautiously in her bed and silently, slowly, began to drive him crazy.

2

In Brown's bar, Lynne suddenly felt like changing her mind about what her favourite movie was, but she didn't want to embarrass herself as a flighty thing. Although he wasn't working in the business any more, John wasn't too short of money. He had some savings and he wrote the occasional article for film magazines and for newspapers. And there was the screenplay. To Lynne, he seemed so relaxed, it was unnatural. They talked for another three hours and didn't mention either the movies or the kidnapping again. As the bar began to fill up, he asked to see her again, a nanosecond before Lynne was about to ask him the same thing. They arranged to meet on Saturday. It was like a date. It just seemed like the most logical move in the world, and neither of them felt awkward. The pair of them just smiled and nodded, and everything went very quiet in that 'ah, well' way that soothes and doesn't bother. As she stood up to leave, Lynne bowed forward and, for about two seconds, rested her forehead on his collarbone. She had only just met the man and yet it seemed entirely appropriate, and she was tired. John leaned in slightly to take the weight, and took a second to close his eyes and smell her hair. Her coat was tweed and smelled a little musty, but her hair was another matter entirely.

Saturday came and they had dinner in a nice Italian restaurant in Muswell Hill, close to where John lived, near the beautiful Odeon cinema. Back at his flat, Lynne wandered about, looking at his pictures and CDs, his plants and books. In the kitchen, Lynne asked about the empty velvet scroll hanging on the wall.

'Are you waiting to fill it up with something in particular?' she said. John flinched a little as he opened a bottle of wine.

'Not sure. The original, along with all my grandfather's war medals, was stolen a while ago. I feel pretty guilty about not having much in the way of a security system. Those medals were all I had to remember him by. My mother wasn't interested in them, so I said I'd look after them.'

John looked at the floor. 'Obviously I didn't do a very good job.'

Lynne was about to say something about her albums going missing and then reappearing, but decided that, next to war medals, it sounded petty. She wandered around some more, went through his record collection and put on Jimmy Buffett and, when John walked up behind her and placed two fingertips on her bare shoulder without saying anything, she leaned back a fraction and didn't say anything either.

Outside in the dark, Tom was perched lightly on a neighbour's fence, watching them both through the kitchen window. He remembered this house. He remembered all the videos. He still had the red felt scroll with the medals, tucked away in his room. So this was the fellow. Tom hovered there until they moved from the kitchen and out of sight. A light went on and, after a while, off in the bedroom upstairs. Tom sat for a little while, while his stomach churned, then he took himself off home. He had a large whisky and played the music he'd stolen, pacing the floor. Now the noises were just a vile paean to numbness. Tom T. Hall sang about how cold it could get in Des Moines, and a crying girl with her cheap suitcase, but instead of filling his heart with a glum hopefulness, and his head with Lynne's busy presence, it just made him feel worse. He turned it off and lay in his bed, listening to the sound of his own breathing. He tried to hate John, but couldn't quite get there.

Then he tried a little harder.

Six weeks later, on what would be their eighth date, a Sunday, John suggested that he and Lynne go down to Westminster and walk the south side of the river eastwards. To simply walk and see how far they got. To picnic and take it at a nice slow pace, and head for Woolwich and see if they made it before dusk. It would be a nice day out. They could get the bus back.

Truth to tell, John Kelso was afraid that he might be in love. He wanted to find out if he was. But he knew he was a spare and skinny proposition for a sensible girl, what with the baggage he'd been carrying around. He was going to have to tell her in full about the nonsense, about the guy with the gun and the accent and the skin. About the missing week.

*

Lynne met him at noon outside the Aquarium. She'd already spent two hours traipsing around inside. It was her favourite place of all. She adored its murmuring dark. You didn't have to look anybody in the eye, it was that dark, but could still absorb the muffled childish squeals as if they were part of the show. The dreamy, mesmerising sharks were her favourite. And, of course, you got to stroke the rays in their waist-high tank, stroking with your fingers right along their sandpapery backs. They almost seemed to like it, and certainly didn't flinch. For a fish to be acting like a cat – that was a nice joke, this time of the morning. So Lynne was in a good mood when John crept up on her. She was leaning over the railings outside, looking into the river. He grabbed her by the waist and pretended to push her over. For a moment she made as if to whirl viciously and clock the bastard, then she realised it was him and went limp, laughing and sprawling her arms around his throat and shoulders, hugging him tight. They both watched the Wheel for a while, and decided that would be their next date, if he could get tickets.

John had brought four cans in a bag, so they set off down the river with a foamy beer and an ice cream each. When they got as far as the Globe, they sat down.

'How come the interview never made it onto a slot on the show, Lynne?' John asked, looking sideways at her.

'Because it wasn't very good,' she replied, gaze fixed on the middle distance. 'We wouldn't have been able to find the right space for it, and they didn't want to spend the money on a crew just on the off-chance.'

She was lying. She'd gone back to Clare and Robert, and reported that Kelso was not show material. He was sensible and reserved and, when you got right down to it, boring. The truth was that Lynne didn't want him going on the stupid bloody show. He was better than that, and she couldn't have borne the thought of him having to sit there and answer their cheesy, inane questions. And a part of her was afraid of listening to the answers. She didn't want him vulnerable. She wanted him the way he was. The way he seemed to be. Strong, calm, in control. It had only been six weeks but Lynne felt as if she had known him for longer. *What a cliché*, she thought. But it felt true. She didn't usually go around tumbling into bed with a fellow on the second meeting (and, technically, first date), but frankly she didn't care. And it was as if it didn't matter whether they fell into the sack or not. As if that was incidental to what was going on elsewhere in their heads. He was thoughtful, not in the sense of being courteous, although he was, but in that he gave consideration to what he was going to say before he said it. Lynne loved that. It slowed the entire evening right down. Talking, and listening, to John was like falling into a warm bath in slow motion. The hackles dropped when she hadn't even realised they were raised, and she drifted into an easier, slinkier timeframe within minutes of seeing his face. Besides, he knew stuff. He was interesting. There had been a few moments when he was distracted and mildly hostile. Lost and thinking about something nasty. She just left him alone when he was like that. Still, Lynne hated lying to him. If he suspected, she hoped he would be relieved rather than disappointed.

'Ah well.' He sounded relieved. They turned around and looked at the Globe for a while. There were lots of tourists around. Business seemed good. The white wall sections were blinding in the sunlight.

They moved on a little way and John sat outside on a tombstone while Lynne took a short walk around the inside of Southwark Cathedral. Most of the tombstones had a skull and crossbones carved onto them somewhere. A lot of people found this morbid and off-putting. But John knew that it was simply an article of faith that, in order for the risen dead to be allowed entry to heaven, they had to be in possession of certain bones – namely, the skull and the thighbone. It was the mediaeval version of 'If your name's not down, you're not gettin' in, pal' for the dead. So the families paid stonemasons to do the necessary. Some of them probably did nothing else and made a good living.

John liked that notion. It was cheerful and optimistic, and not at all dispiriting.

A celestial back-stage pass. Access all areas.

He was still smiling to himself, face up to the sun, eyes closed, when Lynne kissed him lightly on the mouth and suggested they move on.

'Beautiful building, but why does it have to be filled with all those tombs, all that clutter? Same deal with Westminster Abbey. Hundreds of famous dead people. It should be totally empty. Empty and clutter-free is best, if you ask me.'

John took her hand, hauled himself off the tomb and, in that moment, realised for definite that he loved her, and his stomach flipped as he tried to think of how to broach the subject. He knew, even after this short time, that there was something in his demeanour that occasionally made her uncomfortable. Two nights ago, when he'd finished writing an article on the Coens for one of the Sundays, he'd shown up at her flat tense and· uncommunicative. He was okay after a glass of wine and half an hour, but sometimes he remembered what he used to have, and be able to do, and the anger and sense of humiliation would almost stop his heart. After they'd made love, he was quiet and funny and perfectly fine, but Lynne found herself wanting to ask what exactly had happened. And afraid to ask. And he could smell her discomfort. Okay, so he didn't have his TV show any more. Big deal. He still had plenty of money, a modest income on top, a nice flat. And the screenplay. He'd had months to put the incident behind him. Now he had met Lynne. And he was going to do just that. As they sauntered along the riverbank, John felt a sudden rush of hope, hope that he wasn't a neurotic freak, that he was capable of ordinariness, of ordinary love, that everything would fade and he would be left with Lynne and a clean slate.

They walked for hours, slowly, stopping to finish off the beers, to look at Butler's Wharf, the Design Museum, at the view west to the Isle of Dogs. It was around four and still sunny. The river twinkled and a few ferries chugged along, their tinny commentary just about audible. Every time John looked at the river, he wanted it to be ecstatically busy, but it never was. The river would probably never again be as busy as it was hundreds of years ago. They were both slowing down now, so John suggested that they rest at Greenwich. They sat on a bench in the park and watched the squirrels and listened to the sterile, annoying piffle of the pigeons, and smiled tiredly at each other.

'Lynne, would you like to hear what happened when I was kidnapped?'

He could have been asking her if she wanted espresso or decaf. Lynne looked away and nodded. A lovely breeze swept through the park and small children were everywhere throwing Frisbees, shrieking and yawning and tormenting pet dogs by pulling their ears and tails.

*

On the night in question, he had smiled at the young man's T-shirt because, for a moment, he thought the gun was a joke. They looked at each other through the drizzle.

The young man said, 'Hello, I'm a bit of a fan. I have something I'd like you to see.'

He sounded a little drunk and looked a little unhappy.

He jammed the gun in Kelso's ribcage and, as they headed for his car, Kelso wondered what on earth his crew was going to do when he didn't appear to add his comments on *The Kiss*.

He'd never seen a real gun before, just movie ones. He kept turning around to look at it. Kenny snapped at him to knock it off and keep walking.

As John drove the Saab through the deserted streets, he felt as if he was in a dream. He kept trying to say something, but couldn't think of anything appropriate, under the circumstances. Kenny sat in the passenger seat, sweating and giving directions under his breath and trying not to wave the gun around too much. He told John to pull up in the Asda car park at the back of Kenny's flat. As they got out, John gathered himself and looked up at the sky. The last thing he saw before Kenny took the keys and bundled him inside, was a cascade of stars, from horizon to rooftop, a pinpoint, wintry extravaganza of blackness and silver. It was the most beautiful thing he'd ever seen, and at that moment John realised that he was about to pass out from sheer terror. He stumbled over the threshold and up the stairs, with the gun bruising one of his ribs, and tried to ignore his heart's percussive antics as Kenny shoved him into the first-floor flat.

In the back room there were two chairs, a settee with a cushion and some blankets, a table, and nothing else. The room had no windows. There was a door open to a tiny bathroom on the right. John could see a toilet and a sink. The small window was blacked out with what looked like paint on the inside, and seemed to have bars on the outside. It was hard to tell. Kenny motioned at him with the gun to sit down in one of the chairs, then strapped him in with rope and duct tape.

Out of the corner of his eye, John Kelso spotted a potted plant, perched on a shelf. It looked like a tiny version of a nice, tall Mexican cactus, the type that rich LA types paid poor people to steal, so that they could have a big-bastard cactus on their lawn. A big-bastard cactus, reaching for the sky. Stunning, wild-west style, and ten grand minimum.

'What is it you want me to see?' he asked quietly. That's what the guy said. Something to see. Maybe he planned to sit John in front of a mirror while he slowly garrotted him. Kenny didn't answer, but circled the chair, tearing off noisy strips of tape, and sweating and breathing heavily, like some odd breed of silent, conscientious child.

'Do you have sinus trouble?' Kenny asked, leaning over him.

John looked directly into his eyes, and laughed. He couldn't help it. This was ridiculous. Kenny placed a piece of tape over John's mouth, and studied his face for a moment. When he was satisfied that John wasn't having any trouble breathing, he backed out of the room and locked the door.

In the hour and a half it took Kenny to drive the car five miles away, park it in a cul-de-sac, and walk back home, John had plenty of time to think about what was going on. The room was darkish, his nose was getting clogged up and he desperately needed to take a piss. If the guy was some kind of lunatic, then maybe he faced some kind of ghastly death.

At that thought, John felt the kind of fear he hadn't felt in a long time. He started to hyperventilate but he couldn't quite manage just through his nose, so his body just stopped it, and he calmed down a fraction.

The guy said he was a fan. What did he mean, 'something I want you to see'? Then the door opened, Kenny walked in and, after asking if he was okay, began to peel the tape off John's mouth. He seemed to understand that ripping it off is, contrary to popular opinion, not actually the most painless way. So he took his time, and peeled it off, millimetre by millimetre, while John breathed noisily and wetly through his nose, and glared at him, eyeball to eyeball. When he was finished, Kenny stepped back and offered him a paper hanky. John was still tied up so he leaned forward and blew into it, like a grumpy schoolboy, and let Kenny clean up his nose for him, like someone's maiden aunt.

'I'm really sorry about this,' said Kenny, tossing the hanky into a wastepaper basket.

Not as sorry as I am, you stupid cunt, thought John, by now recovered enough to start up some honest trembling. 'What do you want with me?' he croaked.

'I want you to read a screenplay I've written.'

John stared at him. 'No, seriously, *please* – what do you want?'

And Kenny stared right back. His face was utterly immobile, expressionless. 'I want you to read a screenplay I've written. And then tell me what you think of it.'

At that moment, John lost it. He was terrified and bewildered and now, almost speechless with astonishment and the worst kind of impotent anger. He roared, and tried to hurl and shoulder himself around in the chair. He managed a couple of metallic clangs, a couple of inches off the ground, and began screaming and swearing like a maniac.

Kenny was startled and bounced back a step, and pointed the gun at John's head.

John seemed scarcely to notice. He was totally out of it, thrashing around like a madman.

'And you *abduct* me for *that,* you useless *cunt*?!!' John screamed hoarsely – 'you stick a fucking *gun* in my ribs, and you threaten to *kill* me, and you make me drive all *over* the fucking shop, and you tie me *up* – and *all* for the sake of *that,* you *miserable fucker*?!! I should fucking *kill* you, you useless fucking *hack*! You think you're a fucking *genius,* don't you? Well, you're *not* – you're a fucking *moron,* and I don't give a *fuck* if you die *screaming,* so go ahead and *shoot* me, you sad sack, and *burn* your fucking so-called screenplay, while you're at it, you *cunt,* you fucking *maniac*!!'

He screamed and ranted for another minute or so, then stopped and lowered his head, exhausted, and began to cry. He didn't care any more. This lunatic was probably just going to shoot him anyway.

Kenny wasn't pointing the gun at him any more. He was leaning slackly against the table, partly for support. He was genuinely shocked. He'd never heard such language. Not directed at him, anyway. Well, not by anyone famous. He'd never imagined that John Kelso could have a mouth on him like that. Or could weep like that.

All he'd ever seen, and admired, was the Kelso on the telly. The moody, angular, brilliant, quotable hero. He never meant to create something like this. This crumpled, weeping thing – a thing, mind you, he was still scared of, gun or no gun. Kenny moved forward and laid a tentative palm on Kelso's neck, and said he was sorry. Kelso said 'Fuck you!' and Kenny felt a wee bit better.

They both just relaxed for a couple of minutes. John stopped crying and, surprised to find himself still alive, looked up and began to swear again, only this time under his breath. He looked Kenny square in the face. Kenny placed the gun on the table. He turned and leaned in close. John dropped his gaze. Kenny took out another clean hanky, and began to wipe away the tears and the snot on John's face.

'When I said there's something you should read, that's honestly all I meant,' he hissed into John's ear.

Then he unwrapped the duct tape and the rope. John didn't move.

Kenny dragged the screenplay out of the envelope and dropped it in Kelso's lap. It was heavy. Kenny moved to a chair by the table and sat down. John looked at the cover page. Then he looked at the gun, lying a few inches from Kenny's fingertips. Kenny was looking at him with a steady, interested gaze that froze John to the marrow.

He picked up the manuscript. It was very heavy. There was no sound in the grubby room except the sound of his breathing. He turned the first page.

The rustle was deafening.

Four hours later, he reached the last page.

He hadn't looked up once, at first because he was afraid it would provoke Kenny into doing something, and then because, after a while, he couldn't quite believe what he was reading. After ten or twelve pages, John was lost in the world Kenny had created. He was unaware of the fact that his fingers were frozen, unaware of his discomfort in the hard chair, oblivious to Kenny himself, who hadn't moved a muscle all that time, and was still looking at him with an expression that was either devoted or psychotic and possibly both. John couldn't tell.

It was the most brilliant story he had ever read.

John loved it, and right now, he hated this man's guts. He kept his head down, knowing that Kenny was waiting for him to say something. John's fear had evaporated in the telling of that story, in the steely mire of the script. Fear had drifted and been replaced by absorption. Even with a gun pointed at him, John was too much of a professional not to recognise a fantastic script when he saw one.

Yes, this one was a winner. It was not merely a great story with terrific dialogue; Kenny had also paid attention to every conceivable aspect of the film-making process. There were inserts and copious footnotes relating to the set design, the placing of the characters, the lighting and the sound. Every costume was described in detail, as were the specific make-up requirements of each protagonist. There were appendices detailing the names and addresses of catering companies, carpenters, security firms, couriers and all the rest. This film could have directed itself. It was perfect.

John wasn't afraid any more. The fear had been replaced by admiration. And then, as John closed the manuscript and looked up at Kenny, the admiration faded and something else sneaked into his heart.

Jealousy. Something John had never experienced, and he felt his stomach heave with the strength of it. He'd been kidnapped, terrorised and tied up, and all of that was as nothing compared to the anger he felt now. He stared at Kenny's pocked face, and Kenny stared right back, giving nothing away, and in that moment in the silent room, John truly wanted to kill him. He found himself breathing as noisily through his nose as he had when he hadn't been able to breathe through his mouth. This skinny, blank little bastard, with his skin and his cheap aftershave, had done what John had spent most of his life trying to do. He'd gotten off the sidelines, applied himself and written a masterpiece. The earlier humiliation was almost preferable to this. John had tried so hard, all those years ago, and having to give up had almost killed him. But he had suspected back then what the weight in his lap now proved. He wasn't good enough. It was that simple. He had never been good enough, or smart enough, and looking at Kenny's face, and smelling the smell of the sheaves of paper, he knew it was true.

'So,' said Kenny quietly, 'what do you think of it?'

John felt a tear coming to his eye but blinked it back. 'I think it's a pile of shit,' he said evenly.

That was not what he meant to say, but nothing else would come out of his mouth. Perhaps he had a deep-seated deathwish that his conscious mind knew nothing about. His heart was pounding so hard he thought his chest was going to explode.

Kenny blinked, and blinked again. His fingers fluttered on the tabletop by the gun. This wasn't right. Kelso wasn't supposed to say that. He was supposed to swoon with pleasure and forget about the nonsense with the gun and, perhaps, offer some constructive criticism. There was no harm here, for God's sake. This was a diamond, valuable thing and Kenny was offering it to the man for free, a share in his masterpiece. He could be the producer, if he liked, if he so wanted.

But Kelso was holding out the manuscript between thumb and forefinger and glaring at him like some kind of deranged ape, sweat dribbling down his neck. Kenny began to feel a little annoyed. He hadn't mistreated the man. He wanted the answer he expected. He was a fan of Kelso's and he wanted, for the sake of propriety and recognition of a job well done, Kelso to be a fan of his. Just for a while. For the love of *Christ*, it wouldn't kill him, just to pay attention to the pet project, here, and to stop being such a prima donna. Even if he was brilliant.

He picked up the gun. John dropped the script on the floor in fright.

'We need to talk about this,' said Kenny. 'I'm serious.'

John realised, just in time, that he was going to throw up, and managed to avoid the manuscript but not his own shoes. Kenny looked at him for a few seconds, then reached into a drawer and tossed him a cloth. He picked up the gun and the script, reached up and took the lightbulb from its socket. He stood framed in the doorway, a pale light coming from the front room, and waggled the gun a little, its muzzle pointed at the ground.

'Please don't make any noise,' he said, then he left the room in darkness and locked the door behind him.

John sat perfectly still for a moment and closed his eyes. It made no difference, open or closed – the darkness was total. He stood up slowly and felt his way to the sink, gripping the cloth, and slowly tried to clean up his gob and shoes as best he could. He sluiced some water around in his mouth. He placed his hand blindly on the windowpane and, for an instant, was about to scream for help. Then he remembered the harmless, terrifying waggle of the gun. He crept back and lay down on the settee and wondered what the hell was going on. He was pretty sure that the kid wasn't going to kill him. By now, he wasn't sure if that wasn't the best route for all concerned.

He leaned into the sofa, which was more comfortable than he expected, and decided to get some sleep, regardless. He closed his eyes, wondered what time of day it was, and tried to ignore the faint smell of vomit in the room. Thirty seconds later he got up, crawled to the bathroom, and tested the window. It was nailed down. He couldn't even find where the nails might be. And if he could have found them, they were probably six-inchers. He fell back down on the settee and pulled the blankets up around himself. He felt like crying again but then he decided he just didn't have the fucking energy. He could hear faint footsteps in the other room and then he was gone, gone, and out for the count.

He dreamed of the story, and in his dream he was both the

writer and the leading man. Halfway through, the director recasts him as the villain and John burns all the scripts in protest.

It was 9 a.m. Kenny paced up and down in the kitchen for a while. Okay, maybe the man was a little disoriented, but there was no way Kenny was going to accept that verdict. Not without some serious discussion. He and Kelso were going to have to talk about this.

Then it dawned on him, with a bit of a shock, that the station would be wondering where the hell Kelso was. He felt bad about interrupting the show. He rewound the video, and found it fairly easy to pinpoint the moment in the show when the crew realised something was amiss. The Plympton animation was great but he didn't think much of the blonde lassie, flicking her hair and blathering away her nervousness, and pretending that nothing was wrong.

Well, something was very wrong. And right now, it was curled up, smelling like shit, and with its head full of all the wrong opinions, fast asleep in his back room.

Still, Kenny felt that he should let the studio know. He didn't even know what he was going to say, but he couldn't ruin tonight's schedule with a clear conscience.

He put on a heavy sweatshirt and some gloves, and walked down the road to the nearest phone box to make the call. When the receptionist answered, Kenny was momentarily thrown; it was the same chilly cow who had told him that Kelso doesn't *do* phone-in.

'John Kelso won't be coming in to work tonight,' he said, and got a sudden, delightful rush of – what? Power, probably.

'Excuse me – who is this?' asked the receptionist, whose name was Penny and who wasn't so dim that she hadn't noticed the quiet air of panic around the corridors, and the fact that everyone was whispering John's name.

'Never mind. Just tell his crew that he won't be in, for a while. Maybe. They're going to have to get someone else to do the show. If they want the show done.'

Kenny knew that they would probably keep the show going for a day or so. They'd done that before when Kelso had the 'flu. It occurred to him that they might use someone he didn't approve of.

'Are you a friend of Mr Kelso's?' said Penny cautiously, all the while frantically windmilling at the wrist, and making silently hysterical faces at colleagues to call the bosses, or the police, or *someone*.

'No,' said Kenny. 'I'm a fan.'

He realised he was on the verge of giving a lecture, and was about to hang up, when he thought he might as well use the fifty pence to put his tuppence worth in.

'Just don't use the blonde girl,' he snapped, 'she knows next to nothing. It's about films. It's not a fucking beauty contest. And why not do a piece on Cliff Robertson? He's worth it. Or maybe Art Carney and Jackie Gleason – you know, from television to the movies? And Howard and Winkler – same deal! A great piece on parallel careers, right there! Or how about a bit on *Who?* with Elliott Gould?' (Kenny was fed up with people saying 'What?' every time he mentioned that bloody film.) He felt quite excited. He didn't want to hang up.

'You could have a father-and-son thing! Christ, I don't know – Robert and Alan Alda, or the two Arkins!' He didn't hear Penny's intake of breath.

'Or – listen! How's about an item on Bobby Darin films? Well, okay, he only made one, really, so that wouldn't take more than five minutes, so you could do a bit on jazz in the movies at the same time, yeah? Or – country music. Mind you, that's been done ... um ... Or rap, okay? No wait, that wouldn't work – not old enough, really. Sorry. Come to think of it, Cliff Robertson really deserves a season all to himself! Why not show *Charly*, then *Too Late the Hero* – him and Michael Caine kicking seven bells out of each other, eh? Or *PT 109* – him as fucking Kennedy, no less! Recommended by Kennedy, I swear to God! Or *J. W. Coop!* – the world's first art-house western, and –'

At that moment, Kenny's fifty-pence piece ran out. He looked at the handpiece in shock, surprised that he'd carried on so, then dropped it onto its perch and ran from the box into the night. At the same moment, Penny dropped her phone and ran down the corridors, shouting that she'd had some maniac on the line, and that John Kelso might be in trouble.

It took the suits upstairs an hour and a half to even think about believing her. When they finally got round to it, after forty phone calls all over, they instructed the marketing unit to get their arses in gear. Then they called the police. If this was genuine, and Kelso really was gone, then somebody was going to need some training, pronto. This could be horrible.

This could be magic.

Sally heard the buzz in her lunch hour and swerved up to top office, looking fantastic. Just in case. Downstairs in the lobby, the security man glared past the double glazing at the street beyond and bounced, gently and almost imperceptibly, up and down on the balls of his feet. He was as big as a house and, like everyone else, he'd heard about the Kelso thing. He was ready for armed confrontation, and if he was lucky it might come to that.

Kenny returned home at noon, half-expecting Kelso to be gone. He'd never taken himself seriously as a felon. He jammed the gun into the waistband of his trousers and felt embarrassed. It was such a clichéd image. He opened the door and found John lying on the couch, staring at the ceiling.

'Are you hungry?' asked Kenny. Kelso didn't even look at him. 'I can make you something, if you're hungry.'

There was no reply. The atmosphere in the room was arctic.

'Would you like a cigarette?' That got a response.

Kelso sat up. 'I'd like to be able to wash my fucking teeth,' he said tiredly.

His head snapped back when he spotted the gun. 'And yes, I would like a cigarette.' Kenny moved into the front room for a moment and returned with a washcloth, a toothbrush and paste, toothpicks and dental floss, a pack of Silk Cut and a box of matches. He sat quietly while Kelso wiped his face and brushed his teeth. He emerged from the bathroom, lit a cigarette, and sat down facing Kenny.

'Let me go. Please.' He had enough pride to keep the whine out of his voice.

'No.'

'This is insane. Man, you can't go around kidnapping people just because you want them to take an interest in your pet project.'

'It's not a pet project. It's good. You know it's good. I want you to tell me it's good. I want to hear you say it.'

'And then you'll let me go?'

'Yes.'

John opened his mouth. Then he closed it again. He wanted to tell the truth and say it was the best thing he'd ever seen, the loveliest tale. Then the truth snaked nastily around his heart and closed his throat and he thought he was going to pass out. He couldn't say the words. Inside his own head, a silently hysterical voice screamed at him – *Say it, you idiot!!* – but he just couldn't. *This* was insane. He could simply tell the truth and go home.

It was that easy. But his own furious, jealous soul had paralysed his mouth. He felt tears of pure frustration pricking the corners of his eyes. He wanted to tell the truth. But it was no good. He just couldn't make the words come out.

Kenny was looking at him, looking at his twitching face and dishonest eyes, and for a moment Kelso hoped that he might drag the gun from his belt and spare him the agony of answering the question. John bowed his head, leaned forward and spat, ever so slowly, on the floor, convinced he was going to die. And he was doing absolutely nothing to prevent it. A wave of delectable terror skimmed over him. He felt as if he was floating on a blanket of sheer fear, and nothing seemed to matter any more.

He heard a voice, which sounded very like his own voice, say, 'I told you what I thought. Your screenplay stinks. It's shite, okay? Now go ahead. Shoot me. Do it. Now.'

John kept his head bowed and, in that moment of ringing clarity, he realised that, whether he lived or died, there was something seriously wrong with him.

Kenny tapped, silently, the pad of his forefinger on the table twice, adjusted the gun in his waistband and took a good long look at Kelso's head. After about a minute of silence, he cleared his throat softly.

'Well,' he said, 'in that case, I'm going to ask you to help me with it. A little script-doctoring, if you will. It'll be like a project. It will be fun. For both of us.'

His tone was civilised and venomous at the same time. His tone suggested that he knew that Kelso was lying through his teeth. 'It may take a little time,' he added.

John raised his head, and when he saw the script in Kenny's fist and the look of cheerful enthusiasm in his eyes, he almost wished that the guy had shot him. Kenny dropped the script on the table, waggled the gun, again, and told him to read it over. Again. And if he wanted to make notes, here were a couple of red pens and some paper.

And he really should eat something.

John nodded stupidly. It suddenly hit him how ravenous he was.

'What's your name, anyway?' he whispered, expecting a lie.

'Kenny,' said Kenny.

And John just *knew* that it was true.

Kenny went to heat up some pasta and John Kelso silently lowered his head into his hands.

A colleague at the hospital, who just couldn't help himself, had a girlfriend who was a reporter. A woman as old as that, even if they didn't know exactly how old, was news of a sort. So now the Doctor was getting the occasional phone call from the press, asking who the old lady, the mystery patient, was and what was wrong with her. 'There's nothing wrong with her,' he would snap down the phone. 'She's just old, okay?' And then, of course, they would ask how old. And he would have to mumble that he didn't know. But he was telling the truth. There was absolutely nothing wrong with this woman. She was, technically, in perfect health. If she'd been thirty years younger she would've been in better shape than he was. She was just old. Every organ had done its duty and more. And now it was time to slow down, stop and die. But she seemed to have just stopped. Stopped and stayed, before death, fixed at a particular point, in a particular condition, as if to remain so for ever was to be her destiny.

He had gotten into the habit of making sure she was the last one he visited on his rounds. This particular evening, the ward was very quiet. Most of the other geriatrics were asleep and only the charge nurse was around. He sat down beside her bed. She was lying on her side. She opened her eyes and looked at him. There was nothing in those eyes that he could have described. They were full of character but a character he had never encountered. Her skin was so wrinkled it almost fell in upon itself, but she looked like she had been that way for ever, as if his smoothness was, in some way, ludicrous. There was no fear, no annoyance, no love, no anxiety, curiosity, anger, wisdom, shame or discomfort. At least none that he could discern. He leaned forward and stared into her eyes for a full minute. She looked right back at him as if he was a blank sheet of paper. Then something tiny happened and he sat up straight. It was just a small movement of her *gaze, a fractional dilation of the pupil. By doing nothing, she let him know that he was being incredibly rude.*

'I'm sorry,' he said. And before he could stop himself, he leaned in and whispered, 'Please talk to me.' Her expression didn't change and he felt ashamed. Around the other patients he was in charge, he was the man with the stainless touch, the doctor full of glacial reassurance and the crafty geography of medical myths. But when he tried to do something with this one, he was stumped. What was the point to her? She did nothing and said nothing. She simply existed. And that, frankly, wasn't enough. He leant back, shoulders hunched, silently pleading with her to say something.

She closed her eyes and there was not one iota of contempt in the gesture. But she might as well have slapped him across the face.

She closed her eyes and breathed in the smell of the fresh linen. The changing of the sheets was her favourite thing. A vague, gypsy notion of her youngest son drifted into her head. He'd had almost the same kind of brittle confidence, the kind of wet arrogance that had swanned him through his life for as long as it lasted. He was a late child, born when she was well into her forties, and she just didn't have the energy to pay him much mind. It wasn't cruelty. It was a mix of fatigue and inertia. She'd already had three. Her husband Edmund was a silent, hopeless sort, who farmed and drank and wasn't a problem to anyone or anything. He was a sweet, medium-sized nothing, a flimsy cipher of a man, and that's what she'd liked about him. She didn't want a character, big and interesting. She wanted someone smaller than life, a someone who tried to be neither virtuous nor riveting. A man who thought that furry uncertainty was the more interesting option, and who lived by his watery creed, annoying mostly no one.

But Kevin, the youngest, inherited neither his father's sniffing, stupid apathy nor his mother's hard common sense. He was her son and she loved him. But only because she couldn't help it. He got a job on Ireland's railway system, then moved to Birmingham in '39 and joined the Merchant Navy a couple of years later. Every so often, she would receive letters from him, whining about how he was treated differently because of his accent. He jumped ship in Greece in 1941 and inveigled himself into the good graces of the mayor of one of the smaller coastal towns. After two years of working in tavernas, Kevin managed to put his experience on the railways to good use. He became the impeccable Council bureaucrat, the man whose team made sure that every Jew transported north had a train ticket, bought and paid for. It was an incredibly complex operation, lasting months, and he was proud of the fact that every single penny was accounted for.

He was battered to death outside his own front door a week after the war ended, and his body, by some leaky accounts, was dragged aside and left in the Mediterranean sun for the dogs.

She cried when she found out, but only for a few minutes. She was already too old for the kind of energy that authentic grief requires.

Yes, he was her son.

And no, he just wasn't worth it.

Edmund never mentioned Kevin's name again. Sometimes you just have to let things and people go, and stop pretending that blood is more important than anything. A year later, Edmund went in secret to the police station and told them that his own brother was selling tainted poitín, a toxic concoction that was ruining everybody's digestive system for miles.

He ratted on his own brother.

That was the closest she ever came to being in love with him.

That, and the three times he took her to the pictures. Three times, a chance to marvel and drool.

Rita Hayworth and Jeff Chandler.

Hedy Lamarr and Fred MacMurray.

The best-looking blokes on earth, and the women no less astonishing. Watching them made her feel incredibly ugly and amazingly beautiful all at the same time. A decent swagger and some flourishing concerns – that was their lives at the movies. Thrice.

Sometimes in the ward, in relaxed, sunny moments, she thought she might as well talk to the Doctor. He seemed to be suffering in some way. In the meantime, she sniffed the linen and turned over onto her back with a breed of slowness which only time-lapse can detect. When she opened her eyes again, he had flurried off in a quiet huff. He was handsome, insofar as she could remember what good-looking actually was, and, in the quietude inside her own skull in the dark, she was fairly sure that there was no harm in him.

When John paused in his tale, Lynne didn't know whether or not to say anything. The late afternoon sun flittered hither and yon through the trees in the park, here and there, blindingly so, and the last of the tourists were dribbling out of the Maritime Museum. She looked north and saw the tip of the *Cutty Sark* mast poking skywards and, in the distance, the regular flash of light on top of the Canary Wharf tower. Once every second? She regularised her breathing to synchronise with the flash. John was staring at the grass, rubbing the small scars on the back of his hands. Lynne hadn't really noticed them before. He had other marks on his back and arms. She'd assumed they were just natural blemishes. Now she wasn't so sure.

A well-built man jogged past, followed by a man on a bicycle, who seemed to be giving him advice. The jogger had a boxer's build, and he ran easily along the path with the kind of lazy bounce that reminded Lynne of a dingo, or a big fox. He was mesmerising. Occasionally, he would punch the air in front of him in slow arcs, and bob a little to one side. The man on the bike talked and talked, a sterile riff, but the boxer wasn't listening. He was moving in a world of his own, flowing through his own time and space, creating his own louche and graceful boogie. And as they moved away, the trainer's forlorn jabber became more and more faint.

John shifted silently beside her and Lynne suddenly felt very cold.

*

Four trees away, Tom hunkered down and stared at the back of her neck, and he just knew that she was uncomfortable. He resented the fact that this guy, this ordinary-looking fellow with his hunched shoulders and awful dress sense, was monopolising the conversation. His Lynne couldn't get a word in edgewise, the way this bastard was looming in and hogging her space. Tom had tried to stop it, to stop following her and sneaking around like some kind of bogus, shifty bodyguard, and then he had simply given up. He had gone back to her flat one morning last week when he knew she wouldn't be back for a good while, and this time he had headed straight for the bathroom, stripped off and taken a bloody *shower.*

And as he stood there with the suds slithering off him, he began to cry and he couldn't stop. He was lost and he knew it, and he didn't know whether it was the best blessing or the worst catastrophe ever to happen to him.

He stole the CDs of Nina Simone's *Baltimore* and Scott-Heron's *Reflections* as he passed through the living-room, then tidied up a little and deliberately broke the kitchen door lock on his way out. Out of bad temper more than anything. He liked the way she put her little address stickers on everything she bought.

They were black on white with an Amnesty International logo on the left.

That was quite nice. On her coffee table had lain a copy of *The Winter's Tale*, open at the page where Autolycus – the craftiest of all thieves – is described as the son of Mercury, that 'thieving planet'. Was she on to him, or was it just bad-taste-type luck? He ran down the road like a badly frightened dog.

But the worst moment came two nights later, as he was leaving the King's Head. He was winging out and she was swanning in and they collided in the doorway. Tom stared at her and thought *Oh Christ, it's her,* while Lynne thought that she knew him from somewhere. Crouch End was a small place. Could be. Maybe she'd seen him round about. But it was mostly the way he smelled. Tom apologised in a frail shower of small and quietly hysterical smiles, and kept apologising while he veered off down the Broadway.

Lynne hovered in the doorway for a moment, wondering about the guy. He wore a smashing, noisy leather jacket that creaked like a mad thing as he almost bowed in front of her, and he had prematurely grey temples and, well, that was just lovely. There was an addled yet sensible smell to this man. Lynne had a nose like a bloodhound and there was no mistaking that rusty odour. She just couldn't place it, that was all. And she hovered in the doorway for a couple of seconds longer than was necessary, trying to inhale the gentle, renegade bluff of this man, whoever he was. No question about it, she liked the way this guy smelled.

Two minutes later, John arrived and joined her at the table, and after a glass of wine and some sweet, nonsense jabber between the pair of them, she forgot about the guy. At that moment the guy was leaning against the clock-tower, panting like a maniac and trying not to throw up.

*

Two trees away now, in Greenwich Park, he could see the way she was leaning into this man's voice, leaning with a cool and heavy earnestness, as if she didn't mind his talking and talking at all. Tom got off his knees and swerved silently forward and, at one tree away, he could see the hairs on the back of Kelso's neck. He could see the vein on one side of the man's throat. He was staring at that vulnerable nape and balling his fist when he saw her hand sweep up and stroke his head. Tom dipped as he passed, dropping the medal into her handbag. It didn't make much of a sound beyond a muffled tinkle. Tom swept past the pair of them and strode up towards the Observatory, thinking to himself, *that man has no idea how close he just came to getting his fucking head stoved in.*

At that moment, Lynne stopped melting into John's arms and flinched. She caught a whiff of something, of something and she wasn't sure what. She turned and caught a glimpse of a man striding up the hill towards the Observatory. He left in his wake a thing that was almost like a vibration in the air, and for a weirdly horrible moment Lynne heard the creak of a leather jacket and felt an odour rattle around inside her skull, a smell she'd picked up in her own home. She could have sworn that she knew who he was but, the further he got up the hill, the less sure she became. She heaved herself closer into John's chest, and sneaked a look over the crook of his elbow at the hunched figure marching away up the steep slope.

When he got to the top of the hill, Tom parked himself on the grass, and forced himself to look past the museum, at the river, at the broad vista, at all the new buildings going up on the Isle of Dogs, all the cranes. Why did they call it an 'Isle'? It wasn't a proper island at all. Not the way Tom remembered islands. Forlorn, prickly and proper things, with dense undergrowth, broken bottles, blasting heat, twenty-foot creepers, fallen walls, nobody living on them at all and, especially, miles and miles of water between them and anything else. And it was supposed to be 'Ducks', anyway, not 'Dogs'. So Edward III kept his greyhounds thereabouts, but there had been wildfowl on the marshes for centuries before that. When he was small, his grandmother, whom he hoped was still looking after his books for him, used to talk about Rabelais' fantastic 'Isle of Lanterns', where everybody pretended knowledge about, well, everything. And where, actually, nobody knew *anything*. And then she would watch the news on BBC Northern Ireland, and she would laugh her ancient arse clean off.

Tom's gaze was dragged down to where Lynne was still leaning across the man's shoulder. Tom put his face in his hands so that he didn't have to look at it.

John didn't seem to notice Lynne's discomfort, took a deep breath and carried on with his story.

*

He nibbled at the food Kenny had brought him, while Kenny sat at the table opposite and placed the gun in front of him. He wasn't eating anything himself. He stared at John with a look of interested dispassion, and tapped his fingers on the muzzle several times, then realised what he was doing and stopped it. He coughed. John flinched. He finished eating, Kenny moved the plate out of the way and leaned forward.

'Did you mean what you said?' he asked. He sounded hopeful and reproachful at the same time.

John raised his head wearily, opened his mouth to say something else, then just nodded and offered a weak, idiotic 'Yes'.

Kenny smiled warmly, then smacked him hard across the face. John reeled back in shock and pain. It had been a long time since he had felt physical pain of any kind. He couldn't think of anything else to say and now he was too afraid to try.

Kenny stood up, unscrewed the bulb from its socket, said, 'We'll chat about this later, okay?' and marched out of the room, locking the door behind him. His tone was perfectly polite.

In the living-room he sat down and stared at the palm of his hand, which still tingled.

Kenny had always considered himself a reasonable person and yet, here he was, slapping the hell out of a man he actually admired. What was wrong with him? But there had been something in that slap. It had sure as hell shut Kelso up. Kenny sat for a while, tracing the lines of his right palm with his left index finger, marking the track of his long, strong lifeline, and his rather fainter heartline, and feeling weaker and more unsure of himself with every minute, and wondering what he was going to do next. He hoped that Kelso would sleep for a while, to give him time to think about this thing.

Kelso curled up in the darkness, not knowing what to do with himself. He was freezing with fear in the pitch black now, and it was only partly a fear of what the kid might do to him. It was also a nervousness at himself, at his own moronic agenda. Kenny wasn't that big. Okay, there was the gun, but John knew that he could've made a stab at getting free, and the chances were that Kenny wouldn't have tried to seriously hurt him. But John hadn't tried anything. He probably wasn't a coward, but he just didn't have the energy to try anything on. If he was honest, he was stupidly curious about what was going to happen next.

And then, the very thought of what might happen next caused him to shiver and shrink in silent hysterics, down into the sofa, and to try to find the blankets to pull over his eyes, although they made no difference to the pitch blackness. After a while, he was too tired even to be afraid any more. He sank into the couch, into the kind of sleep that only a particular breed of hopeless, skinny anxiety brings.

He slept for twenty hours straight, and Kenny in the next room, fretting and pacing and watching snatches of telly, and afraid to sleep himself, just let him sleep.

On the Wednesday evening, Kenny opened the door, screwed in a fresh bulb, kicked Kelso awake, but not too roughly, gave him a coffee and some toast, then slammed the manuscript down on the table. John ate the food and struggled to come fully awake, hawking and coughing and rubbing his stiff limbs.

'Let's have a look then, shall we?' Kenny said quietly, sitting down. There was no sign of the gun. He pushed the document onto John's lap. John looked up and around and it dawned on him that Kenny didn't have a copy. As if reading his mind, Kenny leaned perkily in, tapped his temple and said, 'Oh, I don't need a copy – I've got a photographic memory.'

It was 304 pages.

Oh God, Kelso thought, *this guy really is a maniac.*

Kenny pushed a red pen into John's hand.

'Right!' he said brightly. 'Page one! What's wrong with that then, eh?'

Kelso looked at the script in his lap. Neither of them made a sound.

He read page one. After four minutes, he read it again.

Kenny stared at him and held his breath.

Kelso looked at Kenny. He raised his red pen over page one.

It was Wednesday night.

By Thursday afternoon, John Kelso had black, fairly bad bruises on his face and neck, a broken left finger, cigarette burns all over his arms and hands, and by Thursday night, three deep cuts on his back, caused by a red pen bring driven in and down about half a centimetre. Kenny was surprised at the difference in hue between ink and blood. There was absolutely no similarity at all. But Kelso had done what he'd done, despite the pain and the noisy nonsense from Kenny, who couldn't quite bring himself to just *stop* him, to simply take away the pen.

John had gone over each and every one of the 304 pages and his red pen was *everywhere* on every page.

To Kenny, each change to his masterpiece was blasphemy – it was like a physical pain. Every time Kelso flipped, raised and applied the pen, he screamed and whirled around the room with his lit fag, and he ranted and objected and landed the occasional punch on Kelso's bowed, unfeeling scalp, and bounced off the walls like a mad thing.

But that's all he did. He didn't have the courage to simply stop the man. To stop the man with a true, grown-up wallop. Or with a bullet. Not necessarily in the head.

He was afraid that maybe Kelso was right and he was wrong. Maybe it was rubbish, like the man said. He hollered and trembled and tried to explain to Kelso, at the top of his lungs, that it was already a fucking *masterpiece*, and that it didn't need this kind of work, okay?

Kelso simply shrugged off the punches and the licking burns and carried on scribbling and scribbling, utterly oblivious to Kenny and his dull thumps and sharp stings, or anything else, for that matter. He went through every inch of the screenplay and he had changed *everything*.

Because it had dawned on him that he could.

Because Kenny loved him.

Because Kenny thought he was a genius.

In the wee hours, Kenny just gave up. He gave up, sagged against a wall and just let Kelso get on with it.

He had turned the good guy into a knowing, smart-mouthed villain, when he was supposed to be simply a good guy with a sensible attitude.

He'd taken out the moral thread, the occasional chorus, the narrative common sense.

He'd changed the dialogue from a set of coherent and connected pieces, into a wilderness of profane and minimalist aridity.

He'd inserted a section about lakes and islands and canal enthusiasts that made no sense at all.

He'd taken out the prison rooftop protest.

He'd killed off the female lead in a way that made Kenny almost vomit when he read it.

He'd taken out huge chunks of all sorts of stuff that Kenny had sweated blood over, and replaced them with a shiny, lumpen series of things that Kenny couldn't even begin to understand.

John had the best, and worst, fun in his life doing this thing.

His red pen was on the verge of running out by the time he'd finished, and when he'd finished, he realised that he didn't give a shit what Kenny did to him any more.

He felt exhilarated and stupid and he didn't even notice the pain any more.

It was Thursday evening and the pair of them had sat staring at each other across the table for two hours.

Finally, Kenny hauled himself out of his chair, and with a gesture of weary menace, leant further across the table than he really needed to, scooped up the bloodied manuscript and walked unsteadily out of the room. He didn't bother removing the bulb, but he did remember to lock the door when he heard Kelso cough behind him.

John ran some cold water over his hands and tried to clean the gashes on his back as best he could. Then he lay gingerly down on his side for a while, and got up when he realised, for the first time, that the lightbulb was going to drive him a bit mad, and that the room didn't actually have a light switch. He wrapped the sleeve of his sweatshirt around his palm, reached up on tippy-toes, and took the bulb out himself. He collapsed back down into the warmth of his sofa without even having to think about where everything was, and, with a feeling that crawled all over him, knew that he was getting into a truly bad habit here.

He couldn't figure out what had happened to him. All his life he'd hankered after the perfect picture, the sweet, lovely story that he could have sold to some huge studio without even breaking a sweat. An immoderate piece of something-or-other that would clank its way into the hearts of the brutes and the boffins, and would mean he would never have to work again.

And he had found it, right here in this dingy room. And the thing wasn't his.

He had taken a thing of beauty and deliberately ruined it. He had bowdlerised and slashed away and he'd done it with a song in his heart. While Kenny was bouncing off the walls, bewailing and moaning every sunk syllable and sentence, Kelso was ignoring the racket and the pain and diving right in with his red pen, secure in the knowledge, more or less, that Kenny could holler and swipe all he wanted, but would not kill him.

That was good enough for John these days, and the notion made him shiver even harder, because it meant that he might not be entirely all there.

He had always thought himself a reasonable person, and yet here he was, a vandal.

A vandal. A hooligan with a busy editorial eye and probably a death-wish.

It was as if the real world had drifted off for a while, and he was left with very little here but a bully genius, an endlessly scarred script and, in the pitch black, in his fist, a stupid red pen and his own mad envy. For a moment, he wondered if anyone was worrying about him, if they were saying anything on the news.

And in the next moment, he realised he didn't care if they cared or not.

As he was drifting off, he could just about make out the tapping sound from the next room.

Kenny sat with his manuscript on his lap and his hands crawling over the keyboard, slowly like worms. He had never felt so bad. As he typed in the red changes, he slowed down to the point where he was using one lazy finger, leaning forward to the point of collapse. He pulled back and the thought occurred to him that maybe he was right and Kelso was wrong. But the thought crumbled, and it dawned on Kenny that he had never put his work to the test. He had never shown any of it to anyone. Ever. And Kelso knew what he was about. The man simply couldn't be that catastrophically wrong. He just couldn't. He was too smart and he was too good.

It occurred to Kenny that everything he'd ever written was someone else's gift, that he'd been plagiarising other people's lives every inch, every word along the way.

It occurred to Kenny that he'd never written an original line in his life.

Kelso was probably doing him a favour.

Kenny took a slug of coffee, hovered his hands over the keys for a miserable minute, then carried on and carried on until dawn, until he was finished. Every red pen edit was in there, in there and done, saved on hard drive, saved on disc.

By morning, Kenny just wanted to lie down and weep, so he did for a while, not that it made him feel a lot better.

By Friday tea-time, he was too exhausted and depressed to think about even feeding Kelso. He left him locked up and alone for half a day, and went for a twelve-mile walk around early-morning Woolwich, head down and quietly seething, and kicking things along the pavement. People, by and large, left him alone, or else veered away sharpish.

Then he came home and stared at the living-room wall for a few hours. There was no sound from the other room.

He turned on the television at Kelso's usual early-morning spot. The station was showing *Pretty Woman*. Kenny froze for a second and contemplated putting his boot through the screen, then decided he didn't have the energy for this shit any more. They had shown *Pretty Woman* two nights ago.

Two nights ago. In the same bloody slot.

That took some balls, he had to admit. Even so, it made his head hurt a bit.

He left Kelso alone for another day, without food, and sat watching videos and drinking beer for thirteen hours. Occasionally he would glance at the manuscript on the desk and his stomach would knot and churn. It was done. To hell with it.

He slotted *Basquiat* into the video with a clumsy violence that made him feel a bit better. After ten minutes of looking at big, balloon, lovely graffiti, he felt sick to his stomach. All he could think about was his old team out on the Scottish rocks, out in the freezing night, clambering and cleaning like a bunch of maniacs.

And the unfair, one-sided brawl that ended with David's ruined face and smashed eye. An antique hatred rose up and almost choked off his breath. Kenny just couldn't stand vandalism. He couldn't abide it.

In the dark, Kelso was keeping still, lying quietly, conserving his energy. He didn't know how hungry he was any more. He had never been a big eater anyway. He lay and dreamed and drank a little water now and again, floating around the few sticks of furniture and flopping back down in the utter darkness. He could have put the bulb in anytime he wanted but he didn't. Pitch was how he had come to like it.

He turned over on his skinny couch and he thought about nothing very much, except his old gang. He thought of Linda's hopeless, helpless face and the awful staccato sounds she made, trying desperately to put together a sentence. It had always been better when she didn't try and just laughed. She had a nice laugh. The best times they ever had, apart from when they were fighting with the other gangs, were when they were wrecking things around the town. Not wrecking exactly, just eleven and careless.

There was a cattle-feed warehouse near Linda and Jason's, and it was a paradise for kids. John's modest mob would sneak in on the weekends and go berserk in this place. It was a huge, plastic-cushioned, mucky concrete cathedral. The roof was miles high and the walls were stacked thirty feet deep and forty feet high with big sacks of pellet feed. He and his gang would chase each other over and around the sacks, jumping from level to level and, amazingly, not breaking their legs, killing rats and bats and whooping like lunatics. Sometimes they would puncture hundreds of bags at a time because there was nothing more satisfying than the feel of a sharp stick stabbed into stuffed vinyl, and the crunchy, criminal smell of the calf-feed pellets, spilling out all over. Then they would troop home, drenched in sweat, Linda probably for a mild hiding from her dad, for nothing in particular, and John to wash himself and sneak off to his bed, hoping that his mother wasn't in the mood for three hours of talking shit.

In the dark, those memories, and a hundred others from his

childhood, had become to Kelso as real as the nice, rotten crumple of the sofa beneath his spine.

As far as he could tell, the best fun he'd ever had, and never had since, was trashing those smelly sacks as a child and just lying back on his high, makeshift, plastic bed, like the princess wincing from the pea, listening to the trickle of millions of pellets falling forty feet and bouncing off the filthy concrete below. When he was twelve he saw his first proper waterfall, and it was nowhere near as good.

John Kelso slept some more and dreamed and disappeared into his past, and the sting of the bangs and the burns, and the best story he'd ever read, didn't seem to matter much any more.

On Sunday night, Kenny turned on the television at the usual time for Kelso's show, expecting another movie in its place.

He had been watching the news for the last four days. Looking for some sign that anybody knew Kelso was missing. Or cared. And there wasn't a peep. Nothing.

He couldn't believe it.

What Kenny didn't know was that the studio had taken the police's advice and had decided to just leave things for a bit. To just sit tight for a few days, because, God knows, the phone call was probably a hoax. Kelso would probably show up shortly, repentant but fine, with a horrible hangover and a booking for three weeks in the Priory, or similar.

Just to be on the safe side, the receptionists had been issued with a short-order memo, to call those friends whose numbers they had on file. And most of Kelso's few friends said the same thing – *Kelso? Yeah, more than capable of a mini-bender, and then some. Lovely guy, though.* At reception, Penny had read the memo and re-read it three times in a silent fit of pure fury. She couldn't believe it. They hadn't believed her.

Penny had been answering phones for a living for fourteen years, and she knew what she was about. She knew the tone and timbre of every voice that slithered onto the line. She could tell almost everything about a caller before they even uttered a word, by the length between pick-up and gabble, the space between syllables, the pitch and song, the difference between the cocky bullies and the merely hopeful. Between those who were hysterically polite on the line and deadpan deadly to, probably, their own families. Penny had ears like a bat and she had been picking her way through the demented aural shambles that is most of the world, for a long, long time.

She could tell the difference between a genuine squall and mere technique, between an honest complaint and some earnest, late-teen sod who just wanted somebody to look at his lousy demo. Penny understood the graphics and infinite fizz and mathematics of the phone, and everything else, by the way of rubbish, that went with it.

When Kenny had first opened his gob five nights ago, with his ludicrous lists and his wee hints of God-knows-what, Penny had known something was desperately wrong but he had hung up before she'd had the wit to think about tracking anything down, and then some other bastard had come through on her line.

But she knew, now, that there was no point in her, a receptionist, trying to persuade the suits of anything.

She got so depressed that she could barely answer the phone in anything approaching a civil manner.

When her lunch hour came, Penny looked up at the ceiling and swore to herself. Then she tore up the memo, went to the pub by herself and got completely plastered.

Kenny was watching the local news and he still couldn't believe the gap where Kelso should've been. He was watching the steam curling out of the near-boiled kettle when he heard the familiar sound of the theme music from Kelso's show. He padded into the living-room and there was Sally, tossing her hair and looking just fabulous altogether.

Kenny realised that he could not bear to watch this alone.

He took the gun out of the drawer, barged into the back room and kicked Kelso, but lightly, in the ribs. Kelso had been sleeping almost continuously for two days and the light and the television noise streaming in from the other room scared the hell out of him for a moment.

'Come on,' said Kenny, 'you should probably see this,' and

waved Kelso in the direction of the door. John staggered forward, blinking. Kenny placed the gun softly against his lower back. *Yeah right*, thought John, *like I've got the energy to tackle anything bigger than a bad-tempered kitten*. He sat down heavily on the couch. He looked to his right at one shelf and saw an Airfix model of what was either a Hurricane or a Spitfire. It was bigger than most, about eighteen inches long and beautifully painted. *That must have taken him ages*, he thought and then the hairs on the back of his neck rose, and goosebumps appeared out of nowhere. He didn't even have to look at the screen. He would have recognised Sally's vowels anywhere. He looked up at Kenny and Kenny looked at his toes.

'There hasn't been anything on the news either,' he said.

Kelso seemed to shrink in front of his eyes, and sat like a chastened child, studying his fingernails. Kenny felt a pang of shame. He hadn't meant to insult the man. He swerved into the kitchen, came back with a couple of beers and the pair of them sat and surveyed the damage.

According to the smiling Sally, John Kelso was still 'indisposed'.

After five minutes of watching what the studio had done to his show, John Kelso sat transfixed. He couldn't believe it. In forty minutes, Sally smiled non-stop, talked a kind of language he didn't understand, and nicely, utterly destroyed the John Kelso Show. Why, he wondered, desolate, were they still even calling it that? They'd even changed the backdrop. Or rather, created one. Kelso used to broadcast in front of a backcloth of black. Sally was perched in front of something mauve and fluffy, festooned round about with pictures of Hollywood stars. By this stage, even Kenny was dumbstruck, and John was leaning, dead-eyed, so far forward he was almost on his knees.

Sally announced the results of the cinema food survey. The Odeon West End was the winner. Best Hot Dog, apparently. Then, having gone into a bit of a hair-tossing frenzy, Sally calmed down and announced her competition.

A competition. John put his head in his hands and clawed gently at his scalp.

The question was, 'What is the connection between *Splash* and *Saving Private Ryan*?'

At this juncture John thought he was going to weep, but he didn't because, despite the fact that he had slept for almost forty hours, he was too fucking tired.

That didn't make any sense at all. He heaved himself off the couch, wandered into the kitchen, fished another beer from the fridge and meandered back into the living-room. He noticed the ragged script, all red-streaked and curled, sitting on the table beside Kenny's PC and, on top of it, three floppy discs.

It was only when he'd leant his weight back onto the couch that they both remembered that he was supposed to be a fucking *prisoner*. He wasn't supposed to be traipsing around like a free man, for the love of *Christ*. John made himself as small and as quiet as possible on the sofa, and examined the carpet, while Kenny glared out of the side of one eye and breathed through his nose, noisily. Honour served, they turned their attention back to Sally.

To finish off her show, Sally announced her classic video review. Of *Pretty Woman*.

God knows, John Kelso knew that he was as big a snob as the next guy, but he truly wasn't prepared for Kenny's vicious yelp of hostility, or the way he leapt off the couch and grabbed the phone, and dialled with the muzzle tip of the gun, as if he was punching someone he hated.

He got through to reception first time and Kelso had never heard language like it. Kenny ranted and screamed abuse for a full five minutes, going on and on about how he had *warned* them not to use that stupid blonde bint, and what the hell had they *done* to Kelso's show? He shouted louder than Kelso thought it possible for a man to shout.

Everything he uttered was shot through with spittle and obscenities.

He prowled around the small room, banging the gun butt against his own head, roaring like no animal John had ever heard.

And then Kenny stopped and stood stock still and, cupping his palm over the receiver so that Kelso couldn't hear, whispered, 'I could kill him, you know. I could kill him.'

When he finally slammed down the receiver and sat panting in a corner, John felt more threatened than defended.

But in the huffy quiet of a few minutes later, something occurred to him. While Kenny was calming down and apologising, by crumpled gesture more than anything he said, and trying, in the corner, to reclaim his composure, something belted silently into Kelso's brain. He began to wonder if someone who was so clever could also be so monumentally stupid.

Kelso had been watching every move Kenny made and he could have sworn that, in his hysteria, Kenny hadn't cancelled the 1471 trace on his call.

Kelso, sitting now almost paralysed with tension, tried to convince himself that nobody who was doing what Kenny was doing could be quite that dementedly stupid. He couldn't possibly make that kind of mistake.

But while Kenny was squawking down the phone, Kelso also knew that he recognised the measured squeak on the other end.

He was certain it was Penny. He had almost asked her out on a date before losing his nerve. But her face was the first he saw every evening when he clocked in at reception and, after thirty seconds worth, daily, of fun and meaningless blather, he just knew that Penny was the smartest person in the building.

After catching the odd bit of measured, near-static calm, he just knew it was Penny.

Five minutes later, Kenny had put the gun down, and was massaging Kelso's shoulders and handing him another beer and lighting his cigarettes for him. John found that even more frightening than the beltings and the burns and the broken finger, but he relaxed into it anyway.

At that moment, Penny was barrelling down the corridor and up the stairs with a piece of paper in her hand, huffing and puffing and swearing to herself that she was going to lose some bloody weight. Starting tomorrow. She staggered to a graceless halt outside the executive office on the fourth floor and stood outside, ready to knock and not knocking. Penny glared, panting, at the bevelled mahogany door for about twenty seconds. She fanned herself with the piece of paper for a moment.

Then she stopped panting, turned around, walked down the stairs, sidled back into her chair at reception and called the police herself. Then she fell head first down onto her console and was sound asleep for almost four minutes, asleep out of pure fright.

Penny knew voices. She knew the difference between a man who said he might kill someone because his soup was cold or his car got towed, and a man who said he might kill someone because he might kill someone.

Kenny and Kelso settled down for the rest of the night and drank beer and watched the last hour of *Movie Movie*. Kenny didn't seem interested in hurting him any more. He looked relaxed and happy. He struck up a quiet, occasional commentary about the film. He could've been down the pub with his best mate.

Now and again, Kelso would take a tiny look across at Kenny's profile. He was staring, rapt, at the screen, the sneaky blue of the television flickering across his face. It didn't seem to matter what movie was on. Not really. The look on Kenny's face was one of majestic perkiness. He was getting to watch great movies and drink beer with his hero. No doubt about it. The rest of the world might as well not have existed. And no real harm done either.

John thought about what it must be like to live in Kenny's head. The man was a miasma of bile and beauty. Yes, he hated his guts, but it was a hatred that lasted only a little while, no matter how hard John tried. He shifted in his chair because his back hurt so much, and he couldn't even get properly angry about that. He felt no less jealous of the script but he had done what he'd done, and he was too tired to feel bad about it any more. Besides, in spite of everything, he was god almighty, here, now. In this poky place, filled with the high stink of something gone bad, with Kenny's hoodlum reverence, with words wounded beyond repair – he was a fucking god. He was basking in the light of the worst kind of love and it didn't matter if nothing happened to him ever again.

Kenny skipped the channels, looking for another movie. He settled on *Reuben, Reuben*.

John leant back, sipped his beer and decided to strike up a quiet conversation.

Well, it was more of a monologue. He began to talk about his childhood because he just couldn't help it and he didn't care if this Kenny bastard was listening or not.

And off he went, murmuring a fraction, then more, and talking things and up and down quietly, then more loudly when the need seemed to arise. Kenny didn't nod, as most people would have done. He just stared and settled deeper into his seat. He actually seemed to be listening. So Kelso just leaned back and closed his eyes and whispered out his early life, between drags and deep breaths, rasping on and out and not giving a damn if the freak was listening or not. He talked and talked and when he opened his eyes and slanted an eyeful sideways, he saw that Kenny was leaning back, mesmerised.

Outside, dawn was just beginning to break. It was the first hint of natural light he had seen in a week. It was almost imperceptible and quite lovely. He might, after all, die in this room. Kenny liked him, but he was capable of it. Kelso, beneath it all, knew that.

Just then, John scratched the burns on his hands and decided that this bloke Kenny was amazing. Just amazing.

That was the thought rolling lazily around in his head when seven armed policemen broke the door down, charged into the room screaming and, in a flurry of gunfire, shot Kenny through the palm of his right hand. The noise was incredible. Kelso threw himself to the ground and stayed curled up there, until a cop pulled him up by the hair and bellowed his name.

In thirty seconds it was all over.

Kenny was taken, moaning, to hospital under armed guard.

And John Kelso was a free man.

He sat with his head in his hands, trembling like a beaten puppy, flinching from the noise and the lights, as the police tore the room apart, and the squad cars pulled up, and a mob of uniforms swirled solicitously around his head, and a flurry of strong hands patted him on the shoulders.

Gradually, he raised his head and looked across the room.

The computer screen was shattered and a rifle round had torn the hard drive apart. A thin and tiny tendril of smoke still meandered in the air around the small wreckage.

The fat manuscript lay alongside, untouched, and the three discs sat perched on top.

John Kelso stared and stared, and stopped trembling.

And began to think like a right bastard.

The sweat froze horribly on his skin and he didn't notice the cold as he staggered forward and slid the discs into the arse pocket of his jeans.

Then, with the proprietorial and slightly embarrassed smile of the father of an obstreperous youngster on the beach, John Kelso tucked the script into the crook of his arm, and mumbled something about his work in progress, interrupted.

The police didn't give a shit, one way or the other. Let the man have his paper. At least he wasn't hurt. Or dead. Most of them had never heard of him.

When things had calmed down a little, two exhausted uniforms took him to hospital where he spent less than ninety minutes getting the gashes cleaned up, some antibiotics, a small finger-splint, and no, they could not remove his jeans, thank you very much.

After that, he was taken to the station for a statement. That took about an hour.

Kelso told the truth. He rattled the truth off like a long, bad limerick. It was actually easier than lying. He blathered and mumbled and stared into space like a reasonable victim, and they got most of it down on paper, and John never once took his paws off the manuscript.

It was something I was working on, when his nibs showed up with the pistol. Just glad he didn't burn it.

He got more sympathetic nods than ever in his life, before or after. Then he asked to be taken home, so the same wilting young cops drove him home. By this stage, the media was getting word and building up a wee mini-squall but right now, in the blinding midday, all Kelso wanted to do was sleep and sleep for about a week.

And then turn over and doze for a fortnight.

He didn't have his keys, so one of the young policemen picked the lock, smiling apologetically. The three of them wandered around in the dark of his house, Kelso in moronic circles. When he was a child, and the family came back from two weeks' holidays, the house always smelled and seemed as strange as his own house did right now. Thankfully, he hadn't left anything burning. There were seventeen messages on his answer-machine. It blinked and winked, redly, at the three of them. The cops scouted out the house. Everything seemed okay. Kelso assured them he was better off at home, and they took him at his word. One of them, Dennis, could feel a dose of the 'flu coming on and, as long as nobody was dead or badly hurt he, frankly, wasn't that bothered.

The policemen left and Kelso closed the front door politely. Then he slapped the manuscript on his living-room table, sank to his knees, and put his fingers in his ears.

After ten minutes he dragged the three discs out of his jeans pocket and dropped them into the cutlery drawer in the kitchen. He walked back into the living-room with his eyes half-closed and stood enjoying what, behind his thick curtains, was just a big, square-ish and smashing pattern of dimness. He picked up the manuscript and tucked it away in a bureau drawer. Then he climbed the stairs to his bedroom, unwashed and all.

He got halfway there, after twenty ludicrous and ape-like minutes on his hands and knees, before sinking so slowly and softly onto the brilliant, thick carpet on the landing.

Kelso lay there for about four hours before the cold really set in and booted him half-awake, and he crawled off, frozen, to his bedroom, where he slept for ... how long, he never found out.

*

The park attendants were tootling around, quietly shooing off the last of the tourists. The temperature had dropped a few degrees and the witless pigeons were fumbling around on the grass in front. The sun was beginning to go down, and the sky was doing amazing tricks around and behind the Canary Wharf tower. The pair of them sat in silence for about five minutes, looking at the lunatic lightshow of streaky colours and shadows to the north.

John had finished his story and Lynne had gradually been sagging gently into his arms. When he spoke of the manuscript, now residing in his house, he felt her stiffen.

The last of the tourists trickled off and Lynne drew herself up and away from him.

She couldn't help it. She stood up and a few leaves crackled under her boot.

She stood away and looked at him. John got off his knees and faced her.

The thing had been optioned by DreamWorks, for the love of God. And he'd stolen it. It wasn't even his. He hadn't written a bloody word of it.

'So,' she said, icily. 'You're a thief.'

That came out a lot harder than she meant it to.

Kelso didn't even blink. His voice was like a razor.

'Yes Lynne, I stole it. Don't you know *anything* about me by now? I've been looking for a break like this all my fucking *life*. And having been kicked, beaten, burnt, broken, battered, humiliated and generally terrified for the guts of a week, I think I *deserve* something for my trouble. What do you think?'

There was no real anger in it. It was an honest enquiry. John Kelso looked at her dead on.

Lynne met him look for look and thought about it for less than four seconds and then decided that she didn't give a damn whether he stole it or not. He was here, and he wasn't dead or crippled. He was here, two feet away and shifting from foot to foot, like a solid ghost with a good sense of humour, and he wasn't going to apologise for a fucking thing.

She stopped feeling like she was made out of stone and sort of melted forward and buried her head in his shirt. John wrapped his arms around her and held her so tightly that she didn't need to hold herself up. The tips of her trainers tickled the grass.

Stolen. Not stolen. She didn't care and she didn't care who knew it.

After a three-second blub, when he thought she was going to shed a layer of skin or something, the pair of them leaned in and took off down the hill and out of Greenwich Park, and tilted in towards each other, holding hands and whispering and talking rubbish, like a couple of sloppy, gossiping children. They headed down east along the riverside walk, towards the pub. The Thames was doing its usual sneaky tidal thing, leaving on the mud a few things in the way of junk but not that much. Cartons and tins and such. The evening sky, by this stage, had gone completely bonkers. Lines of insane blues and something that may have been mauve were fighting, all over the place, with diagonal runs of red and orange. On the way to the Trafalgar Tavern they slowed down and trawled to a stop, still with fingers knotted, and leaned over the river railing to watch both the sky and the river's antics for a bit. Pitching forward, John took a deep, happy breath, fished a cigarette out of his shirt pocket and rummaged around in Lynne's handbag for his lighter.

As they dandered on, the shape and texture of the medal, and the feel of the scrap of fabric against the thickened ridge of his thumb was so familiar that, at first, it didn't register. It felt nice and normal and then he realised where he was. He drew it out in his clenched fist and stopped walking. Lynne turned to look, and he held it out for her to see, laying there with a dull shine on the palm of his hand. Even though she had never seen it before, it looked too much like a war medal to be anything else.

John was looking at her with a weird, stony expression on his face, and the expression said that the medal, beyond question, was his.

'Are *you* a thief, Lynne Callier?' he said quietly, and his voice froze her guts.

She didn't get it, and then a specific whiff and a minor coin-jangle and the creak of a black leather jacket snuck up on her, and she did.

The things came together in her head, and she knew. It was him.

She knew now that the guy storming placidly up the hill was the one. He had been all over her house and all over her bed and swaggering through her stuff, and he had swanned past the pair of them in the park no more than an hour ago, and made her a thief by proxy. It was him.

It was him and she realised, with a churning stomach, that she had seen him too, burbling nicely in a pub doorway, with lovely grey hair, apologising and smelling just great.

Who was he and what the hell did he want? Why hadn't she had the sense to go to the police when she first realised that something funny was going on with her disappearing and reappearing albums?

And bad as she felt, Lynne began to laugh, trying to imagine how that would have gone down at the front desk. Then Lynne's neck muscles felt funny and her head began to wobble and she wasn't sure what was wrong with her.

She stared at the medal on John's palm and he stared right back, but when her legs began to give, he moved forward and caught her.

He hadn't meant to frighten her so. Shit, he knew it was one of his stolen medals, but he didn't care any more where she got the bloody thing. Maybe she picked it up at a flea market or something. He didn't care. He was just scared, now, himself, that he'd said and done something wrong. He hauled her onto a wooden bench outside the Trafalgar and she sat with her head down for a bit.

After another bit, Lynne raised her head and they sat looking at the lights on the Isle of Dogs opposite, trying not to frighten each other any more. John decided he wasn't going to press the matter. He shoved the medal into his back pocket and sat with her on the bench, making soothing noises, and he put his arms around her, and said sorry and sorry and sorry again.

The degree of light was really beginning to get to her. What was the need for it? The question had been burbling around her mind ever since she'd arrived in this hugely nervous place. Everything was white. Or green. And the nurses were so young and shiny. The sheer springy freshness of the ward gave her a headache. Even the decent shadows of evening had an edge and an absence of proper blur that did not belong anywhere. And here he came again. He had begun to make a habit of visiting her last, of all his patients, every evening.

He sat down on the side of the bed and looked at her with an expression that wasn't exactly friendly. This was different, anyway. He'd had a truly lousy day. More phone calls from the papers and now the BBC. They were turning his working day into a freak show. One guy had gone to the trouble of calling a friend in Dublin, looking for some kind of public records information. The rumour was now going about that she was 116 years old. Or thereabouts.

He was becoming a quiet joke and this damp, dozy sow was the reason.

She watched him from under her sheet veil and the antiquely steady, guttersnipe look she was flinging in his direction was driving him crazy. Her eyes were hardly visible in the middle of all the wrinkles. He wanted to say something meaningful. Something that wouldn't annoy her. He had learned to tell when she was annoyed, by the way the crowded landscape of wrinkles shiftily and softly rearranged itself around her face. Sometimes, if he sat for long enough, looking at her face was like watching the kind of morphing SFX they used in the movies; it was a mesmerising face of melting putty. Sometimes he thought it was the best thing he'd ever laid eyes on. And sometimes not.

As he got up to leave, he leaned forward and looked into her eyes *from a distance of about two inches. Then he took off his stethoscope and, as he left, swung it up and across and hit her on the bony upper arch of her foot with it. Hard.*

It was not just a gesture, and nor was it a good, solid tap of either hello or goodbye.

It was a proper blow. And it hurt. She flinched more than she had in months, but she didn't make a sound. She hadn't felt pain like that in a long time.

She hadn't felt any kind of pain at all in an age. He walked off down the corridor with his hands jammed viciously into his pocket, marching and shivering down to his guts and looking from the back like some oversized boy scout.

He looked the way Kevin had looked before he'd hit his teens and gotten nasty.

She felt the awful pain in her foot begin to drain away. The last time she'd felt real pain was when she was thirteen, and she'd broken an arm.

Mind you, the arm in question was halfway up a pregnant cow at the time, and the uterine contractions of a full-grown cow will break anybody's arm, guaranteed.

The calf was the wrong way round, the cow was bawling in distress and both of them were going to die, so neither her father nor the vet had any difficulty in asking her to do the honours. So she did. The thing that bothered her more than the pain of the break was the fact that, when the calf went shooting out past her and landed in a safe, slimy heap in her father's arms, she was still trapped.

While he wiped the snot from its airways, she had dangled helplessly, and he had pretty much ignored them both, her stuck and screaming at one end and the cow hurt and bawling at the other.

She was back at school two days later with her arm strapped up, telling her friends that she fell over. She certainly wasn't going to tell them the truth, but they probably found out anyway. She used to love the walk to school, the two miles that took in a hill with a gradient that nowadays would have been classed as a form of child abuse. Past the fields of spuds and cabbage, past the house of the old man who was regarded as strange by practically everybody. He owned a big cottage just beyond the brow of the hill on the right, and his hedge was something to see. When it was at its most luxuriant, every summer, he would carve into it, not animals, but words. Things like 'Jesus Saves', and other religious mantras, in foot-high, tight and curly-green letters. Jesus alone knows how he managed it. He probably used a pair of scissors instead of shears. But all the kids would automatically veer away off to the other side of the road when passing his house. As if he was dangerous.

Once, on a dare, when she was feeling brave, she snuck into his garden and crouched behind a clump of gooseberry bushes and watched him. A completely bonkers piece of music was blaring out of his kitchen window and he was standing with a soup ladle in his fist, conducting the apple trees.

(Years later, she caught the same mad slice of music on a movie soundtrack and, in the dark, she went away in her head and missed, altogether, a good quarter-hour of dialogue. It was the final couple of minutes of the Waltz from Swan Lake, and she was lucky not to have to go running to the ladies.)

The old man was whirling about like a mad thing in his back garden, waving his misshapen baton, laughing occasionally, but he didn't seem that scary.

He was murdered a year later, and his house was ransacked. The killers were never found. The village was shocked. Nothing like that had ever happened before and everybody was truly sorry, even if the man was a bit odd. After that, the cottage fell derelict and she and her friends gradually began to stop veering off. She sort of missed that swerve, and the demented patterns that the sunlight made on her retinas and on the tarmac, from season to season, through the dense, dancing leaves one month, and the trees' skeletal shadufs the next. The cottage was left to rot, the road was now safe and the rest of her schooldays and much beyond were straight and ordinary, hers and Edmund's both.

Three decades and a bit later, a crew from the BBC came to use the surrounding hills and the ancient, crumbled cottage as a location for a documentary on the Irish Travellers, what they used to call the gypsies.

The village had become a town but, beyond that, not much had changed.

Thanks to the tourist board, most of the crew were offered free accommodation with local families. She and Edmund got Carl, one of the sound engineers. He didn't even tell them what the film was supposed to be about. He would hardly talk to them at all.

Carl was twenty-two, originally from Kenya, and he was the blackest person they had ever seen. In fact, Carl was the only black person they had ever seen. The woman had read somewhere that the Negro was 'God's Image Cut in Ebony', so she was determined to be polite.

When he showed up on their doorstep, with his small crates of equipment, both she and Edmund just stood and blinked at him, wobbling a little, as if blinded by the darkness of the man. But they weren't impolite and, within a wee while, Carl was ensconced in what used to be Kevin's bedroom. He made himself at home, made her promise to bring him his breakfast, and made it plain that he wasn't mad about white people.

Carl's parents had moved from Kenya to Lewisham when he was eleven, and still he couldn't get his head around most of what was going on. At school, the other kids picked on him because he spoke better English than they did, and knew what he wanted to do with his life. He was going to be an architect and he was going to get the A levels to do it, except that he didn't and couldn't. So he left school at eighteen and went to work for the BBC as a general dogsbody. He made tea, sawed bits of wood for sets, shopped for the make-up artists, and finally got some proper training in the sound department, where they decided to let him lie for a bit. He had a real talent for this kind of work, it turned out. Carl had ears like a bat, and after two years with the unit, he could finesse away the gubbins on any set and any soundtrack, leaving only the pure product. Or he could muddy things up. He could do anything with noise, anywhere along the sonic spectrum. All the director had to do was say a few words and Carl was off and running, knowing exactly what the man really wanted. He was good. Sound had become his religion. He could take a piece of murderous piffle and turn it around with just the right degree of twiddling or, if required, he could make a thick twelve-year-old with snot on his sleeve sound like a member of the distressed gentlefolk. Noise, in all its stupid, brilliant manifestations was Carl's comfort blanket and, when he was picked to help with the project in

Ireland, he had no idea of the landscape-shaped abyss of silence that he was in for.

He stayed in his room when he wasn't out on site with the crew, listening to the radio, or eating the meals the lady prepared for him, and not talking much.

The scenery here terrified him. Not because he was overwhelmed by its beauty, but because it swallowed up every sound and syllable and gave little back. It was an aural black hole, with the odd whisper of a breeze and nothing else, and he hated it.

On the fourth night, the rest of the crew took him out to the pub, where they celebrated the wrap of the documentary. They all got drunk and noisy and didn't notice the hostile stares from the locals, who didn't like gypsies much, and liked the notion of blacks even less. Much later, when Carl had gotten separated from his colleagues and been quietly beaten to a pulp behind the pub by four bad-tempered fellows, it took them a good twenty minutes to find him. He'd lost a tooth and one eye was swollen and shut, but given the darkness, their drunkenness, and the colour of Carl's skin, they found it really difficult to tell whether he'd been badly bruised or not. They decided he was probably all right. One of them made a joke about make-up for black folks, as they hauled him up, and took him back to the house. She asked them to help him, by now fully awake and walking more or less unaided, upstairs to Kevin's room.

She wiped his face gently with a clean, damp cloth and, when he leaned forward and buried his face in her shoulder and cried silently and hysterically, his whole body heaving, she wiped his face all over again. When he'd calmed down a little, she asked him to tell her about the documentary, the film about the Travellers, and just let him mumble on to himself, until he was so tired that he just shrank down onto the duvet, drew it around him and curled up like a sick baby. He slept like a nervous cat, twitching all over, and she tucked him in and thought about the gypsies. And about her disappointing son Kevin and the work he had done so well, so meticulously, all those years ago. The perfect bureaucrat in his sunny, dusty, ideal world. Herding his charges off into tidy, miserable clumps, rounded up in the town square, with their furniture and their houses snapped up already, their train tickets in their hands, and most of the other locals

not saying very much at all. Perhaps they were off to a better place.
And they were.

The Blessed Place.
Oświęcim.
Auschwitz.

On his next night out, a week later, Tom decided it was time for some cold, proper thievery. He didn't manage much. He let himself into John's house after he'd been casing it for an hour and had watched him leave. With Lynne on his arm. Tom let himself in and prowled about for a while. He remembered this place now. The smell in the hallway hit him hard. It was familiar from a while ago, but now it was mixed with her smell. It was a pleasant, samey odour, a thing that seemed to work in its combination, and it pissed him off so much he almost struck the hall mirror with the side of his fist. He calmed down a bit and went into the kitchen. He reached into his hip pocket and pulled out two CDs and laid them prominently on the kitchen table. Then he wandered into the tidy living-room with, still, its numerous video players, televisions and DVDs. Tom remembered how he'd felt when he'd first seen all that clobber.

He had assumed that the home-owner was a thief.

Now he knew that the bastard home-owner was a thief.

He prowled around, hopelessly, for twenty minutes, aching to destroy something and afraid to, afraid to shatter something that perhaps she had come to like, even something that, perhaps, she had bought as a present for the man. He helped himself to a mouthful of cooked chicken from the fridge, rewrapped the foil and left.

He was teetering in the cold, hunkered on his spot on the next-door neighbour's fence, when they returned three hours later, laughing together. He enjoyed watching through the window, the way he had before, the way she froze when she walked into the kitchen and saw her Nina Simone CD, and beside it, the Gil Scott-

Heron. With her cute address labels stuck on the back of each, with their gold-coloured, worthy Amnesty logo.

Tom couldn't hear a word and he couldn't lip-read, but he watched her lean away from the man John Kelso and, frowning awfully, mouth short, quick things that made him turn slowly in a circle of confusion, arms fanned out by his sides, palms upturned.

Through the silence, in John's beautiful wood-panelled kitchen, they looked like some kind of dumb tableau, flinching and not knowing what to say to each other. The fence creaked under his weight and it was the only sound. Then her face crumpled and she threw the CD at John's head and her hair swooped down around her face and her shoulders heaved, horribly. Tom was not enjoying this any more. He didn't want to hurt her. He had no idea what he was doing. But he didn't want to cause her pain. He didn't know where he was any more, and he didn't know what he was supposed to be any more. The fence creaked a little more in the cold and the only other sound was that of his own frosty breath.

He watched their slope-shouldered, miserable dance for as long as it lasted, and was almost glad when the bastard John Kelso stepped forward and put his arms around her and their crumpling silhouettes drifted up the stairs, and away on up.

Tom hopped off the fence, blinking hard, landed heavily and rolled over on his back in John's neighbour's flowerbed. He lay there for a bit, looking at the stars, the real thing this time, and they looked exactly like the demented, black-blitzed pattern on her bedroom ceiling. Except that now he was outdoors and cold, and raking dirt with his fingernails. Freezing and filthy and on the flat of his back.

He decided then, at that moment, that there would be no more vain visits to either house. He was going to look after himself, and make some money by whatever means, and he was going to stop this, to stop this thing that had taken and twisted his insides and ruined his heart in the maddest way possible.

It was going to stop.

And this time he knew, even to himself, that he meant it.

He closed his eyes against the insane wash of stars, hauled himself up off the dirt before the neighbours decided to call the police, went home and fell into a bath.

Of cold water, but he didn't care. He lay there, shivering and not crying or anything at all.

A week went by and went along and they decided to put the thing with the CDs and the medals behind them. Neither John nor Lynne knew for a fact what it was about. Perhaps she thought she knew him, he thought, perhaps she didn't. They both felt weird that some guy had broken into both their houses leaving barely a trace, and taking so little. If that's what had really happened.

If there *was* actually some guy. They didn't want to get into it.

Lynne, mostly, didn't want to get into it, so John just left it alone.

A little harmless, fragile bluff wasn't going to hurt anyone.

What the hell. The world was full of criminals.

It was a little thing, a tiny piece of upsetting strangeness which they were not going to allow to get in and dawdle around between them. Now and again, when she was asleep, John would study her face and remember the feel of the medal between his thumb and forefinger and the moment of shock when he had thought, for a nanosecond, that she was someone who might have something wrong with her. He always pushed the feeling away, knowing that she had had exactly the same feeling.

Everything was going to be fine.

*

In the weeks and months following his release, John Kelso had been the object of tremendous sympathy from the general public. Those few members of the general public who had heard of him, that is. His colleagues in the trade were a bit more sceptical, even after seeing his cuts and bruises and burns. It was when he produced his screenplay a month later, and the industry went bonkers bidding for it, that the knives really came out. He exaggerated the whole thing, they whispered. And when it was optioned by Hollywood, that did it.

He was a fraud; they were convinced of it. It was just a stunt to chase up interest in the script. It had to be. This Duthie character had been paid a chunk of cash to act mad, and take a while in a psychiatric ward for his trouble, they were all sure. He'd been carted off to a secure prison, yelping and whining and convincing no one.

No one in the television trade anyway.

No. He was a talented charlatan. No question. The whole thing was a set-up, no matter what the police said. Or the doctors, for that matter.

One broken pinky, for fuck's sake – hardly the most convincing picture of a kidnapping, was it?

They had whispered and quietly bitched for a month, and when John had been back at work for three days, slowly doing some research, some ideas, something, anything that he could work up for next week's show, he was informed, by a memo from on high, that Sally would be fronting his show for at least the next three weeks.

The public seemed to like her, apparently.

Kelso had marched into Sally's dressing room, and, as she sat there brushing her hair, and smiling at him in the mirror, he couldn't think of a single word to say.

The woman didn't have an ounce of malice in her entire body, and Kelso knew it.

He'd turned around, climbed the stairs up to head office and handed in his resignation. His colleagues gave him no leaving do. They seemed too embarrassed even to look him in the eye, along the humming white corridors. He knew that they thought he was a liar, and he couldn't do or say anything to convince them that it had really happened the way he said it had. The marks and blemishes on his hands counted for nothing. They were evidence of nothing, except perhaps a taste for tasteless self-promotion. John knew what they thought of him.

What he never knew, and what they would always and forever be too graceless and jealous to tell him, was that they thought his screenplay was a work of genius. Someone had seen it posted on the net and had clandestinely circulated it.

A week later, they all thought he was a wonder. And they hated his guts.

At the very least, they thought he was just a wonder, a freak and just too talented to be true. But none of them had the courage to actually tell him that both it and he were brilliant, to tell him how good a storyteller he was.

Which was just as well.

John Kelso, the good thief, could have withstood the bad, behind-your-back manners, and the crunchy, envious rancour, but he could not have borne that. He probably would have smashed somebody's face in, if they had been careless enough to throw even some miniature praise in his direction.

Typing up Kenny's original manuscript, extracting it from its mess of red-pen scarification and curled-corner rattiness, had taken John a week of steady work.

He didn't even notice the pain in his hands. In the late evenings, with the curtains closed but with a calm, low glow seeping through, this thing was his nutrition, this thing in front of him. Sheet after sheet, it got sweeter and sweeter, and with every page it became more and more his. It was as if he'd created it from scratch. As if Kenny had never been anywhere near it. With every soft tap and dry papery rustle, the story sank into him, through a process of osmosis, into his larcenous pores, until he felt something close to pride. He knew it was stupid, but he couldn't help it. And the beautiful thing was, he didn't have to change a word. Neither syllable nor comma. He tried to swoop in with a few flourishes near the start, and then thought to himself, *Who am I kidding?* No point in wearing himself out messing with perfection. So he'd sat alone in his house, typing and tapping and talking to no one, except the police on the phone when they wanted him to add something useless to their paperwork, typing and eating now and again and typing, until he was finished. When he was finished, he saved it. Then he saved it again. Then he saved it onto a floppy. And then onto another, with a different title. Then he printed it off. Twice.

John slept for a day and a half and when he was sure that the script was his and safe, he took the scabby, filthy original out to the patio and he burned it on his barbecue.

Chunk by chunk. Twenty pages at a time. It took ages. He sat slugging from a bottle and watched the evening sky, and drank a drink of wine for every section that went up in flames, and was amazed that his neighbours didn't seem to mind the acrid smoke. It smelled nothing like a proper barbecue, but maybe they didn't care. It smelled like harmless office stuff, like Xerox toner or something. He watched every red pen scribble on every page dissolve in the flames, and he could have sworn that the red pen patches sent up a qualitatively different colour of smoke, a smashing stream of watery yellow and a quiff of pink rising, entwined, skyward.

By the end of the evening, Kenny's script was gone, gone altogether, and nothing existed any more but John Kelso's ticket to something. Something else and probably better.

John finished off the bottle of wine with a lousy gulp and tickled the tip of a stick through the ashes, back and forth and up and along, for more than two hours, until he had completely forgotten why he was standing there in the first place.

He came to with a jolt and realised that he was freezing and that it was well into the night.

Only one of Kenny's three floppy disks had turned out to carry the manuscript. Kelso cut it into slivers with a pair of garden shears over a wastepaper bin and scattered the bits into three different bags of rubbish. He felt ludicrous but that didn't stop him. The other two disks held only Kenny's letters home. Almost a hundred letters to friends in Scotland, apparently. At first sight, judging from the file names, they looked like being just big, noisy, sentimental chunks of nonsense, to a bunch of people who, judging by the things that they seemed to be interested in, were probably a bit mad, frankly.

But John read them all, anyway. He'd wanted to know what manner of a man was this Kenny Duthie, this utter loon who had been remanded for psychiatric evaluation and wasn't going to see the light of day for at least a year and probably longer.

Kelso found out all right.

It took him a night and a day to read the letters and he hardly stopped for food, drink or breath. He tried to stop but he couldn't. By the end of it, he was trembling. He felt he now knew another person better than he knew the inside of his own mouth, and it scared the hell out of him. This was a life lived. With proper friends and shared passions and grammar just as it should be. This Kenny wasn't a madman, he was a kind and cool man, with an expansive and lovely acceptance of his fellows, his friends. And he wrote so beautifully, which was no surprise at all.

There were letters to his elder brother, to former workmates in Aberdeen – Andy and Douglas and Mark and David, whoever they were – to, it seemed, everyone who had ever given Kenny the time of day. And every letter was a work of art. The exactitude of the punctuation alone was terrifying for a kid his age, but it was the slant of his stream of thought and the gentle rants against, or for, this, that and the other that really held the attention. Kenny had an opinion on everything, and a deep affection for his friends that his theories couldn't hide.

He warbled on beautifully about building rituals and spirit levels, about graft and booze, about graffiti and vandals and a genius they never caught. The letters were written in the kind of shorthand that assumes you had been there, breathed the same frantic air, been coated in the same plaster dust and lashed by the same murderous and muddy waves at three in the morning. Kenny's letters were glum and gleeful and full of anecdote, as if he was reaching back for something, something like a proper life, sturdy and with some common sense attached.

But in these letters, Kelso saw no space to stroll. No place to mither on about meaningless stuff; no simple bullshit, bright, mournful or otherwise. No room just to say hello, or for necessary and slovenly plainness.

Kenny talked about the loss of the man David's eye as if it had happened on television.

He talked about Douglas and his degree, and his bruises and his daughter, in a warped, three-page passage that made no sense at all, no matter how many times Kelso read it.

In the letters, nasty items which must have been true, were bubbled along and dropped, and things which could only have been perfectly ordinary, Kelso was convinced, were turned into things sheen and cavalier and more snazzy than his own limp life. Kenny's letters might as well never have been posted at all. He was writing for himself and for himself alone. But it was a good act, and there were waves of a desperate, blithering affection for a bunch of people he knew he would never see again, and who didn't think about him at all anyway.

It was as if he was trying to be sympathetic, but the movies just kept getting in the way. Never in a million years, thought Kelso, would he have replied to letters like these. Whoever the recipients were, they were being harangued and lectured.

With more love than most people will ever taste in a lifetime, but even so.

It occurred to him that the writer was possibly the loneliest man on the face of the earth.

The letters scared Kelso almost as much as the screenplay, except, this time, he felt like a real and proper thief.

He sat back from the PC and he didn't know what to do. The thought occurred to him to destroy the disks but, for some reason, the notion seemed like blasphemy. So he dropped them into a drawer and, although the idea of smashing them up kept crawling back to him now and again, he couldn't and he didn't.

And so the months traipsed on and by, and John Kelso and Lynne Callier grew as close as it is possible for two people to grow. Neither of them gave up their flat, but shuttled back and forth, thrice-weekly and more. She went to work at the studio every day, and came back every evening with reports of how the human race was becoming stupider by the minute, while he spent his days on the phone with his agent, talking to producers in Los Angeles – he had never seriously entertained the idea of going there, not even for a short while – and rewriting a few bits and bobs on the screenplay. They were happy together. It was entirely fine, and not a complicated thing.

John Kelso hadn't felt guilty for ages, now. Every line on every page had slithered so deep into his head, he could recite any phrase, line, passage and screen specification as if he had a photographic memory. It was brilliant, canny and brilliantly all his, and everybody knew it. This movie project was moving along. He didn't have to be there. All he'd had to do was sell the thing, which his agent had done without any trouble, take the money and offer some gentle advice from the sidelines. A few grammatical points here and there, a series of quiet and small, small things. The phone rang maybe three times a day, about a little syllable or an accent or some such tiny nonsense, just to keep everything polite, he assumed. The producer and the director were both intelligent, well-mannered men. Kelso was happy to let them get on with it. They would make of it what they could, and good luck to them, because that damn screenplay was idiot proof and everybody in the business knew it. It was going to be huge and everybody knew that too.

Not that it mattered any more. Kelso didn't own it any more.
He never had.
And that didn't matter any more either.

3

On the day of his arrest, Kenny Duthie was bundled off to the hospital to have his hand sewn up. It looked worse than it was. Hardly bled at all. After that, he was kept in a separate cell for seventy-two hours, examined in that cell by the police surgeon, and examined again by the consultant (who only called on Wednesdays and Fridays, and who was sick and tired of pronouncing on mad, bad, alcoholic, thieving, criminal and evil bastards whose first ploy was always to pretend to be crazy, just so that they could avoid prison; but he was professional enough to recognise a genuine nutter when he saw one), then taken, under Section 24 of the Mental Health Act, from the police station to the Intensive Psychiatric Care Unit at Ashworth.

Kenny went, naturally and quite caustically, bonkers as soon as he was hauled through the door, so the staff, quite naturally and sensibly, kept him separate for a bit and sedated him with two sledgehammer 100 mg doses of Acuphase.

That took the temporary madness out of him, but he just kept on misbehaving, miserably and loudly regardless, so under Section 26, they served him an extra four weeks on the ward, and gave him five days worth of 10 mg doses of droperidol.

Which gave him terrifying side-effects – muscle spasms, eye-rolling ('ocular gyric crisis', the textbooks called it), and a near-suffocating tightening of his throat. Several times, ten minutes after a dose, he thought he was going to die. Twice, he got so bad that even the staff thought he might, so they gave him intra-muscular injections of procyclidine as an antidote.

He calmed down a little then, mainly by weeping.

Then for six weeks, they gave him 4 mg daily doses of Lorazepam, and made him aware, dimly, that under Section 58 of the Criminal Procedures Act, he could still be referred back to prison. Or even the courts. Kenny went very quiet.

For the rest of his term on the ward, the nurses gave him, three times daily, 50 mg of chlopromazine. Kenny behaved himself after that. For the whole ten months.

Sometimes at night his old school lessons would come floating into his addled mind. Greek wasn't taught, of course, but his old Geography teacher, Mr Heald, was forever quoting Latin, or whatever. He would explain where words came from. *Sanctuary* was one of his favourites. *Asylum* was another. A place where pillage was forbidden. (From the Greek: *a* = negative, *sulon* = right of pillage.) And here he was. Asylum. And he felt anything but safe.

Kenny had never, ever taken any kind of drug, not even an aspirin, and the feeling of his head, heart, brain and body just slipping away from him, frightened him more than anything had in his entire life. When he came back to himself after the very first dose, and looked up at the face of the charge nurse, and realised where he was and what had happened to him, Kenny cried as if he had been mugged useless by a crowd of thieving thugs, polluted by the worst kind of thing. If he couldn't think straight, then he was nothing. They had taken his mind away from him, for a little while anyway, with the kind of blasphemous aplomb that Kenny scarcely knew existed, and they had done it with infinite care and kindness. So he stopped crying and decided that, if he had to play the game to avoid being really *seriously* drugged again, then he would just have to go along with the whole sucking, mashing procedure. And besides – maybe they were right. Maybe he actually *was* mad altogether, and the nurses' fresh and buoyant concern really was for his own good. Either way, what he had to do was intolerably clear to him. He dropped the act, the brittle panache, the bad tempers and the thin skin, and he tried to be a good and winning boy. It took him two months to accept that the world in general thought he was a complete balloon, but after that he was okay. He slept too much but that was okay too.

Kenny Duthie became a model patient and alarmingly content. He allowed himself to be drenched in the delicacy of the nurses' care. He showed no interest in the outside world, and he never uttered, as far as the staff could tell, one word about the man John Kelso. Not a peep. But they weren't stupid. They had seen clever, mercurial bastards before, and they weren't about to let this one slide under the radar.

Kenny got to know the other patients on the ward. What a crowd. They were an acute and soggy pastiche of the real world, and the funniest, sorriest collection of people he had ever encountered. Over the weeks, his fear fell right away and he gradually took on the role of benign gang leader. In the day room, they began to hang on his every word. Kenny had no idea why. Perhaps because most of what he said had been said before. In the movies. And said better and snootily, and with a proper degree of authority, but his audience wasn't to know that. He allowed himself important silences, which impressed the hell out of them, and he allowed them their own tales, shot through with chippiness, messy and resentful, and tons of obscene, simian scolding, mostly against their families, husbands, wives, whatever. He was truly shocked by their stories and their plastic demons and their sterile confections of pure hate, but he pretended not to be. He just let his fellow inmates waddle on, evening after evening, with their miserable mournings and filthy, staccato tattoos of abuse against somebody or other.

But sometimes it was nice. Sometimes a fellow inmate, usually a younger one, would kick up with a sweet yarn about a girl, or something. And the huge bullion of self-pity would fade for a bit, and they would all just sit and nod and nod, and the loose vocabulary of their lousy lives made perfect sense.

When Kenny thought about it, he realised that he was doing the nurses' job for them.

Den mother. Big brother. Bunch boss. Acoustic king. Whatever. Kenny really began to enjoy himself on the ward.

He was told that his stuff, his tapes, his books, had been sent to his brother's house in Aberdeen. He asked vaguely about his manuscript, but nobody knew anything about that. And in a way, he stopped caring. He fretted in the night for the first couple of nights and then he just stopped. It probably wasn't the drugs, but then again, perhaps it was. Either way, Kenny found himself not that bothered. It was as if a chunky burden had fallen from his shoulders. But he wasn't certain if he wasn't grieving because he wasn't supposed to, or because he just wasn't. Three woozy nights of trying to figure it out gave him a nosebleed, and after a while he discovered that he could only remember some of the plot, never mind any of the dialogue. He tried to get upset. It was his life's work, for the love of Christ. And he couldn't. It must have been the drugs. The whole moody and lofty mess just floated away into the back of his mind and then beyond even that.

Some days, Kenny realised with a jolt that his mind had been empty for he didn't know how long.

But he had his new team and grist, and they began to fill a gap. In the wispy white of the ward, Kenny found a quiet and mangled treadmill that suited him just fine, all replete with pathetic shouting matches between pathetic people, and cut-ups so titanic that even the nurses got scared. He became the groovy and sensible lad, the one the rest of the patients turned to when they wanted to blather aimlessly on and on and on. And, as before, his gift for listening came in very handy. The ward was a place where he could carry on without falling apart, and where he started taking notes again. Where he could pick and choose from the almost unlistenable fucking frazzle of all their sad and fair-to-middling lives.

Pick and choose from the kind of swagger and stagger that just never popped up in the real world.

Ever.

It was as if he'd found a new screenplay. Just waiting to happen. All of it in gibberish, slang, rubbish and nonsense. All of it in Thieves' Latin.

But Kenny Duthie had good ears.

He was going to have to sober up first, though. That was for damn sure.

One of the members of his new-found gang was an awkward chap in his mid-thirties. This guy had been in and out of jail for years, mostly for petty theft but, now and again, for something a bit violent. He had scars on his hands and tattoos all over his back.

The biggest featured a huge red heart, and inside it the words 'Jason and Rita' in a ludicrous baroque font. He was a heavily muscled, slightly hunched figure, with a weird hairdo. Kenny was reminded of Wolverine. Jason talked about his days in jail now and again.

He had gotten religion three years previously and when he joined the creative writing class, at the suggestion of the prison chaplin, he tried to write a story about Judas, or rather about Jesus from Judas's point of view. But when he showed the first draft to the course tutor, the man went a little pale. It was a lovely love story. That was okay. No real harm done there. It was just the way it was written. Its style had the same folksy formalism of one of the gospels, except for the fact that, in it, Jesus was a fucking idiot. An incoherent and impulsive cretin and the ruination of everyone and everything around him. Judas was the sensible patriot and a man of insight and sensitivity. A man who took careful, proper and moody care of the idiot collective, and to hell with the so-called miracles. In Jason's story, Judas spent much more time thinking than Jesus did talking, which made for a bit of a change. Judas Iscariot was a political genius.

Jesus, on the other hand, was a stupid bastard, with all the wit and nous of a carpet swatch. A man who wafted out, effortlessly, damage wherever he went, and didn't pay for any of it until the very last minute. Judas loved him beyond all notions of love, no doubt about it. But the man was a liability, a truly dangerous, lovable and total fuckwit, whose nicely hopeless and puppy-like enthusiasm for moronic stunts was matched only by his own huge sense of self-worth.

The writing course tutor, a solid Christian himself, corrected all of Jason's spelling mistakes, but the story scared him more than just a little. He didn't quite know what to do about this gobby and lofty slice of mini-blasphemy. So he just left it alone. Jason was a committed and intense man who had dragged himself from a state of near-illiteracy up to mere offensiveness. Besides, he spent more time in the gym than almost anyone, and the tutor wasn't about to insult a man with a physique so downright dense.

Kenny admired Jason for his story. It was, frankly, a rubbish and ruptured read. But even so. Besides, he thought it was kind of funny that the guards' peep-holes in a prison door were traditionally called 'Judas slits'. He didn't tell Jason that.

They talked now and again, and now and again Jason would talk about his younger days, about his friends, and about his brother and sister, Benny and Linda.

Kenny could have sworn that those names were familar. Over the weeks, Jason came to feel that he could trust Kenny with his past. So he would talk because it gave him comfort to blather about his nice but useless parents and his brother and sister. And his gang. Jason didn't try to pretend that it was his gang. When he mentioned in passing the name of the charismatic bully in charge of that long-ago crew, the brilliant and funny boy whose parents never knew where he was, Kenny sat stunned and motionless. The coincidence almost made his lungs hurt. John Kelso certainly put himself about. Kenny hadn't thought about him, not properly, for four months. The drugs had a lot to do with it, but when Jason said the name and rambled on happily about the fights over turf and all the other juvenile nonsense, the memory of the man came flooding back.

A week after that, after supper in the rec room, Jason came back from the gym and they got talking again. Jason seemed antsy and upset and, after some gentle goading, admitted that if he ever ran into John Kelso again, he might do something he'd regret. It was all years ago, but even so. The man had raped his sister.

Kelso had raped his sister and gotten away with it. She was thirteen and everybody knew and nobody said anything. She'd had a bad stutter, but after that she didn't. She barely spoke. Jason had fallen away from most of his family but, in the little correspondence there was over the years, Linda's almost total silence was a constant, and a constant embarrassment. Jason remembered finding her crumpled in a corner of the cattle-meal warehouse, an almost invisible line of blood running down her exposed thigh. She didn't look as if she'd been thumped too much, but he knew that something was badly wrong, because her mouth was moving and no sound was coming out. Not a stuttered peep. Nothing. Her mouth was an awful, meandering gash and her eyes were all over the place. Jason was only twelve. He didn't know what to do, so he ran home and left her there. But the next day, he saw his friend and boss and he just knew that John Kelso had done something wrong.

Kenny listened to his story and he could hardly believe it. Okay, John Kelso would have been only a kid at the time, but even so. He let Jason carry on with his ancient, calamitous twaddle, and the more he listened, the angrier Kenny became.

John Kelso had fucked them both. One way or the other. But he decided to let it lie. No point in getting all rowdy. And doped up to the eyeballs for his trouble. So Kenny stored it away and got on with his civilised recovery. Kenny had no choice but to interact with his fellow patients. He didn't have television any more. Or his movies either. So he was forced to face up to the real thing, and he decided that most of it was, frankly, pretty gruesome.

Tim Robinson was one of the more interesting of Kenny's ward disciples. He was an ex-racist. He was forty-seven and one of the original suedeheads in the early seventies. Then he became a skinhead, but not a racist. Then he became a racist, but one with long hair. Then with short hair, but not shaved, exactly. Then, just as he grew too exhausted to be a proper racist any more, and had been in and out of homes for longer than he could remember, he became a skinhead again. It was just so much more comfortable in the hot weather that way. These days, Tim was bounced from ward to ward because he had grown so full of love for all mankind that significant chunks of mankind had grown to hate his guts.

But when he met Kenny, he began to behave himself, and Kenny realised that the man meant every lovely syllable, every noise of brotherhood and harmony between the races, and everybody else, for that matter. Most of what Tim said made perfect sense and the ward knew it. It was just that he made them feel clever and bad, rather than better and oblivious. Especially Adam Ryan, who was from Dundee, adopted, twenty-four and black.

Adam had spent the previous winter following Andy Goldsworthy to a couple of sites around Dumfriesshire and Cumbria, trying to destroy the works before Goldsworthy got a chance to photograph them. But he always folded up with the sheer and miserable cold, long before Goldsworthy had anywhere near finished. He would curl up frozen under a hedge seventy yards away and, by the time he woke up and came to, the work was finished, the snap was taken and the man was gone. Adam had no idea why he would want to destroy a thing of beauty, especially as it was, by its nature, going to melt, dissolve and gently collapse in time, anyway. He had a vague notion in the back of his mind that nothing should be that smart or beautiful, so lovely that a mere photograph of it could move him to the bonework of such sloppy vandalism. So, every time, he would creep off defeated, with no chilly and mad piece of ruination to his name.

It had all started with a photograph he saw in a newspaper of David Mach's gigantic submarine made out of tyres. It just pissed Adam off, it was so fabulous. It was big and boisterous and clever beyond anything he knew he would ever be able to do. And his grandfather had served in the Navy. When Adam was a small boy the old man was quiet about the war, but sometimes he would pour himself a drink and begin to talk about life on board a submarine. The boy never forgot the old man's terse and fractured whisper.

What Adam never realised was that Goldsworthy knew exactly where he was, every single moment he was creeping around in the cold and crackling undergrowth. And he never knew how lucky he was not to have gotten his head kicked in.

The Artist as Fit Bloke. Adam wouldn't have stood a chance.

Eventually Adam gave up and took up with ordinary vandalism in Twickenham town centre.

Still, if Kenny thought he was okay, then he probably was. Kenny was boss. Not because he was a bully, but because everyone else was too tired to come up with an alternative leader. Or too stupid.

Or just too fucking mad.

Either way, Kenny ruled his little tonka-toy kingdom and nobody bothered him. Even the nurses let him get on with whatever his caustic, harmless brain told him he should be getting on with, dealing and doodling and keeping his bereft brood out of trouble.

Richard was fifty-five, a former chef and obsessed with anagrams. Crop circles, mazes and anagrams. Richard could do those magazine, maze-type puzzles in three seconds flat, and Kenny had seen the kind of stuff that could be done on a dozen crappy anagram websites, but Richard was something else. The man took garbage and turned it into poetry, and he did it inside his own sad, under-occupied, over-educated head. Every inmate's name became something else and extraordinary, a pretty litany of something better than their own nature would have suggested. Some of them didn't like it, the way Richard transformed their names, usually out loud in the rec room or in the canteen queue, into things removed from any kind of reality, into sweaty and polite conglomerations of vowels and adjectives that made them look just plain stupid. Or brilliant. Either way, most of the lads enjoyed Richard's weird talent, but some didn't. He never got badly beaten up – this wasn't prison – but after a while Kenny had to take Richard aside and persuade him to stop doing that damn thing. And so Richard went quiet, and after that it was hard to get a single word out of him that wasn't something to do with nursery rhymes or lullabies or Dr Seuss.

Kenny felt bad about that, but even when he relented and tried to softly talk the man back into the world, Richard just avoided his eyes and whispered several princely permutations of the words *Kenny Duthie* (*Hun Deity Ken, Nude Thin Key, Yuh Kind Teen, Ken Yet Hindu* – Kenny was ready to punch him), and curled up in his own wee world, and stayed there for about a month. Kenny made a point of checking in on him, and asking the nurses how Richard was doing, and they were always kind enough to tell him.

And there was Caroline, a woman who was brought in screaming one Saturday night – screaming with an American accent, everyone noticed – who turned out to be an actual, proper nun. In the absence of any identification from Scotland, where she had been picked up, it took the staff three days to piece together who she was. She cried like a subdued banshee for the first two. Wept and moaned and upset everybody. In the night, when she was quiet and doped up, she would tear at her long grey hair with her long horrid nails, and rail and make perfect, rotten sense with every syllable. The rest of the ward heard, off and on, most of what she was on about, and she scared them more than most.

The mad know their own, and she wasn't one of them.

Caroline was sixty-one and, up until sixty, had been the kindest, most selfless person on the planet. She had spent her entire adult life doing vocational work in the community, caring for other people. Tramps, lunatics, drug addicts, whores and all the other debris San Francisco had to offer. When she became a Mercy novice and took the name Aquinas, she had begun slowly to disappear under the weight of other folk's needs. For forty years Sister Aquinas helped and healed out on the streets and froze and just plain put up, hoping, in the occasionally chilly nights, that it was worthy work. She was mugged, albeit not too roughly, more times than she could remember. She listened to bad people telling good stories and decent people telling atrocious ones. She slopped soup into bowls, with feral cats slashing her ankles and slobbering drunks grabbing at her tits, she fed the hungry, arranged shelter for all those without, counselled and soothed and just kept going and going, year after year after unfussy year, for her brood, for her dreary gang, knowing in the back of her mind, for a fact, that none of them cared if she lived or died.

And then, one day, she just snapped.

It happened in Inverness. Her Order was on a coach tour of Scotland. It was the first proper holiday most of the sisters had had in a decade. She and a few others in their street-clothes, which was a treat, were crossing the suspension bridge across the river at night, on the way back to the mission after a day's sightseeing. As the others moved on to the far side, she had leaned over slightly and looked at the river Ness flowing fast and blackly by, less than six feet below her face. As she stared down at the water rushing by in the freezing dark, with only the odd, off-kilter glitter from the filthy orange streetlights seeping into the side of her eye, Sister Aquinas had welcomed the darkness and murky nonsense, because it made her feel as if she didn't exist in the real world. She closed her eyes and breathed in the sharp river air, and then the corrosive and howling truth hit her like a sledgehammer.

She didn't exist in the real world.

She hadn't existed from the moment she took her vow of obedience. For forty years she had been shrinking and shrivelling and disappearing into others' lamentable and lousy lives, devoured by the haphazard and barking hordes who had sucked every fucking ounce of life from her, herself.

She had nothing left to give. Nothing with which to live. Not really.

So it was at that point that Sister Aquinas went completely and utterly berserk on the suspension bridge in Inverness. She screamed and wailed like a mad thing, and roared obscenities against the black sky and against God Himself, and had to be stopped from flinging herself into the river by a couple of guys on their weaving way back from the pub.

Rob and Dave were feeling really pleased with themselves, since their team had just won £300 in the first pub quiz in an age that wasn't for some bloody charity.

The winning question – 'Arthur Q. Bryan, Paul Winchell, Grace Stafford, Alan Lane.'

The winning answer – 'Elmer Fudd, Dick Dastardly, Woody Woodpecker, Mister Ed.'

At this point Rob, already hugely drunk, had got a bit carried away and had started to taunt the other teams.

'Name every one of Top Cat's gang, you bastards!' he shouted.

It was only the fact that he was likeable, when sober, that saved Rob from getting his head kicked in. Dave dragged him outside and in the direction of home, while Rob continued to bellow bolshy shite over his shoulder about Cary Grant and Fancy Fancy and *Guys and Dolls* and Sgt. Bilko. It was only when he started to sing the theme song to *Top Cat*, annoyingly word-perfect, that Dave thought about clobbering him. And then he spotted the woman, weeping and wailing and carrying on, draped over the railings like a mad thing.

They had a bit of a struggle dragging her off the railings since Sister Aquinas, although getting on in years, was as fit as a butcher's dog, and they were both completely plastered. But the pair of them managed it anyhow.

Being totally drunk on a mildly bouncing suspension bridge creates its own precarious brand of equilibrium.

Caroline wept and Rob swore and Dave wasn't quite sure what to do. So he smacked both of them over the head with his mobile phone until they both shut the fuck up. And then he checked that the damn thing was still working.

After the police had taken her up to Craigdooneen's psychiatric ward, still howling like a banshee, Caroline the nun was given a big and blinding bolt of sedative.

That calmed her for two days, but when she started to cry and couldn't stop, hardly even to breathe, she was shipped off to Ashworth in London. On the way there, she wept hysterically every inch. It was only when she came out of the drugs on the second day and met Kenny that she began to calm down a bit, and to tell a few bumbling details of who she might be. So that was Kenny's favour to the staff. A little information, teased out over hours, from her brittle morass of hiccuping misery. An arm crooked around her rounded shoulders, and he got a name. A name. And an address in San Francisco.

By this stage, the Order had been alerted, but it wasn't certain that it wanted her back.

And so Kenny had another fan.

Yes, Kenny discovered a sliver of something resembling power. And the kind of power where he didn't have to hit anyone. It was just kinetic. He was the leader of the gang and his gang was quiet and quietly respectful. Medicated, mostly, but that wasn't the point. He had his prescribed harem and his daily routine and he didn't feel like bothering anyone. For eight months, he kept it that way, because it made him feel saner than anyone else there. He probably was saner than anyone else there, but he didn't want to push his luck.

Jason and Tim and Adam and Richard and Caroline.

Kenny grew to love their stories. Their stories of rotten relatives and even worse schools. Of stuff self-inflicted and stuff not. And later on, their ludicrous yarns of calm and snazzy love, before everything went, invariably, wrong. Of various breeds of pain and utter, utter and awful loss that Kenny Duthie knew, despite everything, he had never and would never come close to feeling.

He didn't even miss the movies any more.

There were more stories here in this ward, and better ones too, and all of them full of something a little chill and slatternly, with illiberal nudges scattered hither and yon. He knew in his heart that he no longer had the gumption to try to write anything ever again. The fight had gone out of him. He knew now that he would never have been able to write anything to compare with this mob. Well, he could, but he'd done it once and it had gotten him nothing but trouble. He wasn't good enough, and that's all there was to it. He was happy enough, these days, to spend his afternoons listening to his comrades' strop and sour menace.

His sweetly ordinary bunch of halfwits, with their loose and collective vocabulary of unimpeachable heartache – Kenny just knew that he was going to miss them all so much when he left.

When he finally did leave, they all crowded around him so, it made him feel guilty. It was his day to go, and there was nothing to be done. He couldn't believe it had been ten months, but it had. He had behaved himself more or less, so, more or less, he was free to go.

Kenny moved into a sheltered hostel for two months. After that he was deemed capable of fending for himself. So he got himself a part-time job with Asda, and a bedsit back in Eltham. After a bit of wrangle with Social Services, he got his videos and his cassettes and his books back.

When he was ready to venture out into the real world, he did just that.

The first thing he did was go to Pizza Hut.

And then he went to the movies. His first movie in just over a year.

He didn't really care which one.

He hadn't read any reviews, so he had no idea what he should go and see.

He just lumbered into Leicester Square with a tenner in his fist and, in the pouring rain, picked the one with the nicest title.

Two minutes into the film, with the steam still softly rising from his coat's shoulders, and the characters beginning to get into their stride, Kenny felt a soft prickle of familiarity on the back of his neck and in the pit of his guts. And the familiar became, horribly, a set of old and personal certainties that he thought had gone from his mind for good. But it was no good. After twenty minutes, he was mouthing every line of dialogue twenty seconds before it even came along.

Kenny sat for two hours plus in the darkness, and for two hours plus, he stared at the screen and barely blinked. After he'd done that, he stumbled out of the theatre into the sunlight, and managed to stop himself from screaming his way all around the slick pavements and thereabouts, by sheer force of will alone.

He vomited, but managed to get to a litter bin first. And then he staggered back to the poster on the cinema wall, and had a long, long and very vicious look at the credits. And apparently it had taken $26 million on its first weekend.

Kenny, with his nose almost pressed against the poster's glass, felt himself being watched. He looked to his left and saw a face he knew. The man stared at him and didn't flinch, exactly. The look in his eyes was one of pity or something close. It was the man from the video shop in Blackheath. The man Kenny had clobbered. He had a tiny scar on his left cheek that just hadn't managed to heal, even with the gift of a good year or so. He and Kenny looked at each other, without rancour, for half a minute. Kenny realised that the man had the most amazing eyes he had ever seen, and was ashamed of himself for not having noticed them at the time.

Back when. Back then. Back when he was decking the poor bastard.

He looked at the cheek-mark and, because he suddenly felt weird at the sight of it, and didn't know what else to say, he said, 'I'm sorry.'

The mildly scarred man smiled in a sensible way, and said 'Yes.'

Just that.

Just 'Yes.'

Then he placed a heavy fingertip on Kenny's cheek, as if he was anointing the dead, and sauntered slowly off without another word.

It began to rain again, a wee sunny shower. A dribble at best.

Kenny stood shivering and stout between the two things, shuddering and trembling between the kindness of the man just gone, and the thief parked here behind glass.

He stood in front of the cinema getting damp and desperate. When, eventually, the weight of a breed of svelte and steroidal sadness crowded around him until he felt that he could hardly stand, he tottered solidly off to the Tube and went home. He went home in a sad and bleary whiff, and when he lay down to sleep, he was absolutely convinced that he would never wake up.

The woman was thinking about patron saints. Trying to remember all the names of the saints who looked after those in distress, or pain. Saint Cecilia – took three days to die, with a bleeding neck, after a botched job by the executioner. Saint Peter – crucified upside down. And dozens of others, all dying horribly. The names that had been hammered into her and her friends at school. Then, as she slowly curled over, under her pristine sheets, it occurred to her that there were saints only for the miserable mob who wanted something. Something fixed, something found. A boil healed, a journey eased, a cancer cured, an argument solved, an exam passed, a sovereign recovered from down the back of the sofa. Either that or, when the game was lost, relief from the pain of loss when death snuck in and did his best, regardless.

Weren't there any patron saints of fine and brilliant things, simply? A patron saint of joy and bliss, to whom people could turn for absolutely no reason other than they had that saint to thank for the fact that air was still streaming in and out of their lungs, and that they hadn't actually keeled over yet? A patron saint of, not the dawn exactly, but of the extraordinary relief she felt when she opened her eyes and saw the creeping beige light through the curtains, and realised that, despite everything, she was still here. Still taking up magnificent space and wasting resources that could be put to better use on diabetics, and young mothers, and on sickle-cell patients. Or the patron saint of tiredness in the streaming dusk, when tiredness was beautiful beyond belief and all she wanted to do, and did, was drift off. Saint Leon apparently came to possess the elixir of eternal life, and the power to transmute base metal into gold. But it brought him nothing but misery. Apparently. And the House of Commons' proper name was Saint Stephen's House, but the woman wasn't sure if that was a good thing or a bad thing.

She would drift and wonder about things that kept popping up from her agile girlhood. The cows in the fields, smelling like hell, and the ewes with the dye-marks on their necks, telling who had been mated and who hadn't, and the rams with their ludicrous dye-balloon necklaces, now all useless and off for slaughter. When she was very small and, on a walk past the fields with her mother, she spotted the red blotches on the ewes' backs, and had cried hysterical tears, convinced that they had been wounded somehow.

The Doctor wandered by, and her memories fled, punctured and entirely ruined.

Real but minor pain was one thing.

Fear of worse was another thing entirely.

The Doctor was different these days. He seemed to be more solid than the boy he was once. And now, he had a mobile phone plastered to his ear much of the time.

The press was driving him insane. They had started to show up every day. Print, so far, not broadcast, but that would come. She had become a story. She had become the living ghost of the hospital. No name. No history. She had unnerved every nurse on the ward. They did the needful, then disappeared.

The Doctor had taken to reading to her from the papers. Usually depressing stuff, occasionally not. He had stopped trying to get any kind of response from her. He just sat and stared and read aloud from the newspapers, in a monotone that wasn't exactly hostile, but chilled her skin anyway.

He told her about the Hindu gentleman who peeled off his own skin to make a pair of sandals for a pilgrimage.

He told her about the American tourists smashed through a Harrods window by a runaway black cab, the wife decapitated.

He sat by her bed every evening, getting meaner by the minute. He didn't know why any more and he barely cared.

In a kinder moment, he recounted the story of how an anonymous bouquet of white roses had been left on T. E. Lawrence's grave every year on the date of his birthday, since 1935.

She took a silent frisson of pleasure in thinking about that. And then he told her that in 1994, the bouquets stopped, and hadn't appeared since.

So someone had died, and nobody even knew who they were to begin with.

The woman shrunk a tiny bit in her bed. He knew she could hear him. He saw her flinch. And so he talked, viciously on and on, in the sterile evenings.

He told her how two stoned, dumb, hippy Doors fans had knifed each other in Père Lachaise cemetery, and bled to death all over Jim Morrison's grave. That made him laugh out loud. Stupid fuckers.

He read from the environment pages. He told her about the new breed of ladybird. With mutant, horrible spot patterns, patterns gone wrong and rotten. Pollution probably. Quelle surprise. *He snickered about how the dingo is facing extinction, with most Australians never having even seen one.*

He laughed his arse off recounting how an okapi in Copenhagen zoo suffered a heart attack and died because the local opera company was rehearsing, at God knows how many decibels, Wagner's Tannhäuser *three hundred yards away.*

How a male kangaroo in Milan zoo apparently committed suicide after the death of his mate, by repeatedly rushing a concrete wall, skull-first. (The Doctor didn't believe that one for a moment. Animals just aren't smart enough to end it all, even when needs must.)

He told her about Granite Mountain in Utah. The Mormon Geneaological Library of over two billion names. The names of the dead. Souls for harvesting, back-the-ways.

'The Dead,' he repeated, just to emphasise the point. The old woman looked him in the eye. He had to tilt his head almost horizontally and lean in very close to catch her expression, and her expression scared him so badly he jolted back and dropped the newspaper. He didn't do that again. And he didn't know why he was being so nasty. He was not an unreasonable person, but he just couldn't help himself. She was supposed to be gone and wasn't, and here he was, being tormented by the media and made a fool of. He was becoming a joke. That's the way it felt, anyway. There had been moments when he ached to tell her that he was sorry for hitting her,

until he realised that he wasn't sorry at all. He was just heartbroken that she was still alive. And he couldn't quite believe it.

The woman read the misery in his poor, youthful, fraught face and, for what she thought might have been about five minutes, she tried to think about how it might be if she spoke to him. Then gave up the effort as a truly bad idea.

So she shrank back under her covers and thought about Gene Kelly and Rita Hayworth in Cover Girl, *and about the dance he swaggered his way through with Vera-Ellen. It was only ten minutes at the arse-end of a bog-standard 1948 biopic of Lorenz Hart.* Words and Music. *Kelly probably did it as a studio favour. She had already been veering well into late middle age when she saw him do that, and she'd never forgotten it. Didn't want to, either.*

While the Doctor mithered on and on with his tales of terrible woe, and his sweaty episodes of bad temper, the woman just burrowed slowly south in her blankets, and wondered what had happened to Carl. The young man, black as soot, from so long ago. The talented child with ears like a bat. The dark and frail kid, svelte and desperate, beaten senseless by her good friends and neighbours.

When, at the war's end, her son Kevin had been dead for two and a half days, and the extremities of his carcass half-chewed by the dogs, the mayor of the Greek town decided to give his body a decent burial. Nobody objected. They were too embarrassed to care. The mayor's aides stripped the rags off what was left of him and went through the pockets. In one pocket they found a piece of paper, scrawled in ink, which read: 'We will humiliate you with our compassion.'

Kevin's hair had been combed and his chin shaved. His six remaining fingernails were clean, he smelled faintly of good wine, and his stomach was full.

He was just dead, that was all.

For some reason the mayor thought that his mother would want to keep the scrap of paper. The woman kept it for a long time. When Edmund died, she burnt it along with a thousand other things. Few things made any sense any more. There were raggle-taggle bits and bobs, niblets of information and globs of memory, and grand things that felt grander than anything, but made no sense at all.

The woman didn't even know any more why she was remembering what she was remembering, and it didn't matter a damn. She thought about the movies she'd sneaked off to.

Escaping to the movies by herself whenever she could. Missing most of that glamour. Relying on the stills in the fan magazines instead. That aside, she'd actually enjoyed the war. Or the Emergency, rather. And Edmund had shown a spark of interest in the newspaper reports. About naval activities, especially. Or was it the Air Force? Either way, until the war ended, and the news arrived about their soiled and ragged son, both of them had managed to maintain a stiff, reasonable and mostly silent enthusiasm about their respective interests.

And just then, into her head popped the story of Mrs Fritz Mandl and the Submarines. Hedy Lamarr and the Torpedo Frequency-Hopping Patent.

Stupid really, that being one of the last things she could remember. And the reasons why. The old woman remembered reading about it in the newspapers, years after the war ended, and it had, quite simply, burnt itself into her brain. Or did she not remember but simply imagine it? She would have written a fan letter if she'd known.

Her very favourite actress, Hedy Lamarr, was married to a leading arms manufacturer who forbade her to pursue her acting career in the 1930s. With nothing else to do, Lamarr had begun to accompany her husband to meetings with his technicians and his business associates, and had, apparently, become interested in the design of remote-controlled torpedoes, and the protection of their radio signal guidance frequencies from enemy jamming.

Before 1940, a torpedo's path, once it was fired, could not be adjusted, so their accuracy rate was low. (For Mr Mandl, a low hit rate would actually have been good for business – the more strikes needed, the more torpedoes sold.) But, for Britain, facing invasion, the deployment of torpedoes that could be steered with pin-point accuracy might have meant the difference between defeat and victory. So his wife, who was vehemently anti-Nazi, made it her business to either create or discover a technology which would distribute the torpedo's signal over numerous, random, individual frequencies, all in fractions of a second.

After she had done most of the groundwork, however, the main problem was one of synchronisation between origin and destination. Enter the avant-garde composer Antheil – a friend of Lamarr's and the man who had solved the riddle of how to orchestrate sixteen console-controlled pianos for the 1925 movie Ballet Méchanique, by using perforated paper rolls. Just like the ones used in barrel organs. And it worked.

The US and British navies actually accepted Miss Lamarr's proposals and, therefore, to ensure that the frequency-jumping patterns of both the transmitter and the receiver – ship and torpedo – were the same, began to equip both with identically perforated paper rolls.

So in the water, the radio signal guiding the torpedoes jumped all over the place, continuously, synchronously and much too fast for the Germans to either detect or jam.

Torpedo hit rates soared. The German ships and submarines were on the run.

The difference between victory and defeat.

Hedy Lamarr.

World War II.

She got a medal for it. The Austrian Association of Patent Holders and Inventors.

And she was so beautiful in her films, on top of everything else.

Hedy bloody Lamarr.

Unbelievable.

The old woman remembered all that.

But she still wasn't sure if she'd actually read it somewhere.

Perhaps it wasn't true. Perhaps she had made it all up, by skinny accident, in her own head, and it was just an immaculate, plausible and jaw-dropping dream, here in her own personal doldrums.

Here on the overlit ward.

And the Doctor, meanwhile, kept on reading to her stories of horror and of love and of both. Stories unholy, skint and stuffed with expert tomfoolery. Stories that were less than stories but more than headlines. Haphazard, immoderate and bossy things that he thought might get a reaction. Then again, he wasn't even trying to get her to *speak to him any more. If she had actually spoken, he probably would have jumped out of his skin, with the kind of antique fright that reeked of his rubbish teens.*

Day after day, he poked and blathered and read from the papers and from magazines and from stupid books.

He told her all about Paul Robeson's sojourn in the Soviet Union, and the blacklisting, and he told her about Gaetan Dugas in 1976. Patient Zero and all the rest of it, and he didn't care if she was listening or not. Well, actually he did, but he wasn't going to let on.

And the young Doctor's voice became harder and nastier with every daft and addled yarn. Yarns of domestic demons and cheerful imbeciles he laid down with no embarrassment whatsoever. The ballad and belch of other people's lives. He talked to the old woman for hours every day, and his voice became, to her, an acoustic trademark of discomfort.

And fear. She was becoming, in her seamless stillness, afraid.

Afraid of this expert, of this caustic and chiding child.

Fear, all her long life, had never been part of her repertoire, but now it seemed to have percolated down, by a lupine and lousy osmosis, into her very pores. She was afraid, not that he might hit her again, but of something much worse. Sometimes he talked to her about his own life, and that really scared her.

She was afraid that she might actually want to talk to this poor and impeccable little bastard. He tried, for a week or so, to read to her from the classics, but the look in her eye just plain shivered the notion away, so he tried some medical textbooks. One of the older ones related a few myths about Melesigenes, the Man of Chios. Better known as Homer.

About how Alexander ('the Madman of Macedonia') always carried his edition of Homer, corrected by Aristotle, in a casket richly studded with gems, and slept with it under his pillow, believing it to be a ward against injury.

About how the old, old superstitions held that the fourth book of the Iliad, *if laid under the head of a patient suffering from quartan ague, would cure him at once.*

The effectiveness of this remedy was vouched for, apparently, by Serenus Sammonicos, preceptor of Gordian, and a noted physician.

The Doctor had no idea what the ague was, but he thought, *What the hell – let's hear it for Homer, regardless.*

And the Doctor just got madder and madder, and in the most civilised manner possible. He took the phone calls and he fielded the press, and he told them, *Yes, she's a wonder all right,* and he just about managed to be a doctor to his other patients, to the point where he wasn't going to lose his job or anything, but beyond the point where he could summon up much energy to think about anything but how wrong the world had gone. Why he shouldn't be so afraid of one old woman, and was. But mainly how awry his own world had gone.

He knew he was losing his mind, but that was a minor thing.

She was getting older and older, yet seemed to stay more and more the same. He was young yet felt ancient and blasted by time. He just wanted to see proper, dull and ordinary diseases but in her could find none. It occurred to him that he should have specialised, younger and earlier. He should have gone into plastic surgery. More money, less grief. But not reconstructive – that would be too depressing. Burns, no thanks. Tits and ass, fair enough. He could cut in and do no damage, and have a look around while he was at it. He was trying to be patient with this old woman. He really was trying his best.

He tried to understand how she was managing to flout every orthodox and luminous rule in the entire lousy book. He really tried.

And he was just awful at it. He kept coming back to the same notion. The one truth he couldn't shake. The truth was that she should have been dead years ago. Years ago.

There was another truth he was trying to ignore.

No two ways about it.

He hated her guts.

He hated her so much that, if she died tomorrow, he would clap his hands and sing around the ward like a mad, mad child, and be not at all ashamed.

So John Kelso and Lynne Callier had fallen in love, and carried on doing so until it just got silly. They began to talk about moving in together, and both of them were thinking, *Sweet Jesus, I have GOT to tidy that place up a bit*, but mainly they just met, ate, slept crazily entwined, and blathered happily and sensibly about love. Not an easy thing to do, but they were both level-headed enough to get away with it. The shivering discomfort of the misplaced medals and the sweet-smelling thief had been put behind them.

Four months before the release of his movie, when the rumours were beginning to fly about potential box office, the station offered Kelso his old job back. They came crawling on their hands and knees actually, along with five other stations, and he just let them all hang for a little while. Sally's foray into the world of late-night movie reviews had lasted three months. The hundreds of written complaints from Kelso fans, orchestrated by precisely twelve insomniac student types – not to mention an inconstant and spluttering stream of low-level irritation expressed on the websites, and picked up by a couple of tabloids – just became too annoying and embarrassing for the station. So they gave Sally a daytime health and beauty slot. And it truly was fantastic. She was stern, prissy, vacuous and utterly wonderful. Huge ratings. Well done Sally.

By now, Kelso could have had pretty much any job in the business, but he didn't want any job. He wanted his old job. When he reappeared in his old early-morning slot – he'd refused a primetime chunk, and the station executives were too afraid to argue with him – there was a decent smattering of congratulations and appreciation from those TV critics who had set their videos for that time of the morning, and most had, but Kelso was old-ish news by now, which was fine by him. He was respected. He was quoted regularly in *Empire*. He got good reviews every once in a while, from the kind of critics who liked *Buffy*. Or Bertolucci. The fans were happy and one of them created a tiny, and very sweet, streaming fireworks display on his website the day the *Radio Times* listings were published. Kelso had his old, lovely job back and a nice quiet life. He had a bucketload of money coming in and a surefire hit film coming out. He had a woman who loved him and whom he loved.

So John settled into his old life at the station, and his new life with Lynne. It took him a while to adjust after months of doing nothing much, but he got used to it. Naomi in the canteen looked at him a bit strangely. And Penny was a problem. In all those months, he had never contacted her to say thank you. To thank her for calling the police and, probably, saving his life. He didn't know why he hadn't. Maybe he was afraid, but the longer he left it, the harder it got. And on his first day back at work, when he walked past reception, he didn't even stop to say hello. He didn't even look at her. His stomach was churning, but he marched right on by. When he got to the men's room he slapped a little water on his face, straightened up and looked in the mirror. He'd never thought of himself as the type to take advantage, or to not give thanks where it was deserved, but he couldn't help it. He just couldn't talk to her. She had, most likely, saved him. And now the sight of that resourceful, clever and sparky woman at reception made him want to throw up. John Kelso was not a stupid man. He did not try to rationalise bullshit behaviour, even when it was his own. But he just couldn't help it. From his first day back until his last, he swanned by Penny at reception with a vicious and daily grace, and he never spoke to her again.

Sometimes he would wake up in the middle of the night, shuddering a little but usually not enough to wake Lynne, and he would lie there trying not to let shards of the dreams creep into his conscious mind. The dreams weren't always the same, but sometimes familiar motifs would come crowding in and around. Child-flung stones winging through the air, and split scalps. Pain and exhilaration too. Near-evangelical gangs and vaulted ware-houses, wary stutters and showers of calf-pellets, a silly load of laughing, and all those brilliant children running away from the cops for no reason at all, screaming like lunatics and whatnot. And the hidden-away, deep and pungent bed amongst the pliant cattle-feed sacks.

And Linda.

John Kelso had never been clear about what exactly had happened that day with Linda, then and there, but he remembered feeling bad about the fact that, the next day, she stopped talking to him. She kept tagging along, slope-shouldered and quiet, on the idiotic and fun night-time raids, but she didn't talk to him anymore. Not even the merest silvery stammer.

Sometimes in John's dreams, the teen Linda appeared and spoke to him and explained, in a voice smooth, charitable and uninterrupted, precisely what he was doing wrong.

With his life then and with his life now. But in dreams, words never make any sense.

Sometimes he would just wake up sweating and depressed. A depression that people sometimes wake with. Feeling rotten, with only a vague memory of rotten and disappeared dreams in the back of their minds and no way to get to grips with any of it. Or even remember it properly.

Sometimes he would wake up and his first feeling would be one of despair, and he had no idea why. A brittle blackness would descend on him, as if a weight was parked on his chest, and he would think about how he had felt when he was at university and trying to write. And failing. The feeling that it would be easier to just knock the whole thing on the head. He had most of what a man could want, and yet the tiny, feral whiff of something truly stupid still snuck up on him when he least expected it. A feeling that he had never tried to describe.

The feeling was not a proper feeling at all.

What it was, was reductively simple.

It was the utter absence of hope.

Which made no sense. His life was just great. Or a corrosive shambles. Depending on what kind of mood he was in. And it had nothing to do with Kenny and what happened back then. In fact, it occurred to Kelso in hindsight that, fear or no, he had never felt so alive as when that skinny, clever Celtic bastard had been pointing a gun at him and screaming like a maniac. But his life was just great.

Thank God for Lynne, his smart, earnest angel. His saving grace.

And Penny at reception felt, daily, her heart breaking under the combined weight of disappointment and, latterly, genuine dislike for the man Kelso. Not a word of thanks. No words at all. At the time, she had refused to be interviewed on television by the news team, because she thought the notion vulgar beyond words, so hardly anyone knew she existed. But that wasn't the bloody point. Kelso knew. A simple hello would have done, and never mind the thanks. She really was beginning to hate the bastard, every time he went, stiff-backed and wrapped up in his greatcoat, marching by. And she disliked herself for carrying on so. This nonsense was not normally part of her makeup. Penny cried occasionally, and mainly, alone. But not on office time.

Lynne Callier got well used to John Kelso twitching by her side and in her bed, in the wee small hours. In fact, she grew to like his tiny, staccato, silent skin-panto, although she felt sorry for his distress, if that's what it was. But mainly, it was a source of quiet fascination to her. She would lie awake in the dark for a little while, not ages, watching her fellow swim the sheets, slow-fast yet gracefully, and not whimpering that much. She loved him enough to let him get some things out of his system, in the night, without having to know the ins and the outs of it.

Besides, she had her own show to think of, and that was becoming more manic by the day. Some of the guests, and thereby the research required, were madder than all get out.

One of them, an otherwise lovely man called Ronald Kavanagh, was invited on the show because he had been lobbying the switchboard relentlessly for four months, and they were getting really fed up with him. Ronald was forty-nine, a proof-reader and utterly convinced of the healing power of laughter. So Clare and Robert gave him a brief slot. Ron did a nice, harmless three minutes about serotonin, and SAD, and case studies of cancer patients who had recovered by watching *Friends* videos, and had just giggled their way to health. Or something. Which was fair enough. But the hosts just couldn't let it go and Lynne gave them the ammo. A list of famous people for whom humour had proved less than useful. Artists, wits, scientists and a load of other folk who were obviously more valuable than the rest of us.

Calchas the soothsayer. Died laughing.

Philomenes the philosopher. Died laughing.

Zeuxis the painter. Died laughing.

Margutte the fifteenth-century, ten-foot-high giant. OK, fictional, but even so. Died laughing.

Lynne's own grandfather. Deputy Ambassador to Singapore. Died laughing.

The hosts tore him apart, the audience whooped with the best breed of vicious glee, and Ronald exited stage left. He lay down in the corridor and cried his eyes out. Lynne passed him, stumbled slightly on her heels and carried right along. In the four-minute interval, on Lynne's recommendation, the house band played a lounge version of 'Soweto Trembles' by Alias Ron Kavana. Sarcasm was not Lynne's forte. She knew that no one would recognise the tune, but it was bright and breezy and amenable to whatever an eight-piece could manage. Besides, it was a cracking tune and Lynne wasn't averse to a little wordplay. Now and again.

The show was brilliant fun these days. The latest guest, by satellite, was a retired cop from Chicago whose website had acquired a bit of a cult following. He was sixty-eight now and it was a miracle he'd made it that far. The site had photographs of every scar he'd acquired in the course of his duties. The man was a mess. And a real hero. Even the dude-anarchists amongst the researchers thought he was pretty cool.

After that, they took a hit. They had decided to introduce a consumer watchdog item, and one of their first 'guests' was a builder from Peckham. Lynne tried to warn them that the guy may have been a lousy builder but he was charm itself on screen. Not just charming but clever too. Disgruntled viewers would phone in with a complaint about ill-fitting door-frames and Andrew would counter with some long-winded treatise on form and perspective and the architectural merits of the Gothic style. Hell, he even answered, or rather failed to answer, a question about damp-proof coursing from Helen in Lewisham, with a windy piece of rhetoric which managed to cover the Bilbao Guggenheim, the Reichstag, the Jubilee Line Extension, his own sitting-room, straw-bale housing in Cumbria, and the unseemly row between Ruskin and Carlyle. And he made no secret of whose side *he* was on.

Clare and Robert had sat slack-mouthed and resentful. But the viewers loved him. They loved mouthy people anyway, but they especially loved Andrew with his big words and his bullshit and his soft Scottish accent. The phone calls and the tabloid nonsense was such that, within three weeks, the studio was practically railroaded into giving him his own show. (Most viewers were probably hoping for a *Marvel Team-Up*-type confrontation, where Andy gets to beat the shit out of Laurence Llewelyn-Bowen.)

Either way, he was temporarily more popular than the hosts. Which is taking a hit.

Clare and Robert sulked. Lynne laughed. She'd liked the man. Easy come, easy go.

The week after that, Lynne had to dissuade them from introducing a viewers' competition, with a cash prize for the viewer who could come up with the greatest number of bands with animal names. Sitting in the café, eyes closed, she'd come up with 123 in 4 minutes, off the top of her head.

This was the type of competition that got skulls broken.

A Flock of Seagulls – okay. Curiosity Killed the Cat, yep. The High Llamas, Atomic Rooster, The Frank Chickens, Eek! A Mouse, Skinny Puppy, The Jesus Lizard, The Penguin Café Orchestra, Thrashing Doves – fair enough, except that hardly anyone had heard of them. And what about Neil Young and Crazy Horse? Which bit truly counts? The 'Neil Young' bit, or the 'Horse' bit? Same deal with Echo and the Bunnymen, and Ziggy and his Spiders. And did she include Def Leppard, Billy Swan, Charlie Foxx, The Byrds, Snoop Doggy Dogg and Gorky's Zygotic Mynci (hell, even the Beatles and the Monkees), although they weren't spelled correctly? And Los Lobos was in Spanish. And Dinosaur Jr. may have been an animal once upon a time, but certainly wasn't now. Including Cat Stevens didn't seem right since it wasn't his name any more, and picking on poor, dead Nick Drake just wasn't seemly. And is Lambchop an animal or merely a dinner? Ditto, the Blue Oyster Cult and Red Snapper. Was Dogstar just Keanu's pet mini-project and not a proper band at all? And all the ones in between, the ones that qualified but not quite specifically enough – The Creatures, The Animals, Mink de Ville, the Jayhawks, Moby, The Fabulous Poodles, Fish, The Afghan Whigs, Atomic Kitten, Voice of the Beehive, Pussy Galore, Super Furry Animals. And Lynne definitely didn't want to include Gil Scott-Heron, as the man was just too dignified for this kind of nonsense.

And she didn't even want to *think* about the Soup Dragons. Or Disco Duck.

After five minutes, she persuaded Clare and Robert not to go down that road. This kind of competition was nothing, repeat, *nothing* but trouble. One of them then suggested band names based on parts of the body, but after being blasted by Lynne with a blistering list of forty-four names off the top of her head, some just plain stupid (Hipsway, Collapsed Lung), some obscene (The Butthole Surfers, The Revolting Cocks – although that one could have gone on the animals list too), and a litany of the problems attendant upon this kind of dumb-arse competition, they decided to drop the idea of band names altogether. Lynne was very, very good at her job. They were actually rather scared of her.

The following week, the hosts had a bash at the subject of celebrity garbage and the sub-paparazzi who spend their wee small hours trawling through bins in Notting Hill. That item was disgusting in more ways than one, but at least Lynne didn't have to get involved much, beyond checking with the station lawyers that they weren't going to get sued. After that they hosted the voice of Bart, Nancy Cartwright, on a promo for her book, and did not disgrace themselves at all. (And for the phone-in, Lynne managed to dig up a chirpy, funny and utterly lovely woman who lived in a semi-detached on an Evergreen Terrace in some town or other in the West Midlands. Everyone enjoyed that one.)

The next two weeks were filled with competitions for the viewers who could quote the most messages – verbatim – from Jim

Rockford's answering machine, the viewer who could tell them what the word *correcaminos* meant (a man from Greenwich won, but since he already owned a complete collection of Roadrunner/Wile E. Coyote videos, he generously declined), an interview with a seventies pop star who was working, very happily, as a staff nurse in an Edinburgh hospital, and a piece on the world's best mazes. And crop circles. Those made everybody, cast and crew, shut up completely. The aerial photographs, from all over the world, were just so impossibly beautiful that the hosts didn't have to say a word for at least seven minutes. On daytime telly, that was not just a first – it was a damn miracle. Seven minutes of photos, huge, sheer and interesting.

Seven minutes lacking, gorgeously, any bull chatter at all. Or even real noise.

That was Lynne Callier's proudest moment. Seven minutes of silence, gobsmacked and wondering, from the lot of them. Utterly unheard of. On *any* kind of telly.

Once in a while Lynne would suggest more serious subjects. Their next guest was a former oil worker from Aberdeen who had been sentenced to death in Saudi Arabia for raping the daughter of a prominent Riyadh family. On the morning of his execution, the family of his victim pardoned him, as is their right. Pardoned him. Just like that.

And the Royal Family not only permitted the death sentence to be commuted, but ordered the man booted out of their country as soon as possible. So the man got to go home, and found himself on a daytime telly slot a week later. But he was not as they expected. His accent was a pure, soft Aberdeenshire where they had expected brisk Glaswegian, and his manner was diffident almost to the point of inaudible. Clare asked him about conditions in Saudi jails, about his previous experience in the North Sea, about the oil industry in general, about his family, about his childhood, about his plans for the future. The man answered politely and cogently and Lynne, watching from the wings, thought to herself that she had never seen a man, suddenly free, more miserable. They never asked him whether he was guilty or innocent, and he volunteered no information in that direction. At one point, he looked as if he was going to pass out, so they cut the interview short, and went to the commercials.

As she headed out towards the car park, Lynne passed a figure sitting in the corridor, and the thought crossed her mind – *I am getting REALLY fucking tired of tripping over weeping guests on this bloody show.* But that seemed to be the secret of the show's success. Strip 'em bare, get their guts, do it with a smile, don't leave visible marks, and only much, much later will they realise the dreadful thing that has happened to them. Maybe the former Aberdeenshire farm-boy turned oiler was feeling sorry for himself and his bad luck. Or maybe he was weeping because he knew that, if there truly was any justice, he would be either in jail or dead. Who knew? Who cared?

But sometimes, Lynne realised how much this kind of forensic televisual wounding was down to her. She was the one who stopped Robert and Clare from looking like fools. She was the one who gave them all sorts of rock-solid stuff to play with; all those facts to spew out and look cool while they were doing it. She handed them an indestructible, telly-friendly breed of cultural permafrost, which protected the entire cast and crew from any kind of comeback from their guests, some of them lovely, some of them just ghastly. But all of them done and dusted, and not a leg to stand on. And a fair few of them crying their eyes out in the toilets. Lynne had seen to the utter demolition of the fair few, and she had never felt bad about it. But these days, sometimes . . . Sometimes, she would crawl into the arms of John Kelso late at night and without a word, she would curl up against him in their bed, in a shivering, shamed and tired heap. Feeling close to truly rotten, not wanting to talk, not wanting to hear the sound of another human voice, really, and not caring if he was asleep or awake.

John Kelso was always awake and he never let on.

The week after the Saudi guy's appearance was Remembrance Sunday, so they did a piece on the War. Or rather both of them. And this is where Lynne really came into her own. It was close to the anniversary of the *Kursk* submarine disaster as well so, rather than going on about nostalgia, Lynne persuaded the producers to do a daily piece on the technological side of things. About the weaponry, the ships, the submarines, the planes. Some commentators felt it was a little chill to concentrate on the machinery rather than the suffering, but Lynne persuaded them that they should brazen it out because firstly, the human angle was already being covered by every other station and secondly, those same commentators were the types of hypocritical bastards who only wear poppies in their lapels on television because they're too terrified of what people will say if they don't.

So they had their week of war-tech stories. Lynne dug up the liveliest ex-servicemen with the best yarns, they got brilliant talking heads down from the Maritime Museum, the Museum of London, the Imperial War Museum. The hosts interviewed (backed up with a raft of colour-coded notes from Lynne) august professors and ex-admirals, cartoonish yet scary NCOs, most of them in their seventies and upwards. They talked to mechanics and to engineers and to designers. Or anyone even close. They talked, day after day, about iron and steel, about rivets and nails, about deafening noise and short lunch hours. Some of the interviewees, old as they were, got so blindingly technical that the twins began to panic. Lynne calmed them down with as many cut-down notes as they needed. Or could grasp. But Lynne was strangely proud of them that week. The pair of them seemed to have grown up recently. They really seemed to be trying to digest this huge amount of information, to do a good and decent job. If only for this week. They were showing up with bags under their eyes. They weren't making much noise. Hell, they were even rushing makeup.

Robert and Clare.

Lynne had hardly ever used their names, even inside her own head. She hardly ever thought of them as anything other than the cretin twins, and now here they were, doing her proud. They did a couple of OBs to a retirement home in Surrey, to interview a couple of ex-'Rosies', and cutting out the swearing from those bad-tempered old biddies took more time than editing the whole piece. In another segment, which caused uproar upstairs, they interviewed three pensioners who had been forced to sell their war medals because they were skint. But the phone-poll indicated that they were right to do it. And Robert was good. He was quiet and respectful, he asked only a couple of questions and mainly let the old guys just talk and talk to their hearts' content. He got the talking right and he got the silences right. At one point, Lynne could have sworn that he was close to tears. And there was a genuine bitterness there which, to their credit, the producers let go ahead. They just seemed to trust Lynne enough to let her ideas fly. Or float anyway. It was only telly. And the war week was a huge success. Because, as Lynne rightly predicted, most people are wannabe-engineers anyway. The human stuff, the parades, the sad and awful stories just left them feeling weepy and helpless.

They were always going to be more interested in the hardware than the software.

But Lynne's *pièce de résistance* was the final interview, on the Friday. She had briefed the pair on World War II aircraft, as far as possible. She gave them biogs and diagrams of the Hurricane and the Lancaster, but saved all her proper stuff for the Spitfire.

And Cliff Robertson.

Lynne had scarcely been able to believe it when she heard that Robertson was in town. She almost peed herself with excitement. She had all his movies, even the Kennedy one – *PT 109*. But *Charly* was the one she watched at least once a fortnight. And the other one – *Out of Season*. The sexiest movie ever set in a chilly, off-season English seaside resort. Lynne was a fan, no doubt. But that wasn't the point. She had done her homework. And she was determined to get him on the show. And not to talk about his movies, either.

If she tried that, he would just switch off and she wouldn't get him. That was for certain.

Robertson was staying at the Dorchester, mostly sightseeing, but also doing some little bits of promotion for Ken Burns's latest documentary, for which he'd done a fair bit of quality voiceover. Lynne wangled herself an interview, in which she didn't actually interview the man at all, but just suggested to him, all innocence, that her show was doing a major piece on World War II aircraft, and would he be interested? At all?

And so the hosts found themselves, on the Friday, interviewing Cliff Robertson.

One of the best actors.

Ever.

About the Spitfire.

Two months previously, Lynne had come across the fact that Robertson was an accomplished aviator and aviation expert. More than an expert. Turned out he owned one of only twelve Spitfires still capable of getting into the air. And Lynne gave the twins all the information they needed to get by. She provided them with a bucketload of notes. Most Spitfires surviving today have no combat history, or have been manufactured from parts. Robertson also owned a Tiger Moth, a Stampe, an ME-108, a Grob Aster and a B-58 Baron. But it turned out that his near-pristine Spit, MK923, was an original participant in the D-Day invasion. After that, it was sold to the Dutch and flew dozens of combat missions in the Dutch East Indies. Later, it was acquired by the Belgian Air Force and, later still, played a starring role in 1961's *The Longest Day*. Around the same time, Robertson was in Britain filming *633 Squadron*, and when he learned that the Spit was for sale, he bought it, and had it disassembled and air-freighted back to California.

In the interview, Robert and Clare stuck to the subject at hand, didn't mention Hollywood once, and even asked some genuinely intelligent questions about Spitfire specs. About the Merlin engine and its unique sound, about its elliptical wing and the distinctive silhouette it produced, and about a bunch of other stuff they weren't absolutely certain about, like the yank Mustang, and the hugely underrated Hurricane. By and large, they acquitted themselves really well.

Robertson seemed to be pleased that they weren't plugging on about his movies, that they appeared to be genuinely interested in airplanes.

Clare blathered on about how, apparently, the Spitfire is regarded as a 'docile' airplane, and won't stall or flick out like a Mustang but has, rather, a graceful way about it.

About halfway through, Robertson cottoned on that this

respectful pair probably had the best researcher on the planet working for them, and that they were actually a bit dim, both of them. But that was okay. He was quite gratified that they'd made the effort. They even seemed to agree with him, as if they would know, that getting up beyond 26,000 feet in a glider was a more thrilling experience than winning an Emmy. Or even an Oscar.

In fact, they seemed to agree with him before he actually said it, but what the hell.

So, Cliff Robertson spent a rather pleasant morning in London discussing, with what appeared to be a very nice couple who had definitely done their homework, his life-long, all-time favourite subject. They asked all the right questions, Robertson was witty, bemused and gracious, and Lynne stood in the wings hopping from left foot to right foot, almost hugging herself with delight.

When Clare pointed out the fact that many of the original test pilots were women, Robertson seemed to tense up ever so slightly and, for a moment, a shadow of what looked like sorrow crossed his face. He looked as if he was about to say something. But then he didn't. They didn't quite know what to make of that. So, with a final flourish, and trying to look cool, despite feeling as rough and sweaty as a badger's arse, Clare and Robert told their guest that, in his honour, the station was going to show one of his movies in its late movie slot – either *J.W. Coop* or *Too Late the Hero*. The choice was his. Robertson laughed gently and chose *Hero*, and went out of his way to say some very nice things about his erstwhile co-star, Michael Caine. Everybody in the studio knew that *Coop*, which Robertson also directed, was by far the better movie.

No doubt about it.

The man was a class act.

That show actually got reviewed in the Sunday broadsheets. As proper television, and not as some snob's skew-whiff distraction, just to fill out 250 words. And it got great reviews. In fact, the whole war-tech week got great reviews. The show was coming up in the world. Lynne was so proud of Clare and Robert. And John was so proud of Lynne.

The Spitfire.

World War II.

Cliff bloody Robertson.

Amazing.

A week later, Lynne and John were in a nearby café, on her lunch hour. And Lynne spotted two faces that she recognised. She was halfway out of her seat before she remembered who they actually were, and slunk, in a horrible, slack-spined way, back into her seat, holding a menu over her face, too shiveringly embarrassed to even say hello. John took in every moment of this pantomime but he was too afraid to ask.

Over his shoulder, two former guests on Lynne's show were having lunch together.

It was the former director of London Zoo and, with him, Lydia.

He had lost his job about five months after his appearance on the show. Five months was too long for actual cause-and-effect. So it wasn't really down to the show. It wasn't their fault, exactly. But his reputation had never recovered from the panda incident. Everybody, including his own Board, knew that that kind of flak was inevitable, especially from the popular press, and they had supported him. But gradually, his colleagues and peers just moved away from him. It was as if he had become, through absolutely no fault of his own, a laugh, a benign embarrassment. He had twenty-three years of academic research behind him, a string of letters after his name, and one of the best records for kind-hearted, committed and resourceful staff management of any boss any-where. But, because of ten minutes on a cheap television show, he was to be forever associated with a happy, howling crowd, a pair of cynical hosts and, let's face it, a viewing public that didn't give a shit one way or the other about animals in general. He'd had enough money to hibernate for a couple of months, then he got himself the deputy director post with the Worldwide Fund for Nature. And they were glad to have him. He landed three huge corporate sponsorship deals within two months.

And he didn't turn on his television again for about a year.

He and Lydia had met totally by accident, in an ATM queue on Charing Cross Road. It was dark, cold and a motorcyclist had slithered off his bike, and bumped into the railings outside the

Cambridge Theatre. He wasn't too badly hurt, but it got strangers talking while the ambulance arrived. So the director got talking to the woman Lydia, and they discovered they both had something in common. Crucifixion by telly.

Well, okay – it wasn't that exactly, but by the time the semi-conscious biker was carted off in an ambulance they both, rather weirdly, felt comfortable enough in each other's company to just wander off to the nearest pub for a drink. The few people still milling about seemed quite glad that the boy in his inadequate leathers wasn't going to die. Lydia had told the man about the fire, about her face and the plastic surgery, but when they went from the relative dark of the street into the bulb-lit bar, she expected him to flinch, the way *everybody* flinched. And he didn't. He took her coat, gave her a big, bashful smile and went off to the bar to get her the Bloody Mary she'd asked for. And that was that. That was the pair of them.

And now, months later, sitting in the café, they both spotted Lynne Callier (whose picture had appeared in the *Media* section of the *Guardian*, as part of a lengthy and fulsome piece on how to turn an ailing chatshow around), and the man, the movie guy, the man who was on the news all those months ago, the one who was kidnapped apparently.

The director recognised Lynne's face, just before she shrank down behind her menu, and flinched. Lydia spotted Lynne's face too, and it didn't bother her in the slightest.

Lynne, at least, had treated her nicely before and after the show, back when, and had been polite about her disfigurement. But Lydia remembered afterwards being so, so glad that she did not work in Callier's telly world. That awful world, full of chesty and occasional rhetoric, of weary and witless menace, of stout, shiny, gormless and profitable crap.

Where a tiny something could turn out to mean absolutely everything.

But not for longer than four minutes, tops.

Lydia, with her ruined and awful face, saw the pretty Lynne Callier flinch and hide. The director saw it too. Then they both looked at each other, looking. And because there was nothing else to do, they just laughed, and ignored the jittery pair at that table over beyond, and went back to their meal. He stroked her face, or rather her scars, in a way that was full of love and utterly unselfconscious.

In a way that she was never totally certain was genuine.

Even when they had been married for fifteen years she still wondered, now and again.

But not so much that it really bothered her.

The Doctor was now getting twenty phone calls a day and three hours of sleep a night. He tried to get the hospital's administrators to grasp the fact that dealing with the press was a specialist skill, and that he had better things to be doing with his time. Namely, being a doctor to his other patients. And still that old bitch lay there. In silence. Hardly moving. Barely eating. Taking up space and looking at him with a look that froze him, occasionally, to the spot. And the more he hated her, the more she frightened him.

She could feel his hatred now and she understood it, for the most part. Not in a way that made sense to her conscious mind, but in a way that she took in every time he walked by. He had long stopped reading to her, but sometimes at dusk, when the ward was quiet and the only sounds were the odd snuffle from the next bed, or a low and dreaming moan from the far side of the room, he would come and sit beside her. He had asked for the lights to be dimmed in the evenings. It seemed to calm them all.

She liked it because it made remembering easier. He preferred it because, even up close, her outline became a comforting blur, a beige, linen-bound mound. And because he couldn't see her eyes. He would sit by her bed and listen to her breathe. Waiting for the last breath, for that beautiful, permanent pause, the one that would make her stop, just stop and go away. Even when she was asleep, the timbre and tone of her breathing did not change one iota. She sank into the sheets and thought about how much he was beginning to remind her of her sour and cruel son, whose death she mourned but briskly. This doctor, this glib and forlorn youngster, with his gallimaufry of newly acquired tics and his ragged body language. But she didn't want to think about that any more. So she just let her thoughts wander. These days, she was just letting things occur, regardless. Senseless snatches of memory slouched in and out, and mithered around in her brain, flitting between moody racket and deadpan blah.

The memory of a mountain floated by. The Isle of Harris. Developers were going to quarry an entire mountain, for aggregate. For roadbuilding. The woman wondered, glacially, about that one. Where did that memory come from? Had she seen it, or climbed it, years and years and decades ago? She couldn't remember. And she almost made a sound that would probably have sounded like a laugh.

How do you kill a mountain?

And suddenly, she remembered a taxi journey she once took from Crouch End up to Muswell Hill. Had she lived there, once? That question floated gently around in her head for a bit. But in the memory, she had never been there before and was alarmed by the sheer gradient of that hill. It was like crawling up a mountain, it was that steep.

But the main thing that she remembered was that the taxi driver cried all the way there. He wept and blubbered, half-silently, and blew his nose, and almost drove off the road several times, because he couldn't see for tears. She remembered thinking that, in the world of taxis, the rules surely dictated that any crying going on should be going on in the back seat, not in the front. Getting out, she tried to give him money, but he just kept on crying, and wouldn't take it. She wanted to ask him what was so dreadfully wrong. But, at the time, it just hadn't seemed appropriate. So off he went, in an unhappy rasp of exhaust fumes.

Lying in her bed now, decades later, she suddenly wished that she had asked why the taxi driver was weeping. But it had been too late. She remembered the rain that night, but not the precise quality of the rain. However, she did remember watching, from the back seat, the rainbow, floodlit prism of the man's tears as they slid down the side of his face.

And the low, gorgeous rumble of the diesel engine.

And about how the exact character of his unhappiness was something she was never going to know, no matter how kindly her questions. There was something about the loose vocabulary of his pain, the solid bullion of his grief, the incubatory and possible ugliness of what he might say, that scared and intrigued her. About *the* way *that he cried. No shame, there. No shame at all. But she had really wanted to know why he was crying, and what, precisely, had lent her driver such a bruised and vengeful heart. She had seen men unhappy before, many times, but the spectacle had always smacked of something fatally inessential, of a sterile confection designed for . . . well, designed for something. Never actually being passionate about anything.* Talking *about passion, yes. She had had a bellyful of that breed of blasphemous and stupid aplomb over the years. But she knew that he would never have actually told her why he was crying his heart out.*

Men being what they are. In all their terrifying and tender detail.

The old woman was awake, and looking at the Doctor with the one eye that was visible. He jumped, almost imperceptibly. Everything about her suggested to him that she was in the middle of a long, long cerebral sulk. And that, if she had been a century younger, she would have converted him, a mere and hopeless child, to something better. Something lofty, lanky and possibly evangelical. But not necessarily involving religion.

Something to do with the speckle and downright stint *of a job well done.*

Beside her bed, the Doctor sat fingering the tip of his scalpel. The blade was brand new, fresh out of the foil, and it had the kind of near-molecule-thin sharpness which causes no pain whatsoever when cutting into skin.

He carried the scalpel around in his breast pocket. To scrape clean his nails, usually.

The gun he kept in his car.

Outside the hospital window, somewhere in the dark and most likely in the car park, a nightingale began to sing, astonishingly so, and neither she nor he so much as flinched, not even once.

4

Tom sat in the pub near the Archway tower at lunchtime, and looked through his cheap, roomy holdall at his latest haul. The more he had stayed away from the woman, the harder it became to go straight, so he didn't even bother any more. He was stealing every night these days, and he just got better and better and meaner and meaner. He found himself taking things like toys and teddy bears and PlayStations, even though they weren't going to get him any money. And just as often, throwing them in the nearest litter bin. He wanted to make an impression, even if it was a rotten one. Because he had been true to his vow to stop the nonsense with Lynne Callier. And it was killing him. He had thought that not seeing her would be easier than seeing her with the man Kelso. And he could not have been more wrong. He knew he was a good enough thief not to get caught, but these days, he was thieving just to fill time between bouts of thinking about her. Her smell, her placid face, everything in and around her – her clothes, her star-lit bedroom, the wet and humid room with all those small and ferocious bonsai. The comics, the music, the books. Everything. Because he was convinced that through these things, he knew her.

Tom took a hefty swig from his pint, just as his guy sat down next to him in the booth. The man had a discreet and quick rummage through the holdall, which contained four portable DVDs and some very nice jewellery. He muttered a decent figure, Tom nodded, the man sidled some money along under the table and disappeared with the bag.

Tom sighed. He was getting so very tired of this. He was twenty-nine. He had never imagined that he would get to this age and be doing what he was doing. He had pinched a copy of *Brewer's* from the last house, a nice two-room semi in Kentish Town, and browsed through it, because there was nothing else for him to do. Apart from get a bit drunk. He missed having his own books around him. Okay, he had hundreds of books in his flat which had formerly belonged to other people, but it wasn't the same. And then he wondered how his caretaker grandmother was getting on. He sighed again.

Under the 'C's, he came across *Cacus*. A famous robber from some mythology or other, usually represented as three-headed and vomiting flames. He was strangled by Hercules, apparently. *Well that's just lovely*, thought Tom. Dead robbers.

Under the entry *Cake*, he came across the phrase 'I wish my cake were dough again.'

I wish I could turn back time.

Tom wondered whether his madman former employer, the genius baker in Belfast, bless him, was still alive. Perhaps he had finally gotten around to it and killed himself.

Another, related, entry described Louis XVI as 'The Baker', and Marie Antoinette as 'The Baker's Wife', because, it said here, a heavy trade in corn was carried on at Versailles and, consequently, there was very little in Paris itself. About which the Parisians were not best pleased.

Tom shivered and closed the book. He didn't know any French people and he just hoped the Belfast baker was still alive. Miserable or no, alive was better. He was busy downing his fourth pint, because he was too bored to do anything else, when a young guy with terrible skin and a put-upon expression leaned over and asked in a pleasant Scottish accent whether or not anyone was sitting here. And no, obviously, there wasn't.

So Tom the thief and Kenny the recent madman got, accidentally, to talking.

About this and that. About music and football and movies. About movies, especially. And, accidentally, about other things, and people too. And the more they both had to drink, the more the conversation speeded up, with both of them having a laugh and finding connections, hither and yon. For a pair of strangers, they got along really well.

And then, after five pints, the conversation slowed down, and the pair of them began, because they couldn't help it, to look for more connections, and just kept it going and going, almost like the way the Irish abroad do. Looking for a connection. Anything. Even if it's only a bar they both once visited. And in the vocabulary of their pained and drunken descent, Tom and Kenny found more than a casual connection. In the middle of all the dimpled and doe-eyed nattering about movies and, well, annoyance with people in general, they found a connection that didn't seem possible. But as the chat wobbled along and along, it became apparent that the man's name simply *had* to emerge sooner or later.

They had a couple more drinks and began to swivel towards, to home in on, the thing they imagined they might have in common.

But they were both afraid, and sat in silence for a bit.

Finally, one of them said the man's name out loud. Twice. And the other sat stock still. Tom and Kenny stared at each other for a long time.

So there it was.

There it was.

A woman stolen. A script stolen. Two lives all over the shop.

Yes, they had more than just little things in common.

Tom and Kenny talked for three hours.

And after three hours, Kenny and Tom had explained everything to each other.

And found out everything as well. Every decked-out, guttersnipe snatch of history.

Every rotten thing, every slight and sliver of pain, every theft and dreadless concern, every piece of grubby and flip tomfoolery.

The ten months of Kenny's pained and interior colony.

Of Tom's invisible, half-steam and idiotic love affair.

The sound of the sea, the hospital mob, the insult of drugs uninvited, and the loss of his script, his life's work.

The insane childhood waterways, her tiny trees, the temptation of violence in the park, and a heavy holdall filled with gadgets, money and other people's misery. The loss of her, mainly.

And the hopeless nights, both.

Everything.

After three hours, they couldn't believe that they had found each other. They could scarcely believe this kind of coincidence.

After three hours, a sweaty and quietly yelping partnership was formed.

And, between the pair of them, John Kelso's fate was sealed.

And then, in the far corner of the bar, Kenny spotted a face he thought he knew. A face he *knew* he knew. And then another one.

It was Doug. The guy he'd worked with, years ago. The guy from Andy's painting and decorating firm in Aberdeen. The boxer who studied English Literature, or the ageing student who got the shit beaten out of him down the docks, at least once a week, depending on how you looked at it.

Kenny leapt out of his seat and ran to the table, knocking over pints as he went.

He planted himself in front of the man, trembling like a toddler.

'Douglas! You bastard – what the *hell* are you doing in London?' he roared.

He couldn't believe it was Doug. He couldn't believe he was looking at that brilliant slab of two-legged idiocy again. He was afraid he might cry.

Doug stood up and gaped at him in shock. Then he laughed, threw his arms around Kenny and hauled him into the air.

He was still as strong as a horse.

'Kenny, you little *prick*! How the hell *are* you? *Jesus*!!' he bawled at the top of his lungs.

He held Kenny three inches off the ground for at least ten seconds, and buried his face in Kenny's shirt. And then he began to blub. That was Doug – tough as anything and ever the weeper. They were beginning to cause a bit of a scene, so Kenny sat down and took Doug, sniffling, with him. Kenny was so glad to see Doug that it took him a while to realise that Mark was sitting beside him. Mark the graffiti-removal guy. And beside him, nursing a half-pint and sporting a black eye-patch, sat David. The same placid David, the marine biology student with the Castellaneta fixation, and absolutely no harm in him at all. Kenny's first thought, bizarrely, was – *Why doesn't he get himself one of those nice coloured patches? Or a glass eye?* Then he remembered the awful, thumping and desperate waves on those rotten, black, paint-covered rocks, and the way the Anderson thug in the pub had rammed that splintered chair leg into David's face, and Kenny hurled himself, almost weeping, into David's arms. David caught him and laughed too, and didn't even flinch too much when Kenny stroked the eye-patch.

'Watch it, pal! I've only got one left,' said David, by way of a gentle warning. He was a lot tougher than Kenny remembered. Much more grown-up. With muscles. Taller, even. His grip around Kenny's back was almost painful, it was that strong. He let go just before Kenny's breath gave out, and smiled at him. The one eye he had left was a penetrating blue. He had spent three weeks in the hospital in Aberdeen, swearing all the way, and he had given up any notion of being a student any more. He couldn't see the point in a half-blind student. David was a very sweet, very smart and very bad-tempered boy these days.

Doug, on the other hand, had been getting along okay, mostly, for the last little while. He had been given custody of his daughter for four months because her mother had gone out and gotten blind, useless and falling-down drunk in Union Street one night and hadn't come home. At all. The babysitter called the police. So Douglas got to keep his daughter and to graduate at the same time. English Literature. He got a decent 2:1.

And then a job in a bike shop, because it was the only job he could get.

And then Social Services took his daughter away again, because Douglas just couldn't stop himself from going to boxing places of a Friday, where he got his ego stroked, his ribs bruised and his head kicked in.

And then he lost the job in the bike shop because, according to the owner, he did not understand the *karma* of bicycles. So Doug punched him in the face and was out the door before the man even hit the carpet.

His entire life was thoroughly, seriously and wholly stupid. And Doug knew it.

Still. Seeing wee, mighty Kenny again – that was a definite and blissful plus.

Even if he'd planned it. Sort of.

Kenny couldn't believe they were here.

The old gang.

He hadn't thought about these guys in ages and ages and now – here they were.

The four of them whooped and hugged and talked a stream of noisy, nostalgic and Caledonian rubbish for ten straight minutes. Just then, Kenny heard a cough and realised that Tom was standing nearby, probably wondering what was going on.

'Oh, Jesus,' said Kenny, by way of introduction, 'I'm sorry. This is Tom.'

Douglas, David and Mark all looked at Tom in a pleasant enough fashion, waiting for Kenny to elaborate on who, exactly, this Tom guy was. When it became obvious that he couldn't, or wouldn't, they all just said hello and sat down.

So the three of them made room, shifted glasses and coats, and then just looked at Tom, again, while Kenny went to the bar.

By the time Kenny had staggered back with a bunch of drinks, Tom was one of the guys. They seemed to like him. And they didn't bother asking him what he did for a living.

So they sat, the four of them, catching up and tripping over themselves to remember all the people and places and sights and sounds of Kenny's former life, and explaining things to Tom when it was obvious he didn't know who or what the hell they were talking about.

But then, as he sat listening to the gruff, bloke-ish and marvellous threnody, now full of laughter, it dawned on Kenny that there was absolutely no reason for these guys to have known each other. He knew them all, certainly, but separately. Aberdeen wasn't *that* small. Doug had worked for Andy's painting and decorating firm, almost exclusively in the suburbs. Mark had specialised in graffiti removal, mostly in the city centre, and mostly for the Council but sometimes out in the seaside.

And David, God bless him, had just been a stupid student all over the place, hired by Mark at the very last minute for that pathetic summer gig on the coast. These guys were not friends, not by any stretch of the imagination.

Kenny couldn't figure it out. Why were these guys together? And here, in London?

So he asked the question, trying to keep his voice as light as possible.

David, Douglas and Mark put down their drinks and turned and looked at him, full on.

'Well,' said Doug, with a jauntiness that didn't seem quite right, 'I went to see this movie, didn't I? And in the pub, afterwards, I just bumped into this pair here and, well, Mark and David and I just got talking. By accident. And we couldn't quite believe what we had just seen. So we got talking.'

By now Kenny's skin was crawling with a small and immaculate breed of nervousness.

'And let me tell you, man,' continued Doug, laughing, 'it is a truly scary experience to see your entire fucking *life* up there on the screen! Especially when it's just a fucking *footnote* to the main action! All those domestic details, just chucked in, like mad. And your friends' and relatives' lives too. Loads of people you know. Like your own children.' Kenny flinched as he remembered the daughter.

'But you just think to yourself that it's a coincidence, that all sorts of people have similar lives. That there is bound to be overlap and duplication. It stands to reason.'

Doug paused, and for a second Kenny could have sworn it was for dramatic effect. 'But that's okay,' he added, calmly, 'that's all right. Hell, it's said that there have only ever been seven stories in the history of the world, and that every story told is just a version of one of those seven stories. Or a combination thereof.'

David and Mark were watching Kenny intently. The three of them leaned in towards him, their collective body language one huge question mark. Aberdeen wasn't that small, but it wasn't that big either. Folks up north remembered Kenny, and they'd heard all about his little stay in the bin. He was the nice-enough kid, the hard worker with the terrible skin and all the blather about the movies. They had heard all about him and John Kelso.

'What's really quite eerie, though,' continued Doug, 'is when you start hearing your own words coming at you from the screen. Things you actually remember yourself saying. Even from a long time ago. Now that *does* feel strange. That's the kind of thing that just doesn't seem possible. Not for all three of us.'

Kenny glanced at Tom, who seemed to be frozen by the sound of Doug's voice. His expression offered no advice. He didn't seem to know what the hell to think. Half an hour ago, his new pal Kenny was the aggrieved victim of a robbery. And now, apparently, *he* was the thief. Tom knew about proper, ordinary thieving and this wasn't it. His thing was electronics, gadgets and, on occasion, small white goods. Not copyright and Intellectual Property Rights. Not plagiarism and frustrated screenwriters. Not this.

Mark and David continued to look at Kenny in a way that suggested that they expected him to say something. He didn't, so Doug kept talking.

'It's amazing how the three of us just met like that. In the pub. On Union Street. In Aberdeen. By accident. Just like that. It's almost as amazing as the way we've bumped into you here. You. Us. Here and now. Incredible, eh? Kenny . . . ?'

He smiled and seemed to mean it.

Kenny looked again at Tom who, by now, seemed almost to be smiling to himself. Whatever little playlet was unfolding in front of him here, there was nothing he could do about any of it.

Tom sort of liked coincidences. It was in his nature. Three weeks previously, he'd watched a riveting wildlife documentary about alligators. Their mating ritual was the quietest, slowest, most mesmerising thing Tom had ever seen. Forty minutes for the male and female to swim a couple of figures-of-eight around each other, snouts barely visible. Humans don't know a damn thing about foreplay. Four hours later, he was still thinking about how brilliant it was when he broke into a gorgeous six-bed pile in Wood Green and discovered an alligator in the scullery. A real, live, honest-to-God baby alligator.

Or possibly a crocodile. It was in a tank, and no bigger than a puppy. Tom had had to quell the impulse to steal it. Or feed it sushi from the fridge. Jesus . . .

Right now, he wished Kenny would stop just sitting there, opening and closing his mouth like a dying trout, and *say* something. Doug and Mark and David were now just looking at

Kenny. Nobody was drinking. There was no malice in their expressions. Just curiosity. Kenny drew himself up and met Doug's gaze. He was expecting to crumple but he didn't, and when he looked into Doug's eyes he thought he saw something close to amusement. And, behind that, something else.

Doug stared at the trembling man in front of him and thought about Kenny's father in the morgue. About how he was so neat, so trim, even in death. About how the man, even with a small part of his head gone, had had a svelte and desperate beauty about him. That's what he had always wanted to tell Kenny.

That his father, in death, was not a hopeless mess, like so many of the other pulverised, dead and dreary bastards poured in of a weekend. That his father's corpse had been a tidy and ghostly thing. But what difference would such a piece of information make here? Here and now? Kenny was obviously trying his best to hang on to what was left of his life, and Doug didn't want to be the one to push him over the edge. Besides, if he was honest with himself – what was there of his own life to steal? Amateur boxer, former. Part-time builder. A reader. Absentee father. Quite mouthy. What the hell was so precious there, that the stealing of a fraction of it made one damn bit of difference, to himself or anyone else? Ever since he'd met these guys, he had been so glad. So glad to find others whose lives had been plagiarised, just like his. They had gotten hopelessly drunk together, then helplessly sober, and had decided that justice needed to be done, and had bought some rail tickets. But what justice? What the hell were they planning to do once they got here? Go looking for Kelso? Or Kenny? They didn't even know which thief to go for. Or who the thief really was. All they knew, when they'd staggered into the pub next door, was that they had seen their own lives, jobs, families and words – right up there on the screen, and it had been the most horrible experience any of them had ever had.

And Douglas wasn't even too sure about that one.

Jesus Christ – maybe they should've just been flattered.

Douglas looked at Mark and David, both looking at him, and he suddenly felt exhausted. Mark had gotten quite excited, coming into King's Cross on the train, looking at all the graffiti on the sidings. He'd lost the Council graffiti contract in Aberdeen, mainly because he was drunk most of the time these days. No reason for it. No big trauma or anything. It was just one of those things. Mark just liked being drunk, and there it was. *Big steal there*, thought Doug to himself. And as for David. Well, Doug reckoned that David had been young and harmless then, and that he was bitter and harmless now, one-eyed or no.

Doug sighed, and looked back at Kenny's pocked and interesting face. He remembered how much Kenny loved the movies and, on an idiotic, internal whim, he tried to remember what his own favourite movie was. And he couldn't. He couldn't remember what his favourite movie was. He used to know that kind of thing as intimately as he knew the inside of his own mouth. And now his mind was a complete blank.

Doug knew that he didn't hate Kenny any more. He wasn't sure if he ever truly had.

But he was angry. And he was very, very tired. And something here needed explaining, double-quick. He looked again at Mark and David, who were looking at him with a chancer's breed of miserable and spooked anticipation.

Kenny was staring at his knees.

Douglas knew that Kenny was a robber. Everybody at the table knew Kenny was a thief.

But what *kind* of thief, however, had yet to be established.

What do you call a robber robbed? It was a tricky one.

'So,' said Douglas.

Everybody stiffened just a fraction, and even people at nearby tables seemed to sense the tension, judging by the way they were burying their heads in their menus.

'So,' said Douglas again. 'Kenny Duthie. Do you want to *talk* about it?'

So Kenny Duthie talked about it.

And for two hours they couldn't shut him the hell up.

When he was finished, they all sat in silence. Doug just let the silence wash around the walls for a while. He could smell the feeling around the table.

Fucking thieves all OVER the shop. NOBODY is safe from these fucking robbers.

Mark and David were slumped in their seats but at the same time seemed quite chipper. Tom he couldn't read at all. Mainly, the boys seemed to be caught between a confusion of mild annoyance at Kenny and a flurry of real anger towards the man Kelso.

'Let's get this Kelso bastard!' snarled David.

Everybody jumped, but nobody said no. Mark hauled himself up and went to the bar.

Kenny found it stunning enough that they hadn't lynched him. But now here they were, not only forgiving him for foraging around in their lives, but also ready to do some serious damage to Kelso. The second-hand robber was obviously, in their books, somehow worse. And Kenny wasn't about to disagree.

Tom sat and said nothing. The thought of Kelso hurting – that was an idea he loved. But she loved the man. There was no doubt about it. Lynne Callier truly loved the bastard.

To hurt him was to hurt her. Tom sighed. He felt tired. He liked Kenny and he liked this confused and clever bunch. But he thought that simply to hitch his grievance to theirs – well, if he was honest, it just wasn't right. Kelso had done those men an obvious wrong. But what crime had he committed against Tom? He had fallen in love with Lynne Callier. That was as much as Tom himself had done.

He stared around him, as Mark staggered back from the bar and slammed the drinks down on the table. He looked at the group of eager and supplicatory faces around him. All those guys with their stupid and adrenal invention.

Kenny and Doug and David and Mark.

And, again, at Douglas's devoutly mercurial face, filled with the worst kind of worn-out menace.

Tom didn't know what to think, but he suddenly felt so very tired that thinking didn't seem to matter any more. So he just let them talk and chatter, and in the midst of the witless and gorgeous conversation of the guys' mild rancour, he decided to be quiet.

In the middle of all the rubbish talk, Doug leaned forward and asked, 'Tom – can you define the word "millennium"?' He was pretty drunk by now, and smiling his head off.

Before Tom had the chance to say anything, Doug answered his own question.

'A millennium,' he slurred, 'is the same thing as a centurion. Except it's got more legs.'

And then he began to laugh. 'My kid told me that one,' he said when he found the breath, and carried on laughing. Tom laughed too. It was a good joke. And it wasn't even a joke.

'I'll make a mental note of that,' said Tom, amiably enough.

'On what?' said Douglas, and all of a sudden, he didn't seem so drunk anymore. He was still angry, but Tom could tell that there was no real harm in him. He seemed more knackered than annoyed.

'Just ignore me,' said Douglas, eventually. 'It's just ... oh, I don't know. *Mugatis labyrinthi*, I suppose. Yeah.'

Tom stared at him. Doug sighed. 'The vapourings of the labyrinth,' he said. 'A million rotten poems about the minotaur in the maze. Bad poetry. Bad prose. Clichés. Whatever. Jesus. I used to be good at this kind of thing.'

Tom looked at his tired face. Yes, he could work with these guys.

Well, with Kenny and Doug anyway. But their lives, insanely annoyed by a clean and livid robbery – that was not his concern. That was not his life. Not any more. He just wanted to stop thieving, himself, and to have a placid, resolute and seemly existence. Until the day he died. That would do nicely.

In the meantime, he and Kenny gave everybody a floor to sleep on.

The ward nurse scuttled around in the quiet. She veered towards the Doctor, perched as he was upon the woman's bed, and veered away again when she saw the look on his face. The ward was serene this evening. Some of the older patients had been watching television earlier on, and the BBC had shown a documentary about sea-horses. That had pretty much shut everybody up. They all tottered off to their beds, their minds reeling, wonderfully, with notions of small and scaly things, gossamer fins whirring impossibly, of the kind of delicacy and beauty none of them had seen since the world was very, very young. The nurses had learned very quickly that twenty-five minutes of David Attenborough quietly pointing at something gorgeous in a forest in Malaysia was worth a tonne of pills.

Trips to the zoo were planned. They never happened.

It didn't matter. Before, the old folks had always watched the Jerry Springer Show, and were very disappointed to discover that most of the guests were fake. That upset a hell of a lot of them. They would sit in the day-room, in front of the television, in a nervous and saggy state of indecision, wondering whose tale of utter heartbreak was real and whose wasn't. The staff had originally thought that watching the show would cheer them up. Snobbery, mainly. Nothing like watching a bunch of trailer-park white trash yell at each other to make this lot feel incredibly superior. But now they were just getting upset, because they could no longer tell what was real sorrow, rage and humiliation, and what was fake. They felt cheated and the more voluble ones started saying so.

So Springer was replaced by wildlife. The really senile ones would've been hard put to tell the difference, but the nurses were disappointed. It had been a bright and nicely vulgar patch in the day, and now they were stuck with snakes in Borneo. Beauty was one thing. Rotten telly was another. And they missed the celluloid heartache, those svelte and grubby vignettes. Who gives a damn if the pain is real or not? Besides, some of the patients were more impressed by Springer's security team, hovering off-camera, than by any of the guests. They just seemed to love the way these huge and muscular guys would wade in at the first sign of a fight, with their conciliatory body language (palms up, always), their gentle, detached demeanour as they hauled screaming and stupid bitches off each other and especially the way in the middle of all that noise they made eye contact with nobody but seemed always rather to be gazing, near-dreamily, into the middle distance. None the less, the wildlife won out.

But the folks were old, and probably all had their own ancient demons to deal with when the lights went out and they were drifting off into a dim and terrifying night, and when the sun sneaked in and they were waking up to a creaking and horrible day.

So the nurses were kind. Which they would have been anyway.

But she never left her bed. And there he sat, perched on the side of it. For hours, every evening, now. He wasn't comfortable and he didn't care. His hips hurt. He fingered the scalpel, and thought about the gun. And because that thought didn't really go anywhere, he told her about his sister. She'd got a divorce settlement worth half a million and cancer, all in the same month. She was dead in four. He had to laugh. Really. He had always hated his sister. Or thought he did until she was dead. And then he decided he didn't. Not that he went to the funeral or anything. But that amount of money and that amount of death – both at the same time. He just had to laugh. Not that he actually did. But still.

And still the old woman didn't react. Not a flicker, not a flinch. She was too far away these days. She was thinking about her schooldays again, only this time she was thinking about how good grammar had been hammered into her and her peers. Here and now, even in the sorrowful and flabby surroundings of the ward, she was thinking about grammar. About how the brittle and unhappy teacher had made the classes a crèche for lovely nightmares, and where getting the right answer was a brush with a scary breed of *redemption. And this wasn't anything to do with life or death. It was just school.*

But the phrases just swam, unbidden, into her head. Words that meant nothing to anyone any more. Words that had ruled her entire childhood.

Words like 'predicate', 'reflexive', 'nominative', 'appositive' and 'intensive'.

Phrases like 'subjective complement', 'elliptical clause', 'predicate pronoun', 'infinitive phrase' and 'dangling modifiers'. She couldn't even remember what they meant, exactly, but she had loved their disciplinary rigour.

And now she was beginning to forget things, things that had been lodged like shrapnel in her mind for decade after decade after decade. But that was okay. Most things weren't worth remembering. She had long since stopped thinking about her age. Memories of her life came and went, now, in a benign and washing jumble, to the point where what was real and what was imagined collided with gentle regularity, and with harm done to neither. She had forgotten her sons' faces long, long ago.

And sometimes, the voices in the ward would insinuate themselves into her consciousness to the point where she was wide awake and listening. Occasionally she would be made aware of the Doctor's voice, and she was sure that his voice had changed. Its adrenal tone had taken on a metallic aspect, and the noise, the spooked and lovely conversation of the ward's background racket – that had changed too. Few people spoke to him any more. The nurses hurried past her bed, as if they did not want to hear what he was saying to her. One evening, he spent three hours showing her his jacket. The one with all the badges. He was especially pleased with the badge he'd gotten from some government-sponsored charity or other. It was small and silver in colour. It was made, along with tens of thousands of others, from a melted-down SS-20 nuclear missile. Or possibly a Peacekeeper. Anybody, nobody in the pub ever believed him when he told them that's what it was. It was incredibly annoying, so he started carrying the Certificate of Authenticity around with him, just to show people, like some keen and witless hillbilly. And then he got drunk one night and he lost it. So he just stopped talking about it altogether.

Lying buried in her bed, she could hear the spare, hectoring edge in the Doctor's voice. And it frightened her. He hadn't struck her again. Perhaps he was planning something more interesting. Or not. Either way, she was too tired to think about it. Pain was nothing any more. Its presence, its absence – these were corporeal things that had begun not to register in her mind. She was more interested in the workings of the Doctor's mind. He had stopped reading stories from the papers and now he just hovered. Hovered with an aura she could almost smell, a presence that was at once pining and frivolous, an aura of civil whippedness. His kindness and cleverness had had their brief sprawl. These days he was a pained and playful goon. The nurses carried on doing their stuff for her in solid swoops of professionalism, but they had more or less stopped talking to him.

The old woman didn't bother them any more. He did.

He did his doctoring job, more or less on autopilot. And he watched her. Day after day. She was an affront. To everything that he loved. An implacable, sheen and thinning insult. Her silent and old, old world was, to him, a place where orthodox songs could not be sung, where the fractured and hugely nervous domesticity of the ward was just ruined, utterly ruined.

The woman burrowed deeper into her sheets, invisible and cavalier.

And the Doctor watched.

He watched this thing, this old bitch, this quiet and malignant vaudeville.

Not much longer now. He was sure of it. He had to be.

And the man, God bless him, went slowly and finally mad.

After two weeks, they had almost consolidated themselves into a gang.

Kenny. Tom. Douglas. Mark. David.

Or possibly a posse. Or possibly a loose conglomeration of temporarily unemployed men with a grudge. But a grudge that was easily transformed into a proper purpose. It wasn't idiotic. It wasn't stupid. And after two weeks Kenny, Douglas and Tom, especially, had gotten to know each other to the point where an unwritten mission statement wasn't totally out of the question.

Sometimes, they'd decided, life was not about money, or reputation, or prestige. Sometimes, it was just about rightfully possessing something. Anything.

Like the story of your own damn life, for example. Or of the lives you created.

So John Kelso's fate was sealed. Again.

None of them seemed upset that Tom was a thief. Or that Kenny had spent time on a ward. And they seemed to have a fair bit of cash between them, for some reason.

Mark, in particular, held no animosity against Kelso. Christ, he didn't even know the man. He'd just wandered into the pub and gotten caught up in other people's stories of theft and loss. And Douglas was a good, if slightly intense fellow. But they were all decent enough company and hell, being unemployed these days, he didn't have any other pressing business. These days he almost felt as if he was on some sort of holiday break, and spent most of his time in the pub.

That was before he went for a train journey north into Charing

Cross, and spotted a startling piece of graffiti on the dirt-blackened siding wall, on the approach to the station. The word was four feet high, as sinuous as a snake, and a mix of at least seven different colours, with silver and gold thrown in around the edges.

The word was *KNOWN* and Mark fell off his seat when he saw it.

The bastard had emigrated. He had moved south. And now here he was in London, as bold and as beautiful as ever. It was early evening, and Mark was a bit drunk, and he honestly didn't know whether to be happy or devastated. The thing was a sparkly piece of home, right there. But it was like a mobile insult too, following him around. Mark was sure that he'd lost his contract with Aberdeen Council because of this guy, and not because he got a bit plastered now and again. He had always been too slack about cleaning this guy off. But he just hadn't been able to help himself. The man's stuff was so damn beautiful. But that's not the kind of thing you say to the Director of Cleansing. Mark always knew that he was in the wrong job, but he never knew what job he should have been in. The rest of the team had had no idea. They just thought that he was a bit of a softie. They had never clocked the fact that, for every rotten, talentless tagger whose obliteration made his heart sing there was a skinny and shining work of art whose removal made him want to lie down and weep. That's why he didn't mind Kenny taking photographs. That's why he'd actually encouraged it, although nobody seemed to notice that either.

He dragged David along on his next train trip into town, so that David could see it too. And as they pulled into Charing Cross, with the sun bouncing off the London Eye and streaming into the carriage, Mark was sober enough to realise that the man had gone rigid at the sight of the huge, lively and lovely word on the blackened wall.

David's whole head wobbled horribly, and only then did Mark remember that graffiti, no matter how sweet and balloon-like, was always going to remind David, with his one good eye, of nothing but pain. Mark reached forward because he couldn't help himself and, while the other passengers floated off the train, he wrapped his arms around David, holding him as tightly as he could, and trying not to embarrass him too much.

'I'm sorry,' he whispered, 'I forgot.'

'It's okay,' said David, a greasy tear seeping down one side of his face. He leaned in and down because now he felt so, so tired, and he buried his face in the shoulder of Mark's creaking leather jacket for a bit, to the point where he couldn't really breathe properly. Then he shivered and drew back.

'Listen – I'm just going to go for a wander about, go to the flicks or something, okay?'

And with that, David disentangled himself, smacked Mark gently on the head, and wandered out of the train and off up Duncannon Street, towards Leicester Square.

He wandered about aimlessly for a bit, biting back tears and cursing the sea and the rocks and graffiti artists and his own lop-sided vision. And he decided to go see a movie.

He didn't give a shit which one. Anything would do.

Day of the Locust, from 1975, was playing in the Prince Charles Cinema, so he wandered in and bought himself a ticket to see that.

After a little while, about twenty minutes in, struggling to come to terms with a screenplay that gave him nonsensical goosebumps, in the dark, David realised that he wasn't imagining it.

Donald Sutherland *was* playing a character called Homer Simpson.

David stared at the screen, his head tilted automatically to favour his good eye but not really paying attention any more, and he thought about his days as a medical student, and the Castellaneta website he'd spent so much time creating. The young fellow he was then, even though it wasn't all that long ago, seemed to him now like a total stranger. A benign and enthusiastic moron. A good student with everything to look forward to.

He had never experienced violence before that terrible night in that town on the Aberdeenshire coast. He'd never so much as gotten into an argument in his life. And then, as a reward for doing a good job in cleaning those god-awful rocks, in the wet and the cold and the rain, he got the shit beaten out of him. And the tip of a pointed cowboy boot rammed into his eye. He had never known pain like it. He remembered rolling around on the floor of the dingy pub and screaming, screaming like a baby, while Mark tried desperately to stem the flow of blood from his crushed eye-socket.

Everything after that was a cold and nasty blur. Everything had smelled of antiseptic. He lay in his hospital bed for what seemed like an eternity. It was eight days.

When his face had healed sufficiently, he was allowed home and offered some counselling. Counselling by a psychiatrist who was seventy if he was a day.

'I actually met Hermann Rorschach once, you know.'

That was the first thing the old man had said as David limped over the threshold.

'I actually went to his funeral, in 1922, I think it was.'

He was so old, it made no sense.

Who the hell uses that kind of old-fashioned, ink-blot stuff any more, anyway? thought David. And besides, since he was blind in one eye, the Rorschach diagrams made no sense. All he could see was one of the butterfly's wings. One of the wine goblets. One half of the fire-breathing dragon. Four spider's legs instead of eight. Half a panda's face. A dwarf throwing punches against thin air. The Nile Delta pouring off only to the right. Ladybirds with all the wrong spots.

He had left the old man's office weeping like a baby. The tear-salt in the empty socket was so painful, it made him cry even more. And so on and so forth.

And so here he was now. Part-blind, angry and utterly, self-proclaimedly useless at the age of twenty-three.

Well, okay then. Fine. Whatever.

David, the good and former student, left the cinema with a sense of purpose and a spring in his step. He did not go home. Kenny and the gang wondered where he was.

They never saw David again.

Three nights later, a young man was found beaten to death on Hungerford Bridge.

He was discovered propped against the wall with some fresh

graffiti and clutching a spray can. Alarmed passengers had spotted the bloody mess on their way home from work.

The cops who attended the scene were treated to the most beautiful sunset the city had ever seen. They and the ambulance guys took their time. They prodded the body and smoked cigarettes, hands on hips, and stared at the hysterical sky for minutes on end.

The story made it onto the news, so ITN taxied a cub reporter down to the river with a link to some bullshit story about engineering work being done on the London Eye. But while the talking head talked, the cameraman made sure he got the sky behind the talking head's head. And as the sun went down, the city just seemed to stop, but slowly. People dawdled in idle clumps in the streets to stare at the sky, simply. London had never seen a sunset quite like it. Drinkers stopped drinking and wandered outside. The traffic didn't stop, of *course* it didn't, but it slowed down, while everyone sat in their cars and gawped upwards. Heart-stopping colours like that surely couldn't exist. Not in real life.

It was without doubt the best sunset the city had ever had, and those with any kind of a half-decent camera went completely mad.

People talked about that sky, dreamily, for weeks afterwards. At this particular moment, however, towards sunset's end, rays of soft gold, intolerably dense, clear and severe, filtered with a percussive and silent surge through the iron struts of the bridge, and illuminated the dead body and made it look almost beautiful. The cop and the medics ambled around the crime scene on the bridge, and took photos. Mainly, though, they just stood around, smoking and looking at the demented sky, looking at the most beautiful thing any of them were ever likely to see before they died. One officer leant down and pried the spray can from the young man's rigid fingers, then stood up and gazed again at the river.

The damn thing, usually an interesting and energetic brown, was actually *twinkling*.

He didn't hurry. There was no hurry. The man was dead.

And he hadn't gotten further than the letter '*K*'.

*

Thievery was almost all he knew, so thieving was what he taught. Kenny, Douglas and Mark were now all camping out on the floor of Tom's flat in Crouch End. A month later, the gang that was left, now minus David and with dwindling funds, listened to Tom down the pub and decided that although they might want to get the bastard Kelso, they also needed money to live on. It was ludicrous, but Tom's little homily worked.

'Either bring in some damn money, you miserable fuckwits, or just fuck off back to Scotland, okay?'

Mark was truly heartsick. He was worried about David. He'd seen the story on the news about the dead man on the bridge, but he hadn't paid any attention because he was outside the pub, staring at that alchemical sky like everybody else and trying to keep from crying. But then again, he also fancied himself as a stylish and proper robber. Given half a chance and some degree of sobriety.

Having somewhere to stay, however basic, was a godsend for Kenny, since his attempts at independent living were variable, to say the least. As far as his appointed health worker was concerned, Kenny Duthie had disappeared off the face of the earth.

So they became Tom's students and protégés, and threw themselves into the blagging business with a pleasing enthusiasm. It was positively therapeutic. For both Mark and Douglas, this was the final cutting of any ties they might have had with home. There was no going back. There was nothing to go back for, and they had both known it the moment they'd stepped onto the train in Aberdeen and ordered four cans of Tennants Extra each from the bar.

And, as Tom had begun to talk and talk, that night in the pub, it dawned on the pair of them that they were born criminals.

They just hadn't gotten around to committing any crimes.

So Tom and his tyro team burgled and thieved and did all right out of it.

Although he was careful to avoid her house, and the pub, and the supermarket, and anywhere else he might see her, Tom did actually spot Lynne Callier twice, opposite the 7/11 on the Broadway, and without her seeing him. And both times she was getting on the w7 bus up to Muswell Hill. She was practically living with the bastard. Probably. But when he saw her, it almost stopped his heart all over again. She looked radiant. And he hated himself for even thinking of such a crass word. But worse than that, she looked truly happy. And in a strange way, although it curdled his guts, Tom was actually glad to see it. On both occasions, the bounce in her step and the glint of her new hairdo just lifted his spirits. He was glad that she was happy.

On Friday, down the pub, Kenny's regular and vicious tirades against the man Kelso just got on Tom's bloody nerves.

'Let's just *drop* Kelso for the moment, okay?' he said, irritably. 'Let's just concentrate on getting some cash, all right?'

They looked at him, surprised, but nobody disagreed.

Sometimes, just getting back to work is the best cure for whatever ails you.

So that's what they did. They got to work, and in no time at all, Tom, Kenny, Douglas and Mark were robbing N8 blind. And for Tom, things came almost full circle, except that this time he had company. A whole and gorgeous world of unlocked doors and absent alarms, of other people's interesting stuff and luminous lives. A world where he could take a deep, deep breath and try to put that rotten, lovelorn past behind him and just get on with the business of being a competent thief.

The first place he and Mark broke into was a neat little semi in Gospel Oak. (Kenny and Douglas were, at the same moment, diving in through the back door of a big brute of a house, somewhere on the Caledonian Road.)

And Tom was again in his element. The downstairs lounge had a safe hidden behind a painting. An actual, honest-to-God *safe* hidden behind an actual, honest-to-God reproduction of a Monet. Or possibly a Manet. Tom began to smile to himself. And in the bureau, he found the safe's combination written on a piece of paper. Taped to the underside of the drawer. At this point, Tom almost pissed himself laughing. The poor bastard had obviously been watching too many rotten sixties spy movies. But he did have to admire the man's timid panache in one respect: the combination was 15 04 26 99. Tom had seen enough BBC2 to recognise Sgt. Bilko's serial number when he saw it. The safe held seven thousand pounds. He took five. It was a very nice house. Mark found some jewellery upstairs and a metal dildo hidden on top of the wardrobe. It seemed to be quite old, and from Japan, judging from the writing on the box. 'Steely Dan' it said in English. Mark was, these days, in a frazzle of delight. He seemed to have discovered his vocation, in a sense, and was doing his best to be good at it. And to impress Tom. He was trying not to drink too much during the day because it just made him think about David, and then he would get all upset.

He wanted to take the dildo, just for the hell of it, for a laugh, until Tom reminded him that they weren't the Antiques bloody Roadshow, and they weren't an Ann Summers franchise either. They were thieves. They had five grand, eight with the stones.

Time to go. Mark always did as he was told, so the pair of them slipped out the back and into the dark. Tom banged his head on the lintel on the way out.

The money was great that night, and would keep them going for ages, but Tom wasn't actually that bothered. In his backpack he had stashed a 'How-to' manual on capoeira, a fat biography of Phyllis Pearsall, complete with original maps, and three framed and autographed prints. One was an animation cel from *Tom and Jerry*, signed by Scott Bradley, no less; the second was an old, black-and-white photograph of Walt Disney and another gentleman, which had the name 'Carl Stalling' scrawled across it; the third was a very old technical drawing of Central Park, with 'FREDERICK LAW OLMSTED' printed in neat capitals in the corner. Tom almost felt bad about stealing the prints, but, oddball music lover or no, the guy was obviously loaded, so what the hell. And he had good taste, after a fashion. Tom liked stealing from folks with what he imagined might possibly be good taste. But mainly he just liked looking at other people's stuff. Always had. Always would.

Tom suspected that the prints were probably worth a fair few grand, and he also knew that he would never sell them. The old magpie instinct had resurfaced and he wasn't even that interested in money any more. Enough not to go hungry, enough to have something to read, enough to acquire a few distracting and beautiful things – well, fair enough then.

Sometimes he wondered if his grandmother still had his boxes of books in her loft, or if she had gotten rid of them. Or if she even remembered who he was. He'd never been a great one for phoning.

Back home from the Caledonian Road, Kenny and Douglas had done quite well too. Five hundred quid in cash, five DVDs, three cards and, for some reason, a wedding cake.

An actual fucking wedding cake. Three tiers. The pair of them had humped it out of the scullery and out the door and all the way home, laughing like a pair of maniacs. Just because they could.

They were learning. And the notion of cruelty was just that and nothing more.

Back in the flat, they all got drunk, celebrated their winnings, congratulated each other on their stuff, and threw bits of icing and marzipan at each other until four in the morning.

Much later, after Kenny and Mark had passed out on the carpet, Tom sat staring at the ruined cake, thinking about suicidal Belfast bakers.

The plastic bride and groom figures were still, miraculously, perched upright on the top. He felt faintly, a feral notion tickling the back of his brain, and he wondered if that creative, decent and weeping baker had succeeded in dying, since that was how he had seemed to be heading. Hopeless memories of flour-clouds, bilious artistry and screaming grooves of sheer bad temper all kicked their way into Tom's mind.

Perhaps, and the thought alone was exhausting, the mad baker had succeeded in living. Now that would be something.

And Douglas sat on the floor, staring feebly at the bruise on Tom's brow, thinking about his own fighting days. His own terse and lofty boxing days. He was sobering up fast now, and looking at the tiny scars on his knuckles. He'd had a laugh these last months, but it was beginning to dawn on Doug that perhaps he wasn't as comfortable a thief as, say, Mark. It just didn't sit well with him. He was quite skilled and Tom knew it. But his heart wasn't in it. Sneaking around wasn't his style. Marching right up to people and punching their lights out – that *was* his style. Showing off whatever skill he had, and bleeding afterwards, if that's what was required. That, apart from his Literature course, had been the only thing that Douglas had ever cared about. Well, that and his daughter. She would be three by now. Or thereabouts.

Douglas was fed up, keen and as fit as a butcher's dog. He needed a fight. A proper fight. Tom could almost feel the vibrations of misery flitting across the room, so he just decided to leave it alone. The last thing he wanted right now was a fight with Douglas.

He staggered to his feet, laughed to himself at some private joke, patted Doug affectionately on the shoulder, drained his drink and went off to his bed feeling beguiling and scrappy, in himself. Feeling quite happy, actually. He wandered off to his bed, flopping helplessly in, and didn't wake up for seventeen hours.

He never saw Douglas again. But that wasn't his fault.

What Tom could not know was that Douglas's last minutes were the happiest of his entire life. He had gone down the pub, gotten gloriously drunk, and then propelled himself, happily and unin-vited, into the middle of a bunch of English Literature and Philosophy students and their tutors. But they didn't seem to mind too much, and let him sit down. They all got to talking like maniacs and after an hour, were buying each other doubles, and arguing the toss about their favourite books, their favourite movies, their favourite boxers, the 'Laturnalia' website one of them had discovered (which had the best toilet graffiti from around the world), if Anthony Perkins' best movie was *Winter Kills* or *Remember My Name*, how the hell you were supposed to pronounce Enver Hoxha's surname (one of the kids was convinced it rhymed with 'Roger', and got his lager in his lap for his trouble), and whether or not a second-best bed is a compliment or an insult.

Douglas was so happy. There's nothing quite like being around young people, especially students. He hadn't had a decent, drunken blather for ages. He almost felt as if he was at home and back at college, studying *Othello* and off fighting for fun.

Even when he bumped into the big guy, on his way to the bar, he was in such a good mood that the torrent of abuse spat into his face just struck him as funny. Even being invited 'outside, pal' made him laugh. Douglas was an excellent and skilful fighter, but sometimes that simply is not enough against bulk, cruelty and sheer bad temper. The big guy and his even bigger friend probably didn't mean to hurt him that badly, and the students were so drunk, they didn't even notice that he was gone.

In the alley, Douglas boxed beautifully and brilliantly, and a million awful things went through his mind as he lay bleeding from a real bad abdominal stab wound, on top of the pub's wooden barrel-drop gate. (Like most people, he had always avoided stepping on the things, convinced that they would give way under his weight.) Mostly it was just vague notions about how pain of this kind simply couldn't be possible and, minutes later, with his shattered face plastered to the smelly wood, how beautiful that shade of dribbling red was, but when the cold finally took him, seven hours later, Douglas was thinking only of his daughter. Of his daughter and of marzipan. He felt bad about stealing that cake. That wasn't right.

Research has shown that extreme cold can keep alive people who are badly bleeding.

Not this time.

Two nights later, Tom was asked to identify Douglas's body. After almost jumping out of his skin at the sight of a cop on his doorstep, he realised that they weren't after him. They weren't after any thieves at all. They just hadn't been able to find anything on the body apart from a piece of paper with Tom's address on it. No wallet, no nothing. Just an address. It was as if the man had been afraid of forgetting where he lived. As if that piece of paper was the only thing he had left. Kenny was out, thank God, and, besides, had displayed a studied lack of interest in Doug's whereabouts. As if he was afraid that something bad had happened. He had gone down the Broadway with Mark to do a food shop, and that had been seventeen hours ago. The pair of them had probably gone on a bender. Still, Kenny had a sensitive stomach.

So Tom gave the police a couple of names in Scotland and agreed to go down the morgue. He stood in that awful space, shivering horribly, and when he was shown the body and had quelled the urge to vomit, he was so, so glad that Kenny wasn't there. Douglas's face was barely recognisable as human. He had only known the man for a little while and now he didn't know him at all. He had been hoping that Douglas would look presentable. No and no again.

Outside the hospital, he tumbled to his knees on the pavement and almost fell into the traffic, like some dumb and lumbering toddler. This was ridiculous. He hardly knew the man. But even so, he had liked him. The man had been smart and intense and funny. It had been like having a partner.

And nobody deserved to go into their next life looking as grim as that.

When Kenny and Mark finally fell home, Tom sat them both down and told them what had happened.

Kenny heard the word 'morgue', stood up, and marched unsteadily from the room.

Mark wobbled around in circles in the living-room for a bit. He was totally plastered but he could still recognise fat, proper and true sorrow when he heard it. And he didn't like the feel of this at all. This wasn't fun any more. They were just supposed to have a laugh, blag stuff, give it to Tom for fencing, and generally have a good time. People weren't supposed to die in a pool of blood, in an alley. He was trembling like a freezing kitten.

Tom stopped talking. No point in upsetting the man any further. Mark stared at his toes.

'This was a mistake,' he burbled, to no one in particular.

Tom went into the kitchen to see if Kenny was okay, which he was, just about, and when he came back, Mark was gone.

Mark had wandered, miserable, back to the pub and when closing time came along, he wangled his way into a club, and when that closed in the early morning, he staggered back into the pub at opening time. And so on and so forth. And when he was good and drunk, he wandered to Euston station and bought himself a ticket north.

And that was that. He had nothing but the clothes he was wearing.

And he was so drunk, the staff were tempted to throw him off the train at Preston.

But they didn't.

And then there were two.

Kenny and Tom.

The gang had gone from a five-strong, brazen and peppery bunch, enjoying themselves madly, to an unhappy and lonesome two.

A little subtle robbing kept them both in food and cash for two weeks. But they both knew that something was wrong and missing. They didn't talk about it but they both now felt nervous and pointless.

Kenny and Tom.

They had once had a common purpose. Something beyond rent and booze and making new friends. They both knew that a sizeable chunk of both their lives had been stolen, and they still hadn't done a damn thing about it.

On a Friday night about a week later, they went into town for a wander about and a movie and there, outside the Prince Charles cinema, were posters for Kelso's film.

Well, Christ almighty – after making a decent fortune on the blockbuster front – now it was doing the fucking *art house* circuit? Four months and it would probably get its terrestrial debut on Channel 4. Some of the blown-up reviews, under glass, were going on about possible Oscars, not least for Best Screenplay.

Beside the poster was a small black-and-white photo of John Kelso, looking cool and almost handsome. Kenny flinched at the sight of the man's face. The bastard looked so happy. Kenny thought about all the movies he had seen in his life. About how, if he was truthful, movies had been the most important things in his life.

Ever, pretty much.

The rain began to pelt down and Kenny just couldn't tear himself away from the poster. And then he lost it. He began to punch at the poster, helplessly, like some kind of screaming lunatic. Tom grabbed him matter-of-factly by the scruff, to spare the man's knuckles if nothing else, and looked at the photograph. Kelso had lost weight. And he was wearing a truly beautiful suit. And he did look happy. And Tom knew that his happiness had nothing to do with the damn movie. The image of her face swanned into Tom's mind, and he almost took a vicious swing at Kenny, simply because no other target was available.

But he didn't. He just wrapped his arm around the rapidly crumpling Kenny, and there the pair of them stood, staggering exhaustedly in the rain, almost falling but not quite. Leaning into each other, utterly drenched now, and feeling as if they were choking. As if dying for something or other, and wondering what the hell had happened to their lives.

Dying for something lurid and gifted to sneak up on them, unbeknownst.

Dying for lives of even dreary and arctic utility.

Dying for some damn justice.

For someone to hurt.

Dying for someone else to take up the damn *slack*.

That day was coming and it was coming up fast.

*Now it was three in the morning and he was standing by her bed —
she had been moved to her own room for some reason — cleaning his
nails with his scalpel. He stared at her unblinkingly for the three
minutes it took to scrape through all ten and, since he wasn't looking
at what he was doing and, because the scalpel was very sharp, by the
time he was finished, blood was dripping from his fingertips onto the
floor. He stared at the thin and harmless flow for a bit, then raised
his hands and let them hover over her. The blood dripped onto her
impossibly wrinkled forehead, and onto her awful eyelids and onto
her ghastly mouth.*

*With his left hand, he slowly planted the scalpel into the pillow,
millimetres from her face, and cut through the fibre all the way around
her head. Feathers puffed, miraculously, up and out, and a few of the
tinier ones floated down in the dim and lovely light and stuck to the
blood on her skin. And this time she flinched. She opened her eyes and
she looked at him and she flinched. But in her eyes wasn't even the
glimmerings, or the beginnings, of a question. She stared at him, and the
look she gave him this time really opened him up.*

It opened him up and it opened him wide.

And in his shock, he stayed that way.

He knew now what was going to save him. And his sanity.

And, in that moment of utter shock, he knew what he had to do.

*In that stunning moment, although his own heart had become a
precarious, glossy and glacial thing, he felt as if, suddenly, he knew
where his life was going, and what his purpose was.*

*He had earned the right, dammit. He had earned the right to a
little bluster and hollow conceit, a small and lurid piece of crusading
mousiness. Just some resistance to all the things in his life that were*

frightening him. All the things that made him feel that he was good but not good enough. Talented but not talented enough. Just the wrong side of genius. Lacking in the kind of arctic tactics that got people ahead these days. Apparently. And definitely lacking in 'people skills'. So he'd been told.

The old woman continued to look at him with a stern, ho-hum and splendid melancholy, and she still never budged a bloody inch. It was obvious now that she would never speak to him. He knew that. There would be no winning, wailing, anabolic or stout stuff from this old cow. Not a word of either mean and predatory education, from which he might have benefited, or of a bleary, boo-hoo and rotten supplication. Nothing.

She would never beg. And he and she both knew it.

But in the meantime, he thought he'd better clean up after himself, and so he got on his knees in the half-dark, and, with a moistened towel, he slid to his knees and began to gently clean the blood from her face. This was the first time he had actually touched her skin in an age. It was surprisingly warm. When he got as far as her mouth, he was tempted to cover it with his hand and never to let go.

But he knew, now, that there was no need for that kind of thing at all.

What he had to do was what he was going to do.

He laughed gently just then, because it was as if a huge and unfathomable weight had been lifted from him, leaving him just mad and rosy-cheeked enough to get by without getting caught. And if he did get caught, just mad enough not to give a damn one way or the other. Life seemed to be streaming along so fast these days. Things were just going to have to come to a head. Or something.

In the corner of the room was a tiny potted plant. That caught his attention.

He hadn't noticed it before.

He finished cleaning up the bits and bobs of blood and whatnot, and looked at it for a bit. The leaves were so small as to be abnormal. Was it a Fig of some sort?

It was truly and terminally pretty.

He hadn't authorised that.

5

So, John Kelso and Lynne Callier were in love. That much was certain.

And judging by the intensity with which the pair of them said hello of a morning, they were going to be an item for a long time to come.

Both their jobs were going brilliantly. Kelso had managed to take his show from cult to almost mainstream. Without even changing his slot. He now had 750,000 respectable working people either watching his show live at 3.00 a.m., or taping it for the next day.

The BBC even pitched the occasional nibble for his contract, which the studio, to its credit, studiously ignored. And so, John Kelso just carried on his familiar and nightly joust. And on and on he blathered about his favourites.

His favourite this and his favourite that, and his favourite the other.

The week *Episode One: The Phantom Menace* was released, he didn't review it.

He didn't even mention it. The execs went berserk, the fans laughed themselves silly, and Kelso went about his merry bloody day. He presented father-and-son profiles, he presented notions for a jazz-centred season (*Too Late Blues*, and *Pete Kelly's Blues*, especially), and he pitched a few other ideas he'd heard somewhere. He suggested a double bill of *Spinal Tap* and *Fear of a Black Hat*, and three weeks later, it happened. As did most of everything else he recommended these days.

He was a player now. And he didn't even have to put on a suit (or meet one), to do it.

And these days, since his show was now ninety minutes long, they allowed him to play lengthy clips from pretty much whatever he fancied. Bad taste or no.

Sam Neill delivering the most gorgeously blasphemous monologue that the Church (and the right wing) ever missed in *Omen III*.

A delirious man (almost?) deflowering his own daughter in *The Crazies*.

A getting-on but still pretty Tony Curtis being executed, horribly, at the end of *Lepke*.

The Monkees commiting suicide in the final moments of *Head*.

Ron Moody coining it with fake displays of epilepsy in *The Twelve Chairs*.

The future Lois Lane getting her heart cut out in *Black Christmas*.

And so on and so forth.

John tried for a chunk of *Man Bites Dog* but even the studio drew the line at that one.

Which was fair enough, considering that some gore just doesn't bear thinking about.

And *Seconds* – they wouldn't go for that one either. Mainly, and probably, because it involved a very negative portrayal of plastic surgery. And much else.

But it wasn't all nasty stuff. Some of it was good and nice. Like the moment when Mr Rochester, played by a splendid George C. Scott, sits blind in the garden and Jane, a suitable and willowy Susannah York, comes along and places a gentle palm on his shoulder, while John Williams goes beautifully berserk in the background.

Or the utterly gorgeous Jeff Chandler sacrificing life and limb for a bunch of bad-tempered, rock-bouncing, yodelling, nineteenth-century French immigrants and their precious bloody *grape-vines*, of all things, in *Thunder in the Sun*.

Or Joan and Sterling going even moodily madder in *Johnny Guitar*.

Or, better yet, cartoons. Getting *right* back to basics.

John Kelso was so happy these days, and so happy with his job. And the best part was that he was able to help Lynne with her job. And she helped him with his. When it came to the dumb and dusty detail of popular bullshit, they were both walking encyclopaedias.

And they both had a love of order, of routine, of the kind of disciplined mental stamina which made both their lives worth living. And which they both had the sweet common sense to know was worth absolutely nothing at all.

Lynne Callier was content. She hadn't thought about the guy, the guy with the leather jacket and the grey hair and the great smell, the guy who had been in her flat, for quite a while, and there had been no sign of him anywhere. John's twitching unhappiness in his sleep had almost stopped, and they spent their time these days cooking and making love and talking. And working too. They would sit at their laptops in adjoining rooms of both their flats, yelling ideas at each other all afternoon, typing like maniacs and laughing like idiots. Their different schedules meant that they got to spend almost all day together, after Lynne got back around noon and before John left around midnight.

And her show was going so well. The hosts had become almost respected. It was now acknowledged within the industry that their tech-specific shows had been the best thing about the whole Remembrance week, and their ratings were now pretty much trashing everyone else in sight. And they trusted Lynne enough now to just let her keep going; whatever she suggested usually got done, sooner or later. And so Lynne did her stuff.

She organised interviews with three stern Creationists, got them good and riled about the exact date – was it really 9.00 a.m. on 23 October 4004 BC? – and then gave Clare and Robert a bunch of other anniversaries for 23 October. The first appearance of the Teletubbies, for example (big cheer from the audience, there), the date that *Jurassic Park* passed the $100 million mark (even bigger cheer), celebrity birthdays, celebrity deaths, and the date that Bull Durham tobacco went out of business in the US.

And a dozen other pieces of utter nonsense, until the deeply decent, deeply stupid and strictly suited Christians just couldn't stand it any more and exited stage left, pursued by a work-experience teenager with a clipboard. She had been tempted to get the twins to follow that item with a piece on a talented South London jeweller who called himself Cain, and rub it in with the fact that the word meant 'metalsmith'. But they ran out of time. Even so, the audience laughed itself silly.

The following week was 'Music Week for the Over Sixty-Fives'.

And the result of the phone-in was just stunning. It was one of their best shows ever. Everybody expected the interviews with minor celebs to be punctuated by boring Broadway showtunes, sturdy Vera Lynn, Nat King Cole and cheesy 'Sing Something Simple'-type tunes. Wrong. When the figures were put together, there were an equal number of votes for Jimmy Buffett and Randy Travis. Val Doonican got slightly fewer votes than Jimmy the Hoover.

Tom T. Hall, Charles Trenet and the Shakin' Pyramids came up even. The Blue Nile, the Virgin Prunes and Neil Sedaka all got equal numbers, as did Richard Rogers and the Undertones. As did J. J. Cale and the Buzzcocks.

Some of the oldsters voted for specific songs, like 'Edelweiss' by Christopher Plummer, 'Morning Train' by Danny Doyle, Loudon Wainwright's 'I Wish I Was a Lesbian' and, bizarrely, 'Something's Cookin'' in the Kitchen' by Dana, of all people. Brilliantly clever rhyming, according to one old fellow. And there were seventeen votes each for Rick Astley and Toots and the Maytals.

One old guy phoned to nominate Alyssha's Attic, Kitchens of Distinction and Daryl Hall. Lynne got one of her staff to call him back and point out, as gently as possible, that they weren't looking for band names based on parts of your house. Just your favourite artist, sir. The old man thought to himself, coughed for a bit, then nominated Glen Campbell.

What sounded like a teenager sniggered in the background.

Good choice, thought Lynne.

The kids counting the votes in the back room almost bust a gut laughing and, when Lynne saw the results, she sat down because she had to. Most old people weren't supposed to be this interesting. Okay, so some of the votes would, naturally, have to be put down to antiquated belligerence, and to sneaky grandchildren running up bills, and to just plain lies. But even so. It was a startling show and got great reviews, and started bullshit debates in the broadsheets, no less, about how we treat our old folk.

Lynne Callier hadn't spoken to her parents in years. And didn't intend to.

So be it.

And so on and so forth.

After three weeks of soap-star interviews – that had become the natural limit beyond which the twins went running to Lynne for something actually interesting – they ran a show about robbery victims. That one was tricky, but she got through it. All those interviews with all those tainted people. Not like herself, with just a wispy thing following her around, and taking and leaving things, like a loving and scary wraith.

No, these folk actually had horrible things happen to them, and had had beautiful and significant things taken and gone, and gone for ever. And obscene graffiti scrawled on their bedroom walls and small heaps of human shit left on their duvets and in their kitchen sinks.

Tom always watched the show, and always made private bets with himself as to which items she had done, because they were interesting, and which ones she hadn't, because they weren't. He was preparing his lunch when he saw the item on robberies, and it almost stopped his heart with the embarrassment of it. Of course he would never do anything as horrible as that.

But he was a thief, all the same.

The next three shows were the hardest work Lynne ever did. They featured interviews with a perfumer, the owner of a garden centre and the man who compiled the crossword puzzles for the *Express*.

Smells and plants. Lynne felt a nosebleed coming on just thinking about them. She tried to get Süskind of course, but wasn't even remotely surprised when his agent called to say, rather politely in the circumstances, that his client didn't do daytime television. Or that kind of thing. At all. Actually.

Lynne replaced the receiver with a small smile, and they made do with one of the *Ground Force* gardening team.

Mazes and riddles. Tom actually *got* a nosebleed when he saw that show.

And in the middle of the show about mazes, crop circles, UFOs and the like, the hosts took a call from an elderly man who wanted to make a comment about the piece, several weeks ago, on the Spitfire.

'Yes,' he said, in a voice as frail as dust, 'there were women test pilots. But not for the reasons you lot think.' Clare threw her eyes to heaven, but they let him blather on anyway.

'The reason was that trained fighter pilots were valuable. And expensive. A limited resource, if you will. I used to be one. And we were all men, right?'

'Er, yes,' said Clare, uncertainly, 'we had gathered that.'

'Well, women weren't . . . a limited resource,' said the old man, and his voice was full of embarrassment. And suddenly the studio went very, very quiet.

'Test pilots had to be . . . dispensable, sort of. Because they were more likely to get killed. So that the *real* pilots, the men, like, didn't. Later on.'

At this point, the old man paused to cough, and the truth of what he was saying seeped around the studio.

'I'm sorry,' he croaked, 'but it had nothing to do with equal opportunities. It's just that women were regarded as a bit . . . well, dispensable. I'm sorry. I know. I'm sorry. It wasn't very gallant, was it?'

At this point, his voice gave out and he hung up. The audience was utterly silent, and probably horribly embarrassed. Clare looked at Robert and then they both looked at Lynne in the wings. Lynne shrugged back at them. She couldn't be expected to know everything. And then she remembered the way Cliff Robertson had flinched when Clare had mentioned the subject, weeks ago.

He had known – of course he had – but had been too well-mannered to go there.

Well, good for him. Lynne smiled to herself.

You win some.

Clare and Robert gawped elegantly at each other for a moment, but in a kindly (and professional) way, as if realising for the first time that one of them was actually female, and what a terrific thing that was. Then Clare, recovering brilliantly, introduced the next item, which was an interview with the great-great-grandson of James Finlayson, the rotund actor who appeared in most of Laurel and Hardy's earlier movies.

The man whose expression 'Doh!' had travelled down and down the decades. It was a good interview.

The following week was an ordinary, movie-type week and, amongst other pieces of nonsense, viewers got to phone in with their faves. The number of people who voted for Jerry Lewis's *Cinderfella* was positively alarming. But alongside that were votes for *Cube*, *Trigger Happy* and *Smile*.

Lynne suspected that John and a colleague, perhaps, were involved in rigging the poll, but – what the hell – it made the show a bit more interesting. And the hosts didn't seem to mind these days. In fact, Clare and Robert were getting so damn relaxed at this, bless them.

And sometimes Lynne caught them looking at each other in a way that had something to do with something more than just the job.

They were both married.

To other people, obviously.

But sometimes the pair of them sat on that stupid, chintzy sofa, while the grips and the gaffers and the best boys scurried around them in an industrious and hurtful flurry, and just stared at each other. For no real reason and with nothing to say.

It would make no sense. No sense at all.

Oh, Jesus, Lynne thought, *the red-tops would have a field day with that one.*

But even so.

Robert and Clare, these days, were beginning to look at each other with a look that lasted no longer than three seconds, but in a way that almost stopped Lynne's breath right there in her throat, and that nearly made her laugh for the sheer frisson of seeing something so sensible and lovely.

And nearly cry for them, and for the inevitable and stupid misery that they were going to bring upon themselves.

But people can't help the way they feel.

They just can't.

And that's all there is to it.

The next Monday's show was all about language, or slang, or whatever.

An expert of sorts – some English professor Lynne had booked – dragged himself on and, despite a colossal hangover, actually managed to talk colossal sense about various bits and bobs that actually held the audience's interest. The man was a card, and no misake.

Viewers were invited to call in and ask him where words came from. It was like *Notes and Queries*, only noisier.

People wanted to know things. They wanted to know, for example:

Where does the word 'checkmate' come from? *(Persian: 'Shah Mat' = 'The King is Dead'.)*

And the word 'hooker'? And no, I'm not talking about rugby. (*'Corlear's Hook' = a brothel-packed area of nineteenth-century New York.*)

What does the expression 'Saffron from Ireland' mean, exactly? (*'Shit', exactly. Mediaeval shit, to be more exact.*)

Why 'batty', to mean crazy? (*Fitzherbert Batty. Lawyer in Spanish Town, Jamaica, 1830s. Utter, utter lunatic.*)

And the word 'ghetto'? (*'Foundry' – Venice's seventeenth-century Jewish community lived next door to one.*)

I'm addicted to *Who Wants to Be a Millionnaire?* What am I? (*A 'mataetechnician' – an expert in useless knowledge. And you're a moron. Sorry.*)

At this point, the Professor had the decency to begin to sweat.

And then someone called in, laughing, with the question 'What is love?'

The audience burbled happily to itself, with that gorgeous roll of quiet and shared hilarity that exists only within the sturdy ranks of a television audience.

Nothing better than an unanswerable question.

The Professor, who was from Maine, fifty-five and whose name was Kip Simon, and whose wife of thirty-five years had died thirty-five days earlier from pancreatic cancer, exactly thirty-five days after diagnosis, looked at the carpet for a full half-minute.

Which on television is practically an eternity.

And then he looked up, stared straight into the camera and said, 'What is love? Good question. Why don't we talk about that? Let's talk about love, why don't we? Yes. Let's do that. Let's talk about love.'

And, because neither Clare nor Robert nor even Lynne had any better ideas or, indeed, the gumption to stop him, that's what Professor Simon did. He overran the next three items and, for thirty-five minutes, he talked and he talked and he talked.

He talked about love.

Quietly and with a gentle authority. And he brooked no interruption. The producer went silently bananas, waving his hands in the air, the boom guy didn't know where to go so he just stayed where he was, and the two cameramen, well, they had both taken a liking to the Professor, so they weren't going to budge a bloody inch.

Lynne held her breath. The man sat there, heartbroken and sensible, and he talked about love and nothing but.

Love and nothing but.

And the studio just let him, to his miserable heart's content.

Thirty-five minutes. That was another first.

Unbelievable.

And everybody was watching.

A million fed-up, heartbroken and post-maturbatory housewives were watching.

Another million stoned and happy students were watching.

John Kelso was watching. John Kelso, that organised and stable soul. He was watching and suddenly, watching, was stupidly scared.

And Kenny the utter madman, of late, was watching. He

watched and he wondered what was wrong with this Simon guy. He knew damn well but hey – what the hell.

And Tom, the calm and reasonable thief, was also watching, and he gave it seven minutes before he turned it off and weaved off to the fridge for a huge drink.

And Lynne Callier was watching from the wings.

She sucked on a carton of Ribena and just let the Professor do his thing.

For longer than a half-hour, the man spoke the most ragged, awry and dented kind of sense, and none of it mattered a damn.

It didn't matter that he actually *was* speaking the truth about love.

The truth, actually, is neither here nor there.

While his hosts sat and stared, Professor Simon talked about the Gods and man and everything in between; he talked about Camadeva and Cupid, and about Eros and Freya. He talked about William Shakespeare and Ali MacGraw, about Geoffrey Chaucer and Jeff Stryker, about Edward Gorey and Gore Vidal. About Bob Newhart, death and Stiff Little Fingers. About *Frasier* and the Poohsticks and Dolly Parton.

He went on and on and on, in a deep and attractive voice and, just at the moment everybody thought he was going to break down in tears, he didn't. He gathered himself, didn't mention his wife once, couldn't believe they hadn't stopped him, and finished with a short monologue from Raymond Chandler. The one about blondes.

Sarah, his wife, had been a redhead.

The audience erupted. They hadn't a clue, mostly, what he'd been going on about but, boy, they just loved someone who could talk like that.

That evening, the Professor took a phone call from the *Sun*.

They were offering him £34,000 a year to be their house psychiatrist.

The Professor told them to fuck off.

Then he replaced the receiver, curled up on the floor and cried like a baby.

But he felt better, even so.

John Kelso and Lynne Callier, then.

They enjoyed better and more interesting yarns, and finer and finer weekends in bed, and a squall of mini-fights that, over the months, only served to illustrate how much they needed each other. He floundered around in garden centres, where he felt like an alien, and bought her plants, including a twenty-year-old bonsai. And she spent hours traipsing around comic shops and spent £120 on issue 137 of *The X-Men*. They did that kind of thing a lot. And knew, now, that love was a grand and excursive thing. A terrific racket altogether.

But sometimes they both felt absurd brushes of, well, something else or other.

As if they were being watched.

It was probably just a result of being minorly famous. One morning, when Lynne mentioned that her show was going to be featuring an item on a kid who worked with the police when his friend disappeared – well, John Kelso almost jumped out of his skin.

He'd been a doppelganger once, as a child. Although the tatty and furry uncertainty of that piece of scary nonsense was so, so old, it still gave him nightmares once every five years or so. Never mind.

He looked at Lynne, said nothing and kissed her as he walked out the door.

That particular afternoon, John was off to prepare his pieces on airplanes in the movies (Spitfires, obviously), endangered species in the movies (he wanted pandas, but all he could manage was gorillas; cue boring clips of Sigourney Weaver), interesting plants in the movies (*Day of the Triffids* . . . like, duh . . .), and deafness in the movies (never mind *Children of a Lesser God*, what about Alan Arkin in *The Heart is a Lonely Hunter*?), and a few other bits he hadn't decided on yet.

And Lynne was off to interview a doctor at Moorfields Hospital in Shoreditch, for a fifteen-minute slot on the show.

There was an old woman. She was one of his patients. She was the oldest person alive. Or supposed to be. Well, the oldest person in Britain, at the very least. Well, nobody actually knew, since they couldn't find any papers, so nothing was official and she sure as hell wasn't talking. That was the other thing that had gotten the papers going; she wouldn't talk. One of the nurses had heard the old woman talk in her sleep. It sounded like Gaelic or something, but there was definitely nothing wrong with her vocal chords.

Whatever – she was so old it just made no sense, apparently. Nobody knew anything. There had been nibbles from a swarm of other stations, apparently, but their requests for interviews had all been turned down. Clare and Robert thought that Lynne was probably the best girl to send, given that it was a situation that required some tact and delicacy. Lynne thought it was a stupid, intrusive assignment. Old folks shouldn't be treated as bloody freaks, just because they've managed to avoid dying for a certain amount of time.

But she got on the phone regardless, and spoke to a youthful and fragile voice on the other end of the line.

And the interview was confirmed.

John called to say that he was finishing up early in the studio, and would swing by the hospital to drive her home, before going back in.

Yep, thought Lynne, smiling. *A couple of hours at home in bed. Excellent.*

The Doctor was alarmingly young. But, more than that, he had an unnatural calm about him that gave Lynne the creeps.

He met Lynne outside the old woman's room, sat her down in a chair outside the staff room, and trembled his way through the first sixty seconds of the interview.

This time, the studio had actually given her a camera crew. In other words, one guy.

'Just relax,' said Lynne. 'Listen, we'll turn off the camera, and you can just gather your thoughts, and talk at your own pace, okay?'

'Okay.'

The Doctor was as white as a sheet. He looked as if he was about to pass out.

Lynne studied his face while he gathered himself.

He couldn't have been more than twenty-six, but he looked about forty.

He had his fists jammed in his pockets. Like a dumb and shamed schoolboy.

Lynne put her hand on his shoulder, and she could actually feel the sweat through what was probably three layers of cloth.

This man was scared. And he was beginning to scare her. What was wrong with him?

'Come on, pet,' she whispered, 'everybody gets stage fright. You don't have to talk about the old lady if you don't want to. It's just television. It's stupid. You don't have to.'

'Yes,' he whispered, 'I do.' And his voice was like a razor.

He was twenty-five and he felt like an old man. Whatever old and orthodox songs, of sheen and common sense, he used to sing inside his own head had long now been distorted. His life no longer seemed to belong to him. The soothing vaudeville of ordinary fatigue had been replaced, replaced by a bunch of impure and ringing stings in his brain, as if the siren wrench of the old woman's sheer awfulness was something that was *not* his fault. But was going to have to be dealt with anyway.

He had watched his own life go away. And neither massive, decked-out or sterile guff, nor sheer and teary hard work was going to help him. Ever again.

He felt like crying, perhaps, but he just didn't have the energy. His fear and misery, these days, were things both replete and mathematical. He had nothing left.

Not one scrappy, beguiling or rotten idea to save his own life. Not a damn thing.

And so, because he was exhausted and dented and because his mind felt like the scruffiest place on earth and because he wouldn't, couldn't give in to the criminal gesture of sleep, he leaned into this nice-smelling woman and whispered his story into her ear.

It took two minutes and when he was finished, Lynne was the one who was trembling.

'Listen –' she began, and didn't get any further, because at that moment, he took her hand and led her ever so gently down the corridor and towards the old woman's room.

Behind them, two men marched down the corridor.

One was scrawny and pock-marked, the other was grey-haired but young none the less.

Lynne didn't even have to look over her shoulder to know, but she did, briefly, anyway.

And there he was.

The bastard thief with the young, grey hair, the most interesting face, and the best and loveliest spring-heeled smell on the planet.

An odour like a treadmill. A smell like a cul-de-sac because, after it, there was simply nowhere left for a sensible person to go.

It was that good. That smell. That addled, pussyfooted and moderate slice of jouissance.

It was that good, and that stupid.

My God, it's him.

In four nanoseconds, Lynne thought, simultaneously, of her tidy kitchen, her starry bedroom ceiling, the loud and daft doorway of the King's Head pub, and a broad and smashing stretch of Greenwich Park.

And of the creak and smell and creak again of that damn leather jacket.

Lynne knew it made no sense but, hell, it was definitely him. He'd already been all over her flat and all over her stuff. All over her plants and her vinyl and her books. It was him.

And despite all that, she was actually glad for the glossy glimpse of him.

And honestly so. She wavered for a moment, there in the corridor, inhaling the smell and the gorgeous, reasonable pallor of the man.

And Tom stared right back at her. He stared at her and, for a moment, he forgot to breathe.

At the sight of her, he became, again briefly, a polite and dinky guttersnipe, a beatific child with nowhere to go but to her. He almost fainted at the sheer sight of her, and at that moment both she and he were thinking the same thoughts.

For the love of Christ, this makes no *sense*.

He is just a thief. And worse (or perhaps better) than that, a thief tamed.

And there is nothing more boring (or scintillating) than a remorseful robber.

But what the hell was he *doing* here? Here, in this hospital. Now. Right *now*.

What the hell was *wrong* with him? Surely he had more sense now, after all these months, than to try anything. More sense than to start this stalking bullshit all over again. He was the enemy.

More or less. Didn't he *know* that?

Didn't he know that he was the enemy? These days at least.

And why was she trembling like a drenched cat?

And who the hell *was* this guy with him?

The skinny man with the bad skin and the nervy manner?

Honestly.

As the Doctor tightened his grip slightly, and led her down the corridor, Lynne began to feel more than a little afraid. Something cut-up and stupid was happening here. She wanted to escape from the Doctor's grip, but didn't want to face the thief, the man who had rifled through her house, through her life. With a purpose more frightening than ordinary thievery and more comforting than ordinary affection.

The notion of him hadn't scared her for a long while, but it unnerved her more than she would ever admit. And now here he was, ten yards away from her. And walking towards her still, but slowly. And she couldn't take her eyes off him. Him and his mate.

His eyes were green, she noticed, as he ambled forward but nervously so.

John, whom she loved and loved beyond all else – his eyes were beautiful but brown.

Right now, she hated this man's guts.

But only after a fashion.

Tom looked. And Lynne looked.

And the expression 'no love lost' does not even begin to describe it.

Tom and Kenny were here to *get* Kelso. That much was certain.

That was all. One way or another. They hadn't even discussed what they were going to do with him once they'd got him. Nearly kill the fucker, maybe.

Neither of them was entirely sure. They had been following him, on and off now, for a sad and pathetic week, usually after an afternoon in the pub.

They knew only that they wanted to confront the bastard. To call him a thief.

To call back into existence their own lives. To take back what he had stolen.

And not just for their own sakes. But for Mark and David and Andy and the rest.

And for Tom, because the bastard just didn't deserve the Callier woman. Simple as that.

But how? How to do that thing for which they were aching?

And having been there – then what?

And then what? Seriously.

Then what the hell were they going to do with the rest of their lives?

But for the moment, however. Well, whatever.

Keeping up with Kelso wasn't exactly rocket science.

Wherever she went, he followed.

There you go.

Love and nothing but.

Bastard.

And just then, as the Doctor and Lynne and Kenny and Tom all bundled to a shivering and ragged halt, and stood in a ridiculous breed of tippy-toe stasis outside the open door of the old woman's room, he appeared.

John Kelso appeared.

Behind them in the corridor.

He had parked on a double and he didn't want to wait. Not for too long, anyway.

He had meandered down and along the corridors – he was in no hurry – looking for his Lynne, his woman, and had spotted this hopeless and mildly menacing mob, stuck together in some kind of stupid tableau outside one of the patients' rooms.

And in the middle of this hugely nervous scrum – there she was.

There was his Lynne.

Kelso smiled.

And there was Duthie.

Kelso froze.

Kenny Duthie and John Kelso stood and stared at each other, with a bunch of apprehensive and adrenal background noises from the hospital bunging up their ears.

John Kelso had promised himself – if he ever saw that fucker again, he would kill him.

And Kenny Duthie was thinking exactly the same thing.

And, what with the double breed of both hatred and terror they both had going on, backwards *and* forwards, they barely noticed that the Doctor had taken a gun from his pocket and was pointing it at all of them.

A gun. An actual gun.

At all of them. In turn.

Well, pointing vaguely, like some kind of unhappy, wavering and half-asleep moron.

But it *was* a gun. An actual, real and *big* fucking *gun.*

The Doctor waved the gun around, silently and with elbows askew, as if he was, baton aloft, conducting a particularly curly and disobedient strand of thin air.

His face was the colour of dirty snow, and his expression managed to be stunned, authoritative and ghostly all at the same time.

They stared at him.

He was a Doctor.

And here he was.

Pointing a gun at them.

Amazing.

And because there was nothing else to do in that miserable, brief and yet interesting breach, they all just moved around in imbecilic circles and stared at each other. And stared and looked.

Kenny at John.

Lynne at Kenny.

John at Tom.

Lynne at John.

And Tom at Lynne.

Oh, Jesus. Some things just aren't worth getting into.

And, besides, there's no arguing with a gun.

Not in any serious sense.

The Doctor waggled the gun in the air, like a sweating and lethal toddler.

He motioned maniacally, with the kind of amateurish body-language that quietly said, 'Would everybody please move, please, into the room, thank you very much, or I will blow your fucking heads off right now, awfully sorry, but there you go.'

He had always tried to avoid any actorly rubble but the tired slattern in him was enjoying this shit. No two ways about it. He was enjoying himself.

He was now, at once and apparently, the cleverest and the filthiest goon on the planet.

And he knew it.

He had all sorts of perky and acid notions to his name right about now and, by *God*, there was nothing better than having a bunch of folk with (at the very best) mercurial and mottled virtue, here and hostage.

He, in the middle of his misery, had still managed to graft together something stout, in thrall and still sensible.

And, besides, he had this huge gun.

He had this big, damn gun.

And these various fuckers were all truly terrified.

Excellent.

And so, under the shadow of that gormless, squalid but very valid threat, the four of them sloped into the old woman's room, exactly like the quartet of very frightened people that they were.

The memories were coming thick and fast now, but made less sense, somehow. When she did open her eyes these days, it became apparent that the room was filled with flowers. Flowers of every species and colour and shape and smell.

As a young girl, she had always been told that flowers should not be allowed in a hospital room. It was probably a myth.

Edmund bought her flowers, once. Many years after the war. There was neither reason nor occasion. He just came home one day with a bunch of tulips. And, as he stood there in the doorway, with neither of them saying a word and both of them frozen with embarrassment, it dawned on her, and probably him too, that it was the worst possible thing he could have done. He didn't cross the threshold. He just turned around and walked away down the path, tossing the tulips over the hedge as he went.

So quiet. So stupid. Both of them.

But now her room was full of amazing and extravagant blooms of every possible sort.

And now, noise. This was a puzzle. The walls were covered with shadows of the most ruffled and viral beauty, a riffling manifesto of strobed and strange shapes, bobbing aloft and talking and talking, and now shouting. The old woman blinked, hard, to clear her vision, and there he surely was. It surely was her Edmund, with his grey hair and his youthful face.

But such a thing wasn't possible. Edmund was long, long gone.

And now, stood here, instead, was this handsome and sweet-smelling young man.

And beside him stood a shivering and pretty woman, and beside her, a thin and scarred boy who was trembling almost more than is

228

possible. And behind him was a nondescript sort with a nice enough face.

And behind all of them was the young Doctor and what he was holding was surely a gun.

He was talking in a voice she no longer recognised. It was shrill and flinch-worthy and truly horrible. He talked and pointed the gun at her face, and all these other strangers in the room seemed, simply, to shrink by degrees.

Well, this was interesting.

And now there was more talking and more shouting.

The Doctor leaned over her and touched her papery cheek with a touch that was at once gentle and uncharitable and, as he brought what might have been the muzzle of this interesting gun up to her head, other shadows crowded in and around, all of them screeching and dreary.

And now the Doctor was pointing the gun at the pretty woman and at the nondescript type. They both seemed to move forward but their progress was impeded by the swoop of something handsome and grey-haired.

The old lady couldn't make out any of this any more.

She closed her eyes and squirrelled her way slowly into the blankets. This was none of her business – this vague and ridiculous tableau, with all these over-excited people.

She was going to slide into sleep now, hopefully for ever.

She drifted off, twitching imperceptibly, and her slow slide into skedaddling, shindig-type and lovely dreams was so, so nice that she barely noticed what were probably gunshots.

6

The Present Day

John Kelso shifted on his ledge, sucked on a Benson & Hedges, took a swig from his fourth beer, looked at the twinkling windows opposite, shielded his eyes from the glare and filed his nails for a bit. The view was so gorgeous. He had pretty much exactly the same view as the tourists in the London Eye, except that he hadn't paid for it.

He sat there, perched on that ledge, and he thought about his life thus far.

He had always loved order and, more to the point, he had always had it. More or less.

And then his world of order had been turned upside down. And not by the man Kenny.

By Lynne Callier and by everything about her. Being held hostage under threat of death by a lunatic film buff whose idea of a love bite was a cigarette burn on the arm was as nothing compared to the things she had done to his heart. To his life. And the gratitude he felt for that made everything else seem like stupid and stony pieces of choppy nonsense.

Cliché or no, she was the best thing that had ever happened to him. The filthy and bleating convictions of a lad like Duthie were, now, neither here nor there.

As he gazed out over the river, he noticed that the tourists seemed to be taking photos of him. Well, okay. Whatever. He just stared right back. He could almost hear the tattoo of their ludicrous jabber and he didn't care. They were pointing their cameras at him and gesturing with the kind of polite and impeccable disbelief which tourists seemed to display pretty much everywhere. Kelso loved tourists. He adored their warm enthusiasm for, well, everything. He even liked the tired and bad-tempered familial fights they had in the pubs of an evening, with their sore feet and their mute disappointment with, well, everything.

Kelso lit another cigarette and finished off the can of beer. He stared at the 'scrapers and at the far horizon. God, it was such a beautiful day. Warm and with the very air humming. No car fumes this high. The city was just a sweet and dinky little creature from this height, a gentle and half-steam thing that wouldn't hurt a fly. It reminded him of his days as a kid, when he and his pathetic gang would go hollering around the fields, and his head was filled with guttersnipe images of the most ruptured, hot and downright silly evenings. With pictures of him and his gobby and so-called gang running, mad, through the streets, jubilant for no reason and roaring for no reason either. And fighting like demented ferrets against a bunch of kids who were just as fizzily bonkers. Jesus . . .

He thought about his addled mother. He was getting a little tired now. The sun was beginning to hurt his eyes. It was probably the beer. What a stupid bitch.

Did he mean to be that mean? Did it even matter?

He closed his eyes and tried to shake the memory of her looming over him in the middle of the night, reeking of sheer craziness, the most sublime smell and idiotic notions.

And talking. Talking and talking and never shutting up.

Kelso looked down, down the fifteen storeys below him, at the mixed and mobile pattern of pedestrians and cars, and he decided that it really didn't matter. Then he remembered that he didn't like heights, so he pulled back, took a deep breath and thought about some of his old stories, the stories he used to create when he was much, much younger. Especially the one about Leonardo and time travel and cardiac arrests.

Da Vinci terrified and as dead as a doornail. Ah, well.

His television shows, over the last seven weeks, had become more and more strange, and Kelso hadn't needed his producers to point that fact out to him.

The staff were tiptoeing around him as if he was made out of glass.

In fact, ever since that incident at the hospital, most of them just did their jobs, kept their heads down and tried not to talk to him at all.

John Kelso was galvanised these days. He threw himself into his show, did what he wanted, and didn't really give a damn any more what the studio thought.

He did an item about plastic surgery in movies (and mentioned Rock Hudson only once).

He did an item about submarines in the movies (*none* involving Petersen, Hackman, Connery or McConaughey).

He did an item covering decent teachers in the movies, and good grammar, to boot.

He did a piece about robbery victims in the movies. Not the robbers, just the victims. Robbers would have been a hell of a lot more interesting. He was tempted to talk about war medals and vinyl LPs, but he resisted the urge.

He did a bit about architecture in the movies that was supposed to last two minutes, tops. Kelso blathered for at least a quarter of an hour about William van Allen and Wallis Gilbert and Sixten Sason, and it took him a while to realise that his producer had long gone to the commercials.

He did a whispy and atonal piece, and he had no idea why, about coroners and their forensic examinations, but for some reason he couldn't fathom in his own heart, he wanted a comedy bit, and so, resisting Foster and Hopkins, all he could come up with was a very young, but none the less cracking, Michael Keaton in *Night Shift.*

Over those seven strange and unwinnable weeks, he went home often shivering, fed up and with absolutely no idea where his notions were coming from.

He was getting less than three hours' sleep a day.

He lay in his bed and thought that perhaps he might do a show about guns.

And when the full impact of *that* idea sunk in, he laughed until he threw up.

John Kelso was falling apart and he knew it.

His last show came around. He knew it was going to be his last show.

Because he knew he wasn't going to be around to do it any more.

And on his last show, after a rambling but not entirely incoherent treatise about his old favourite – cartoons – he left his tired, worried and beloved audience with the thing he had always despised the most. He left them with a quiz.

Larry Fine, Joe de Rita and Shemp Howard. And no – there were no prizes for guessing.

Then he walked out of the studio into the rain, without even a coat. The staff didn't know what the hell to do. There were another fifteen minutes of the show to go. One of them slapped in a tape of *Tex Avery's Screwball Classics* and nobody seemed any the wiser.

Kelso stood in the car park in the soaking drizzle, his face raised to the black sky. A couple of his new researchers, both of them under twenty-five, hovered around the fire escape. But he just stood there, head up in the night to the heavy rain. In the absence of instructions, and afraid that he might get violent if they tried to persuade him to come back, the poor, timid things crept back inside instead.

Kelso just stood there, head back and arms outstretched, until he was truly drenched.

And then he walked home like a see-through, soiled and sodden ghost.

Now here he was, finally, on his ledge and gazing out over the city. No going back now.

The town was looking especially perky today. The sun kept shining, the windows kept twinkling, *there* swooped another falcon and there died another pigeon. Good.

Kelso lit a cigarette and looked at the river. There seemed to be a bit of a commotion building up on the pavement below. He ignored it and looked at the river again. Ludicrous visions from movies and comics and cartoons swanned in front of his eyes but he just banished them from his mind.

He banished them in a way he had never been able to do in his whole life.

He dismissed the lot of them and, with them, all of his past life.

All of it. All that love of organisation and neatness and things as they should be rather than as they are. And with them, all that hopeful and hoodwinked energy, that he could better have spent elsewhere. He smoked his cigarette and swigged from the half-bottle of whisky with a trembling hand.

The tourists in the Eye were still taking snaps of him, perched, noticeably, on the edge of an unsafe-looking rooftop and with what looked like, even at a distance, an unsafe look in his eye. Kelso smiled ferociously at the pod, flipped them all the bird, swigged another swig and went back to enjoying his own skint unhappiness.

He thought about the man, the thief, the grey-haired, young and handsome bastard who had stepped between him and a bullet in the hospital room. He thought about him for at least two minutes every day if he was honest.

The way the man had looked at Lynne had frightened Kelso almost more than the sight of the gun being waved around by the young Doctor.

But not as much as the look on Lynne's face.

She was looking at this man with a look that spoke of *something* that Kelso just couldn't track, or even make out.

When the noise had died down, and the Doctor had been dragged by security, screaming, from the room, Kelso had found himself on his knees with this guy's head in his lap and his blood pouring all over the shop. The man was dying and there was nothing anyone could do about it. His chest was a mess and he was losing so much blood that he could hardly whisper. But he tried anyway.

Kelso held the grey-haired youngster in his arms, as if enacting some ghastly *pietà*, while the pair of them sloshed crazily around on the floor in a glossy pool of blood.

But the dying man never stopped whispering.

And what he whispered about, in the last ninety seconds of his life, was love.

Love and Lynne Callier. Her name was the last thing on his lips.

After a bit, John Kelso had let the slippery and limp body slide from his grasp.

He turned slowly, blinking moronically, in both sorrow and shock, and in search of an explanation. Of a solid story from her which would, right now, make sense of his world and bring his woman back to him. But there was no sense to be had. The man had died in a slow and gentle rasp, but with time enough to spill his heart, and with love to spare.

Lynne Callier, on the other hand, with a bullet in her brain, had died instantly.

*

Kelso had done all the crying he was going to do. He finished off the half-bottle, moved a little further forward on his ledge, and just couldn't believe the hooligan tricks the sky was getting up to. It was a wash of imbecilic colours that really shouldn't exist. The car sounds and the slovenly chug of the riverboats drifted upwards and Kelso, more than drunk now, decided that this was definitely the second-best sunset that there ever was.

Over to his right, swooping in narrow circles above another, shorter building, a bird began to sing. It whirled in tight and difficult loops and sang its wee heart out.

It was a nondescript creature, as plain as plain could be. The bird sang, but beautifully, and as Kelso stared at it, he realised that it wasn't a nightingale.

It was a bloody *lark.*

Oh, now, that is just not possible, Kelso thought to himself. *Not an actual lark. Not here, not in a bloody city.* Not in a place swamped with eight million people.

Kelso laughed with something that might, in another life, have been called relief, lit his last cigarette and listened to the bird for a while. Yep, it certainly was lovely. He hadn't heard the high and uncertain trill of a lark's song since he was a kid, but it was thrilling none the less, and unmistakable too. He was so glad he'd thrown the air pistol in the garbage last week.

He rose to his feet, raised his arms to the heavens and stretched every muscle in his body. That felt good, and the corrosive beauty of the city was, below his feet right there and then, a beauty he could just about comprehend.

John Kelso's entire life had been swamped and swamped utterly, right from the start. He knew that now. He had never stood a chance. He knew that too. His life had been, from the outset, the best ever exercise in running away. He had been surrounded, and had surrounded himself, with the kind of acute and near-corporeal distractions that generally stop a man from getting hurt. Ever. Or so it goes.

With a comforting network of facts and figures and obscure nonsense that he had never shared with anyone. Except with his television audience.

And, latterly, with Lynne, but in laughter and only briefly so.

With all this armoury, then – an entire life's chorus's worth of the correct, the colonised, the tidy and the telling – his life should have been sorted, surely. All he'd had to do, all his life, was to get flush with the interesting and detached folk and to avoid the nutty dullards. Or so one would have thought.

And then she had come along and changed everything.

And now she was gone.

And everything was changed again, and there was no comfort to be had.

None at all.

All those films. All that haphazard and self-centred bullshit. He knew that he hadn't defrosted enough for her. But over the months he had gotten close, and both of them knew that it was going, brilliantly, that way.

They had been creeping silently towards a rapprochement decent enough to carry them both beyond ordinary love.

And they had been getting there. Yes, she'd had the presence of mind to have the odd immaculate bitch about this, that or the other, and John was nervous sometimes, but by and large it was turning into a properly nifty love story.

A story that they were both, shyly, beginning to believe in.

And now she was dead.

He had spent less time with her body than with the thief's.

There isn't much to do over a corpse except cry, and even the most heartbroken have to give up after a decent interval.

It took him three times as long to wash the blood off his hands in the hospital bathroom and it occurred to him, as he watched that mesmerising crimson swirl in the tub, that he was very abruptly, and absurdly, annoyed by the fact that he couldn't tell the thief's blood from hers. But it was only when, five minutes later, one of the doctors had forcibly stopped him from sucking miserably on his still-wet and reddened fingers taken hold of his sodden sleeve, pulled him discreetly aside and made discreet mention of blood tests, that Kelso had gone berserk. By the time he had calmed down, he had nothing left to explain to the police.

God knows – he had tried, but there are some things a man just can't fight.

Ever since Lynne died – well, there are some things a man cannot beat.

John knew now that every single moment of every single day, from now until the day of his own death, there would be a world of svelte and unfussy desperation hammering at his head and at his heart, until he just wouldn't be able to stand it any more.

He was exhausted, exhausted with weeping.

Nothing was going to be right, ever again.

It was all wrong, all of it, and every stupid sad song ever written was right.

Bastards.

But listening to that lark's amazing song, he was more grubbily happy at that moment than he had been in a long time. Perhaps the pair of them, he and Lynne both, would find some resolute and angelic nonsense to bang on about in the afterlife.

Whatever.

He lowered his head into his hands, rubbed his eyes – and came up smiling.

You never know. He took off his shoes. And then his socks. And he wondered to himself why on earth he'd ever felt the need for dental floss. Now that was just downright silly.

John Kelso tiptoed forward, stepped up and stood hovering on the edge of his ledge.

His arms were outstretched, his eyes were closed, and his bare toes were curled around the lovely crease of the concrete. With the sun shining, wonderfully, on his face, he didn't open his eyes and look down. He'd already done that. The air was wonderfully warm and surprisingly clean up there.

It was fifteen storeys down and he didn't give a damn any more what the tourists thought.

He could hear faint voices of civic commotion from below. Fire engines, probably, and the murmuring and distant cackle of a mob probably itching for him to topple.

And a specifically Scottish voice, shouting up at him.

He definitely recognised that accent.

But everything now in his world was shiny, gone and freshly ludicrous. Nothing really really mattered any more.

In fact, nothing mattered.

At the precise moment John Kelso jumped off the ledge, he was neither happy nor sober.

He was drunk and miserable.

But he wasn't stupid either, and he wondered, in his heart of hearts, if perhaps this wasn't a mistake and premature.

No.

It wasn't.

He knew, in his heart of hearts, that justice was being done.

But after about three seconds of freefall – about halfway down, and around the seventh floor – John Kelso found himself wondering and wondering again.

Did he jump like a proper person, or did he just stumble, like a fucking amateur?

241

In his own unique and heartbroken way, of course. And, of course, much too late.

By the time Kenny Duthie had made up his mind about whether or not to go to the funeral, he'd taken delivery of a new bunch of lodgers.

The media had collared him for a day or so and then, amazingly, decided to leave the poor ex-loony alone. Kenny hid behind a mask of tic-ridden vulnerability, insisted he had nothing to say about that kidnapping thing, about that part of his life.

It was all ancient history, he said.

He'd been rehabilitated, he said.

It had nothing to do with him anymore – he hadn't thought about the man John Kelso for a long time. He was over that now. He was over it and he was trying to get on with his life, so please . . .

And it actually worked. The press backed off and Kenny found himself, on the day, with just enough space to sneak off to the fringes of John Kelso's funeral.

It was a disappointingly ordinary, soulless affair. Lots of work colleagues in deliberately bright-coloured suits. Lots of burgundy and mauve.

Morons, thought Kenny to himself. *Bastards. What the hell is wrong with black? Why can't these people show some respect?*

A slightly overweight woman was hovering on the edges of the crowd. She looked as if she didn't know whether to cry properly or just grimace with grace. Or perhaps laugh, even. She looked at Kenny but not as if she recognised him. Kenny had no idea who this unhappy creature was but he had, at the least, the good manners to speak to her briefly. In the end, she just leaned against his shoulder, eyes closed, and sobbed like a baby. It turned out her name was Penny.

Kenny was embarrassed but curious also, so he let this sad woman lean in there for a bit. Besides, he had moral support these days, so he was able to relax a little.

Kenny's old gang was there with him.

His gang from the Ward.

They had shown up on his doorstep, in an utterly barking but handsome clump, one night the previous week and, when he had gotten over the shock, he had almost wept with joy to see the lot of them. It was only when he saw that gormless bunch of faces that he realised how horribly lonely he was.

And now here they all were again.

Jason the bodybuilding blasphemer.

Adam the young, black and would-be dark destroyer of great art.

And Caroline the mad nun.

And a fragile and skinny thing called Linda who, apparently, was Jason's sister.

Oh, Jesus, even Richard the anagram king had shown up, along with Tim, the full-of-love skinhead. They had all gotten together months after Kenny had been released, and had decided to go visit their old, wrinkle-free mentor.

The boy with all the best stories and the kindest words.

They missed him. It was as simple as that.

Amazing.

Kenny let them all stay for a week.

And when they'd eaten all his food, he kicked them out.

But right now, here they were – all Kelso's colleagues, friends, near-enemies and various hangers-on, hovered around the edges of his funeral in the pouring rain. And while the vicar mumbled about days to come, Kenny found himself sneaking a look at Linda and thinking about that rotten and irresistible story about her and the teenage Kelso, down amongst the cattle-feed sacks.

Jason had gotten in touch with his sister, after five years without so much as a word between them, and had brought her down to

London with him, just so that she could see the bastard Kelso put into the ground.

Kenny had offered her a slice of toast in his overcrowded kitchen two days previously, and had almost gotten a 'thank you' out of her.

She was still near-silent these days, apparently, but Kenny couldn't miss the look of quiet satisfaction in her eyes, right here and right now at this interesting funeral, as she stared at the dull-coloured coffin wood, and at the churned mud all around.

And then she looked up and smiled a smile precisely in Kenny Duthie's direction, and for the next little while, while the vicar continued his routine and dreary blah, they never took their eyes off each other.

Just like the Everly Brothers when they sang on stage.

Those brilliant brothers and their ruthless harmonies.

Eyes locked, always. They simply couldn't afford to take their eyes off each other.

Kenny and Linda stared at each other a bit like that. For a bit.

And off to the left of the funeral crowd stood a woman easily in her sixties. She was beautifully dressed, but she hovered uneasily, and flittered like a quiet and demented moth, as if she knew that she was supposed to be there, but definitely didn't want to be there. She looked at the scene through opera glasses, talked to no one, took Polaroids of the casket, made copious notes in a sturdy, ring-bound folder, and didn't shed one tear.

Mothers the world over are *not* of a piece.

*

After Kelso's funeral Kenny invited everybody across town to Tom's memorial service, which was being held later that same day. Amazingly, everybody accepted.

And it was so much more fun, everybody ended up drunk and crying.

It was properly and expensively paid for too. Everybody wondered about that. Afterwards, of course. The flowers alone were amazing. Great, gorgeous bowers of roses and tulips and God knows what else, and with ferns besides. They were so beautiful.

This was a real expensive service. Which made no sense at all.

(Many, many years later, Kenny Duthie learned, from a minor aside in a *Telegraph* obituary, that Tom's extravagant memorial had been paid for by a rich, reclusive gentlemen who, many, many years ago, had owned an island in Fermanagh. He didn't recognise the man's name. And that fact annoyed him for the rest of that particular Sunday morning.)

After the service, they all went to what had been Tom's favourite pub in Crouch End.

Adam and Caroline danced until she couldn't stand it any more, Tim and Richard argued about lousy song lyrics, peanut butter and *Mr Ed*, and about whether chain gangs would ever have worked in Blackburn. Then they made the landlord drag out his son's school atlas, so that they could see what kind of a watery and excellent place this poor, dead lad had come from. And decided that the small, wet and complicated county of Fermanagh was too beautiful a shape to be true, and probably much more trouble than it was worth.

And in the middle of that half-sad muddle were the signs of lousy, best and brilliant recovery. Kenny and Linda had a slow dance, the first slow dance he'd had with a woman since he was a teenager. He read her face as they sashayed around the tiny dance-floor and, as they twirled, rather exhaustedly, what toppled then into his mind and into his heart was a plethora of thoroughly stupid notions. He thought about thievery and, as he looked more closely at that damaged and interesting face, he could feel a story coming on. A proper story, with complicated and hurtful bits bolted on. A bloody *story*, regardless. Christ, maybe he would even find another script here with, and from, her, something else to replace what had been taken from him.

Kenny was slow-dancing and thinking, and staring and thinking of a brand-new screenplay. An honest-to-god brand-new story. A keen and slinky script for life.

He decided then and at that moment, that he could steal yarns with the best of them.

And if he had to steal from the likes of her – well, fair enough.

And as they danced, this woman, the quiet and lovely Linda, was looking right back at him, with an expression interested and then some.

A thief is just a thief. Calm down, all.

Even the telly twins were here, having been accidentally dragged from one service to the next. And now here they were – Clare and Robert, in tears and handsome both, downing pints of snakebite, dancing drunkenly across the floor like a pair of undisciplined wraiths, and declaring utter and undying love for each other.

Which would have been almost funny if it hadn't been completely true.

Robert and Clare were divorced from their respective partners (obviously) three months later, and got married to each other (obviously), about four weeks after that.

And then, well, the pair of them actually lived happily ever after.

So. True love, then.

True love, of various and undeserving sorts, slithered along its own implosive and chippy path, all that night. And for a long time beyond that night.

True love made its mark, like an ignorant and brilliant scrawl on a wall.

True love made vulgar inroads hither and yon.

True love got its head kicked in and punched well above its weight.

And at the very least, didn't do too badly at all.

The room was dark these days. The nurses would occasionally draw the curtains to gaze out over the lawns but, mostly, she lay in a soft and pleasant gloom.

The young Doctor seemed to have disappeared a long time ago and been replaced by an older man, whose voice was calm and whose palms were warm. He would touch her on the shoulder sometimes, as he spoke, and his touch was feathery and respectful. Everything seemed to be much quieter too. The staff moved by in a slow and ruffling blur.

She was as healthy as ever and easy to look after. Even if she was as old as the hills.

People had lost interest in how old she was. It just didn't seem to matter any more. She was as old as time and that was all there was to it.

She was no longer truly aware of the passage of time. She was floating, now, on a river of memories and the world had drifted away.

She lay in her bed and thought about the past and the notion of love came crowding in. She thought about her parents and her brother, and about her husband and her children. And about everyone she had ever met in her long, long life.

All dead and gone. Every single one. Even the memories of them were now strange and precarious things. But their very fragility was of comfort to her, because now there was no wearisome battle to keep them alive, no struggle to love them any more.

They were gone.

Love was gone. Her world entire was gone.

Everything was gone now.
And everything was precisely as it should be.

And now she was thinking of music on a summer's day, and of an old man, in his back garden, waving his arms at the trees, and she wondered if that had really happened, or if she had imagined it.
Everything else in the world was gone away now.
All that was left was a picture of blinding sunshine, and an old and crazy man conducting the trees, and music she had never heard before.

The old woman burrowed into the blankets and listened to that music while the whole universe, all around her, shivered placidly away into nothingness.
Everything at that moment was thin and perfect and ghostly and gone.
She smiled to herself.
She was going to live for ever.